Too COOL
To GeT MaRRieD

Too COOL To GET MaRRieD

and other true stories

DaViD SEELeY

PERENNIAL LIBRARY

Harper & Row, Publishers, New York
Grand Rapids, Philadelphia, St. Louis, San Francisco
London, Singapore, Sydney, Tokyo, Toronto

"The Shaggy Club," "Cruising," "Too Cool to Get Married," "The Gods of Padre Island," and "The No Decade" originally appeared in *Texas Monthly* magazine. "Cruising" was originally titled "Dear Parents." "Modern Girls," "Night Life in the Age of AIDS," and "A Today Kind of Marriage" originally appeared in *Playboy.* "Boys' Night Out" originally appeared in *Mademoiselle.*

A hardcover edition of this book was originally published in 1989 by Harper & Row, Publishers.

First PERENNIAL LIBRARY edition published 1990.

The Library of Congress has catalogued the hardcover edition as follows:

Seeley, David.
    Too cool to get married and other true stories.

    1. Young adults—United States. 2. Young adults—United States—Social life and customs. I. Title.
HQ799.7.S44 1989   305.2'35'0973   88-45057
ISBN 0-06-015944-8

ISBN 0-06-091632-x (pbk.)
90 91 92 93 94 FG 10 9 8 7 6 5 4 3 2 1

to lee and rich—
many monday nights.

contents

1. j.b. and me   *1*
2. the shaggy club   *35*
3. cruising   *60*
4. boys' night out   *72*
5. modern girls   *80*
6. too cool to get married   *94*
7. desi   *108*
8. the gods of padre island   *142*
9. night life in the age of aids   *160*
10. the no decade   *183*
11. a today kind of marriage   *195*

EDITOR'S NOTE: Except for "J.B. and Me" and "Desi," all the stories in this collection are true. No names or identities have been changed. "J.B. and Me" and "Desi," however, are to a large degree fictional. The only real-life characters in "J.B. and Me" are Cherry Blair, John Branch, and the author; the story's other characters are fictional creations that reflect Mr. Branch's fatiguing and stressful love life. In "Desi," the only real-life characters are Mr. Branch and the author. Desi herself is actually a composite of various Manhattan residents the author has known and loved and carried home on cold winter nights.

Too Cool
To Get Married

1

j.b. and me

One day about a year ago, my friend John Branch peeled a note off his bathroom mirror. Written in smeared ink on a piece of faded yellow paper, held in place by a gnarled bit of crusty tape, it said: WORK ON THAT PLAY TODAY! It was marked by ancient spots of shaving cream, a smear or two of some girl's lipstick, and yellowed shadows of other bits of tape, which had fastened it to other bathroom mirrors over the years. John wasn't replacing it with a fresh note; he'd always been partial to things that suggested a history, a romantic past. Instead, he crumpled up the note and dropped it in the wastebasket. To a casual observer, John might have been housecleaning, sprucing up the place for expected guests. But that moment was enormous: on that day, with that gesture, John stopped being a writer.

When I discovered this, it was like hearing news of a tragedy. Because writing—and by extension art and romance and love— were all that John had ever lived for. It seemed that giving up on writing was, for John, like giving up on water or faith or God. We had been best friends for ten years, and in a way he was also giving up on us. We could never be the same friends again, because I'd always fear he was betraying his vision, betraying the dreams we'd both nurtured so long ago.

When I landed my first newspaper job I was a naïve twenty-one, so ignorant of the business I'd accidentally applied for a job in advertising. Luckily, personnel recognized my talents—I could type, and I knew my Social Security number—so I was shuffled off to be a clerk in features. Within a few months I was writing little stories, usually about women's club meetings or baby gorillas at the zoo. It was a stretch for me to mingle with the reporters at the paper—I looked about eighteen, didn't drink much, and besides being a technical virgin (the result of years of Catholic girlfriends), I attended a Southern Baptist church three times a week. Not for religious reasons.

There was this girl there. I saw her one Sunday when I dropped off my little sister, and I fell desperately in love. She looked like a young Mia Farrow and had the unlikely name of Cherry Blair. At the *Times Herald,* I would sit at my desk and write love stories about Cherry, typing her name over and over on my VDT, filing them lovingly in my queue. But I never had the nerve to talk to her—at ice cream fellowships and Monday night youth volleyball, I merely swooned from a dozen feet away, terrified even to approach her.

One day at the paper, I was so enthralled by Cherry I made a mistake. Instead of sending an account of some women's club meeting, I sent one of my stories about Cherry from my terminal to the copy desk. A few minutes later, a young man appeared behind my VDT, clutching a printout. He was a part-time editor on the desk, and though I'd never met him, I thought he was rather odd: he was tall and thin, with very pale skin and a face that looked like a Greek statue's, chiseled and wise and a little sad. His eyes were dark and piercing, and he always had a Dartmouth scarf thrown around his neck. He came in each morning with bicycle clips on his ankles and windblown hair; sometimes he even wore a beret at the desk.

"This is a very interesting story," he said, handing me the printout. "I'm trying to convince Clark to put it on page C1."

My face must have screwed in terror; it was one of the syrupiest Cherry Blair stories yet. "White chargers" and "flaming sunsets" leapt up from the page. I stammered an explanation, but he laughed and waved it away.

"It's stunning prose. A bit thick, perhaps. But it's certainly better than a report on the Nellie Day Trigg Garden Club. By the way, we haven't met. I'm John Branch."

After that, John took an interest in me. I was an unformed kid badly in need of a mentor, and I'd already been lucky enough to cultivate one—a novelist named C.W. Smith, who wrote film reviews for the paper. C.W. had read my Cherry Blair stories with undisguised horror. One day he dropped on my desk three assignments toward becoming a Man and a Writer: One, forget about Cherry Blair. Two, date a racy girl on the city desk named Marcy, because she seemed to like me and was "eminently beddable." (C.W. felt losing my virginity, technical or otherwise, was of tantamount importance.) Three, and most important, I had to move to New York.

But C.W. had a wife and a house and ten-year-old twins. He couldn't offer me the day-to-day (or night-to-night) tutelage I so desperately needed. John Branch stepped in to fill that void. We went out for a drink after work that very day, partly to soothe my nerves. Thanks to a less sympathetic editor, the Cherry Blair story had been sent to "all terminals." It had even been posted. But John said to put it behind me. "That part of your life is over now. I'm taking you on as my protégé, see? First, we'll order still further drinks."

John's theory was that after losing my virginity, getting drunk a lot was my next step toward being a Man and a Writer. After four rounds we were a little boiled, and John began my first lesson. He quoted William Blake: "Sooner strangle an infant in its cradle than nurse an unacted desire."

"Hmmm. I see." I looked at him quizzically.

"That means you should do what C.W. says. You must seduce the girl on cityside. It'll do you wonders, and who knows? She might even enjoy it." He asked me what I was reading.

"Oh, Fitzgerald, Hemingway. I just bought big collections of both their letters."

John rubbed his temples and sighed. "Those two. All right. What about Spinoza?"

"Who?"

"Henry James? John Hawkes? Joseph Conrad? T.S. Eliot?"

"Well . . . I guess I should read more."

"I'll make you a list. I've an extensive library at home—I don't normally loan out my books—people always lose them, or spill

Coke on them, or write silly things in the margins—but I'm going to trust you."

Two girls came into the bar; they might have been dance majors from Southern Methodist University. One wore a resin-dusted Danskin under a pair of jeans. "They're like orchids," John said. "Excuse me."

He walked over to the girls and bowed slightly, taking their hands in turn and grazing his lips delicately across their knuckles. I couldn't hear what they said, but after a moment one of the dancers laughed and ran her fingers through John's hair. When he came back to our table, I asked how he knew them.

"I don't know them *yet*. But the dark girl—the one in the leotard—I have enormous plans for. Isn't she lovely? Do you see how her back curves as she stands at the bar, delicately, like a gesture? I only met her a week ago, at a party, and I've been utterly transfixed since. I hardly sleep at night."

We mused about the girls, who had settled into a booth, indeed like two orchids. The vodka warmed me like a blush, and I suddenly comprehended a future that included ballerinas, late nights in dark bars, interesting people, and high art. We discussed grand plans for the future of Western Literature.

"Sigmund Freud said, 'All that can survive you is your work,' " John whispered. We vowed to begin great novels that very weekend.

We were tutor and student; we soon became friends as well. John's oldest friend, a high-school classmate named Duncan Becker, had moved to Mexico three years before to live and write in the artists' colony in San Miguel de Allende. He occasionally sent John letters that would take weeks to arrive and were full of strange messages, hieroglyphics, bits of Mexican dust. He was living with a fiery, tempestuous Mexican woman in her forties; his letters detailed their constant battles over other women. She was violent, scary—she often pulled knives on women she suspected of looking at him with lust. "Mexico has the highest murder rate in the world," John told me. "The women there are very passionate. Maybe too passionate." He missed Duncan a great deal. It had been years since he had someone on his wavelength to hang around with all the time. So in a way, I had stepped in to fill a void for him, too.

After only two months, I had fulfilled two of C.W.'s three prescriptions. I'd forsaken the lovely Cherry Blair along with her congregation, and I'd launched a dizzying assault on Marcy, the girl on the city desk. Before, our dealings had been marked by mild flirtation and one awkward lunch. But with John's guidance and advice, I unleashed upon her a phalanx of romantic weaponry: snippets of Victorian poetry sent to her computer queue, a ribbon-wrapped cassette tape bearing love themes from *Tristan und Isolde* and *Madama Butterfly,* and inducements to dine with me by candlelight at a little bistro John had selected near downtown. Marcy was unprepared for such an onslaught: she didn't know what hit her. When our affair reached its zenith, I took some lines of a Lord Byron poem John had trained me to memorize and whispered them against her ear as we struggled together with a passion I'd never dreamed of imagining with Cherry Blair:

> *She walks in beauty, like the night*
> *of cloudless climes and starry skies;*
> *And all that's best of dark, and bright*
> *meet in her aspect, and her eyes.*

John liked Marcy, but he didn't want me to go all mushy over some dame and neglect my studies. Stubbornly, though, I developed a deep crush, and for a few weeks my whole world was Marcy, Marcy, Marcy. Then she threw me over for a sportswriter and I saw with crystal clarity that the road John had laid before me was more important. Of course, it took several screwdrivers for this road to come into focus.

"It's okay to feel sad," John said. We were in our favorite bar, a place called Piaf's, where mostly actors and dancers and students from the S.M.U. arts department worked and ate and drank. "It's experience for your writing. Think of your heart as a muscle—Marcy is strengthening it, even now, as she lies beside some baseball writer and smells his beer and whatever that stuff is they put on the bats."

"This isn't making me feel better."

"In any case, you're a free man again. It's the best possible of events. You can make love with any woman on earth. Every night will be a romantic adventure." He moved his arm slowly to take in the crowded bar. "There are girls, girls, everywhere. Each one has a story. Each one is a novel, a play, a poem. Each one is a work of art, waiting for us to appreciate it. If we try, if we always aspire to a state of aesthetic bliss, we can discover things about these women no other men will ever know."

"Waitress!" I yelled toward the bar. "Another round."

John smiled at me proudly. "There's my boy."

But this sounds like we only thought of women. No, there were so many other things to love as well, things I'd never known before. There were Richard Strauss's "Four Last Songs"—written on his deathbed, at eighty-four, when he hadn't written such songs since he was our age! As we listened to the beatific Elisabeth Schwarzkopf perform Strauss's enchanting music, we sat limply on John's carpet, our eyes closed, and John translated the German, up to the last word of the last song, which was death.

I would go to John's place, leaving behind my singles complex in North Dallas as I headed for his artsy neighborhood near downtown, and we'd stay up late, writing in our journals at his old oak dining table, sipping cognac as he unveiled for me the music of Wagner, Sibelius, Puccini. We saw Baryshnikov perform with the Dallas Ballet, attended poetry readings at a bookstore on Lower Greenville. We went in my Firebird—John didn't have a car, and he's never had one since. It was yet another thing about him that was slightly Elizabethan. Late every night, we'd make forays to Piaf's in a state of aesthetic grace, and our flirtation with this dancer or that actress could not be denied. After a lifetime of loving women from afar, I was suddenly loving women all around me. There were so many of them, and they were all so wonderful.

To better coordinate our literary and woman-worshiping pursuits, we rented an apartment together in the summer of 1979. In his neighborhood, of course. My belongings were meager, the standard array of mismatched glassware and wicker furniture accumulated by a twenty-two-year-old male in the '70s. But John's holdings were massive. It took two weeks just to unpack his books—we constructed shelves to line every square inch of wall space, even along a wall in the bathroom. John arranged his library carefully, alphabetized by author, and categorized by genre—fiction, nonfiction, dance, film, theatre, poetry, and reference. Closer to the floor were hundreds of albums, mostly classical recordings. These, too, were carefully laid out, alphabetized by composer or band. Our apartment was an impressive place to walk into, and live in. Our plan was to write great novels and great plays there, and become famous and make love to beautiful French starlets.

In the spring of 1979, we saw the Sex Pistols at a shit-kicking roper joint called the Longhorn Ballroom. Punks were spitting on each other and breaking bottles, and we were in their midst as surely as we'd have been at the opening of the opera. "All forms of artistic expression are to be embraced!" John shouted, drunk on long-necks, in his combat boots and beat-up jeans. Then he pogoed into the crowd, banging away at skinheads. The very next night we were at the symphony in ill-fitting corduroy suits, listening to Rachmaninoff. We were live wires, tuned in to the world, up for anything. John had begun to write dance reviews for the *Herald* and I was reviewing rock concerts. "At this rate," John said, "by 1980 we'll be ruling the world."

We had a list of sacred things—at the very top: books. We copied a line out of John's journal—"Books are sacred"—and posted it with important notes by the phone. There were sacred events, too. The most sacred of all was the S.M.U. Literary Festival, where every November, a host of literary luminaries lit up the auditoriums and lecture halls. We'd sit rapturous, listening to their amazing prose, and every night there would be glamorous parties at some rich S.M.U. alum's Highland Park home. Bartenders with white gloves would pour the best liquors; fine food would be spooned from pewter trays. And of course all those wonderful S.M.U. dance and drama girls would be hovering everywhere.

At the Literary Festival in 1980, we heard John Cheever give a reading of his short story "The Swimmer." It was just after he won his Pulitzer. Sitting in the darkened auditorium, John and I were electrified, as much from the promise of the party to come as from the reading. Hours later, we were milling about the library of our third Highland Park mansion that week when a woman walked up to John.

"Do you like girls?" she said. She was an amazon—nearly six feet tall, with flowing dark hair, stiletto heels, and a short black dress. And she was staring into John's eyes.

"I beg your pardon?" John said.

"My friend and I were just discussing you and so I wondered whether you were the kind of person who likes girls."

"Well, certainly, most of them. Especially the inquisitive ones in black dresses."

She smiled, surprised, and took his arm. "That's wonderful." She looked at me, nodded toward a nearby redhead, said, "That's Jill," and pulled John into the crowded room outside.

The redhead sighed. "That's the last I'll see of her tonight. Say —where did you get that drink?"

John Cheever was drinking a glass of club soda in the kitchen, surrounded by undergraduates. But no John Branch. Jill and I were making a tour of the house an hour or so later, emboldened by drinks. She'd taught me a useful lesson about open bars: "There's always a long line at these parties, so when you get your turn, don't just ask for a drink. Ask for two doubles, shoot one right there, say 'Thank you!' and walk off with the other." We'd repeated this process three times, and soon we were bumping against a door in a dark upstairs bedroom.

"I'll bet a million dollars they're in there," Jill said. "I can hear Sarah breathing." No light came from beneath the bathroom door. "Shhh!" Jill said. We listened and heard a faint giggle. Then a gasp, and something like perfume bottles falling in a sink.

"Sarah! Let us *in!* It's Jill!"

A moment later the door opened; the amazon shushed us in and closed the door behind us. "I can't see a thing!"

"Jill, you're always interrupting me," Sarah whispered.

"Is that you, John?"

"Um, yes. Uh—huh!—how's the party?"

"Well . . ." Jill squeezed my hand, and we leaned against the inside of the door, listening to the sounds of John and Sarah making love. I felt Jill's lips at my ear. Her tongue stabbed inside and my head went *thwack!* against the door. Then Jill giggled and whispered, "You know, Sarah's husband is *right downstairs!*"

"You're kidding me!" I hissed. "We should get down there!"

"No way. I'm hiding from my husband, too."

A beat. "Oh."

We held hands, listening to the dangerous moans in the dark.

That night Sarah became our first asterisk girl. In a hallowed place on the oak dining table we kept a list of all the girls we loved, or wanted to love. "It's unseemly to just slap 'Sarah Alexander' on a list of mere mortals," John said. So we devised a new system: "transcendental" girls would have asterisks placed beside their names, a simple icon representing the inexpressible. Sarah Alexander was the first—her name had a certain regal formality, and in fact she led a not unserious life. She was an architect at a big firm downtown—she'd done some associate work once with I. M. Pei—and she was married to someone on the S.M.U. faculty. But Sarah was not the staid matron this brief résumé suggests. She was wild. She traveled constantly in her work and had a string of lovers strewn about the states. She was partial to tightly rolled marijuana cigarettes and anything that reeked of trouble.

There was one problem: the fact that Sarah's husband was an S.M.U. professor troubled John's conscience. John's scruples were such that he could readily launch an affair with any man's wife—even the wife of a friend—but screwing the wife of, say, a dedicated professor of Greek philosophy seemed somehow cruel. We imagined some doddering older man, his entire life wrapped up in the dubious joys of ancient study, imparting his wisdom daily to bored, spoiled rich kids. Imagine John's glee, then, when he bolted through our door two days after the party, with this bit of wondrous news: "Guess what? It seems that a Mr. Alexander is indeed on the S.M.U. faculty—but in the *business* school. He specializes in *corporate accounting*. This isn't an impediment—it's a *justification!*" John commenced to plunder Sarah with relish, his conscience clear.

Not long after John's affair with Sarah began, he and I bolted from the *Dallas Times Herald* in favor of a fledgling weekly. The *Dallas Observer* was an arts-oriented tabloid distributed free throughout the city, modeled after the Boston *Real Paper* and the Chicago *Weekly Reader*. We were offered $1,000 a month—to us, a staggering sum—to come aboard as contributing editors. John particularly was ecstatic—no more editing "Dear Abby" columns, no more layouts of the food section! He would be granted much more than his customary six or eight column inches for his dance and theatre reviews, and given the opportunity to direct the *Observer*'s arts coverage. It all sounded great, and in many ways it was. Few gave the *Observer* more than six months to live, but we would write for it well through the 1980s, seeing it through lean and green times.

Within a few months, the *Observer* was losing so much money its staff was trimmed by dozens, and soon John and I were just about the whole editorial staff. We worked sixty, seventy hours some weeks, staying up all night at typesetting machines, proofing pages and writing headlines. Cute young freelancers would drag in at 4 a.m. with late stories, reclining atop our desks as they watched us peel off line corrections. One girl was so persistently tardy with copy that she drove us nuts, but she made up for it by occasionally bringing us heart-shaped Mexican speed pills, which helped spur us on to another ten hours of typesetting.

When he wasn't wrestling with the *Observer*, John was wrestling with Sarah. Before that night at the Literary Festival, all of John's love affairs had been marked by a certain civility, a studiously observed beginning and end. He seduced his classical girlfriends—the ballerinas, the serious actresses, the bookish poets —with much handholding, hours spent listening to Schubert concertos, and steady supplies of wine and cheese. Sarah blew all that away. If John's life was all about order, hers—at least her chaotic social life—was about its opposite.

One night, fresh from a rendezvous with an oiled lifeguard in L.A., she appeared at our place with an early birthday present, four bottles of champagne. As she pulled to the curb she saw John—who thought Sarah was safely on the coast—leaning into an open car window, kissing some casual girlfriend goodnight. *Boom!* went the first bottle, narrowly missing John's feet. His other *amour* burned rubber, narrowly avoiding a new paint job as *Boom! Boom! Boom!* the other three bottles of Moet & Chandon exploded up and down the street, while poor John zigged and zagged, like a soldier dodging grenades.

Another time, Sarah used her husband's season tickets to lure John to the opera. He was interested in the work—Wagner's *Götterdämmerung*, part of the *Ring Cycle*—but Sarah had other ideas. John strode purposefully down the aisle just before curtain, knowing that Sarah's husband had excellent seats. She tugged him to a halt.

"I don't want to sit up there. Let's look for something quieter, in the back."

They ended up in the last row, which was shaded by a balcony and nearly empty but for them. Before the overture even got under way, Sarah had removed her panties and hooked a long leg over John's. When questioned later, John could recall little of the performance, but every detail of Sarah's. An elderly couple two rows ahead kept looking over their shoulders because Sarah had a habit of squeaking as she came. Finally, at the first intermission, they fled the Music Hall to screw unbridled in Sarah's car.

Their affair was intensely passionate, but it also had an edge of cruelty and gamesmanship. Sarah would sometimes phone him during out-of-town trips as she lay in bed with other lovers, making smacking noises as she said how much she missed him. At other times, she could be as dreamily romantic as John. As presents, she gave him first editions of some of his favorite books, and once a ribbon-wrapped stack of plays they had seen together or discussed. It was hard to imagine her as a serious architect during the day, but she was—that next Christmas, she gave John blueprints of their "dream home," featuring a wet bar the size of a swimming pool and a bedroom with built-in night-club, featuring cages where '60s go-go girls danced in the nude.

"Where's the nursery?" I asked John when he showed it to me.

"Don't kid me."

He had no illusions about a future with Sarah. He certainly didn't wish for her to get a divorce and marry him. "Better a few months of great romance than a lifetime of drudgery," he'd say. He felt marriage was a hollow, hopelessly bourgeois institution, unfulfilling and doomed to either banality or destruction. "Some people like to feel roped in by marriage," he said, "because otherwise they feel no reason to restrain themselves. But as Shaw said, 'If the prisoner is free, why lock him in? And if he's not, why pretend that he is?' " He considered great loves to be too blazing in intensity to withstand mortgages, yard work, and the squawking horror of small children. Romances were works of art, and we were artists; the trick was being able to accept it when the time came to move to the next canvas, to the next cool block of marble.

To be honest, Jill and I egged them on in their battles. Jill looked up to Sarah just as I did to John; like me, she was three years younger and existed in the shadow of her friend, admiring her but never quite living up to her exploits. Mirroring our idols, we naturally fell into a mini-affair of our own. Nothing like John's and Sarah's—we didn't fall in love and we didn't drive each other insane. We merely wrestled within earshot of our mentors, hoping they'd hear us and investigate. "I don't want her to *beat* me this time," Jill said, peeling her sweater over her head and collapsing drunkenly on my Posturepedic. "She *always* beats me." But we were a pale imitation of a real romantic war. After a few ineffectual attempts to convince our friends that we, too, were passionate lovers, we kept our shirts on and became allies in the struggle to stir up John and Sarah. We wanted fireworks, and on the nights—two or three a week at least—when Jill and Sarah evaded their husbands and partied around town with us, they rarely disappointed.

Through all of this, John was undergoing—not a metamorphosis, exactly, but a kind of evolution. Sarah was one symptom; he'd been drawn to her just as he'd been drawn to the Sex Pistols at the Longhorn Ballroom. Now a whole range of rough-edged, modern influences encroached on our rather stuffy writer's lair. His supply of "popular" records had expanded, in two years, from half-a-shelf to three, with other punk and new-wave albums scattered neatly beside the stereo. He rarely brought home classical albums anymore (he had the pick of review records from the *Herald* and *Observer*). If he did, they were by Steve Reich or Philip Glass—another deconstruction of the placid norm. He wasn't rejecting his more conservative passions—he still read literature, followed the arts—but he was no longer limited to them. Where once he required drawing rooms, intermissions, and glasses of sherry to woo women, now a stretch of asphalt outside a punk bar could suffice.

Sarah wasn't the only sun in John's romantic universe that year. They were apart weeks at a time, waiting each other out, battling and loving from afar; within these gaps John placed tiny samplers of affairs, romances like bite-sized chocolates—some sweet, some nutty, some spiked with liquor and wrapped in glittering costume. Mostly, they were in the vein of his old, classical girlfriends: artsy types, dancers and actresses, a girl who worked in a bookstore. Many of these affairs were chaste, involving little more than conversation, a book recommended and loaned, with a fetching note pressed within the dust jacket, a drink at cocktail hour on a rainy day, a decidedly John Branchesque kiss on a shy girl's hand. But chaste or not, John could be found most nights at his oak table, often till 4 or 5 a.m., smoking and recording his adventures in his journal.

It was about that time that John pronounced me "done," excused me from reading *Middlemarch* because I found it "hard to follow," and set me free upon the land. He rented an apartment in the Argyle, a converted 1920s red-brick hotel, and I moved into a tree-shaded duplex a few miles away. With this move our lives diverged a bit. For nearly four years, we'd been close, day-to-day friends. But now I was falling in with a gang of friends I knew from my *Herald* days. Perhaps I was growing weary of living the ethereal artist's life seven days a week. With these guys, I could watch Cowboys games instead of "Live from Lincoln Center." I could shoot baskets instead of write poetry, see the Yankees instead of the Joffrey Ballet. My diet became more balanced, but John and I would never be as close again.

I got out just in the nick of time. November 11, 1982, loomed directly before us—a date that went down in John's journals as the Night of the Great Calamity.

"I'm crazy for imagining this, if I am imagining it," John told me one afternoon, blowing on a cup of coffee. "But I think she may actually leave her husband. She calls me often in the middle of the night, with her husband asleep right beside her, and whispers 'I love you.'"

"Watch it, John. She must be up to something."

"I know, I know. But just suppose, mind you, just suppose she really does love me? Enough to leave him, I mean."

"You know how she is. She's just excited by the danger. And how do you even know it's her husband she's in bed with?"

John had it bad for her, worse than ever. In the last several weeks, he'd abandoned his *petites amours;* when Sarah wasn't around, he merely slaved at the *Observer* or sat smoking at his table, waiting for her to call.

November 11th came—how innocuous that day seemed in the dawn! How ordinary were our movements as we read our papers, called each other's answering machines, met at the *Observer* for the drive to John's. He'd just returned from a dance critics' workshop at Duke University, and Sarah had suggested a rare quartet reunion. By that evening, something portentous was in the air. Brooding clouds rolled in, dark as bruises; there was the sound of distant thunder. "It's Dostoyevsky's birthday," John said. "Almost anything can happen." Sarah and Jill arrived with odd promptness, and obviously had a good start.

"We've been drinking margaritas at Moctezuma's," Jill announced. Sarah just walked up to John and ran her tongue across his adam's apple.

"Well!" I said brightly, rubbing my hands together. "How about a nice liqueur?"

Sarah pulled away from John and fished around in her cavernous purse. "Aha." She pushed her fist out at us, turned it upward, like a kid in a Cracker Jack commercial, and unfolded her fingers to reveal four white tablets.

"Oh, Quaaludes!" Jill yelped. "Yay!"

John and I rarely did drugs—a glass of brandy and Prokofiev was all we needed to transport us—so we barely appreciated that these were among the last Quaaludes on the face of the earth. But within an hour or two, we were appreciating everything.

Sarah decided we should have a night of secrecy, so we avoided our usual haunts. Instead of a nice Piper Heidsieck at the Melrose, we settled for two bottles of André champagne ($2.79 a bottle), pulled by Jill from a gleaming, whooshing refrigerated case at 7-Eleven. John took the wheel of Jill's husband's Mercedes, since Jill wanted to be in the back with me, popping the plastic corks at passing cars. The first one careened off the lip of her door and ricocheted around the interior, setting loose a wave of cheap bubbly on her silk blouse.

"John, you *bumped* something," she said, slipping off the blouse. She wore nothing underneath. "David, be a darling and hold this out the window, okay? That way it'll dry faster. John, go really fast so the wind will get stronger."

We zoomed around awhile, chugging the André while Jill's blouse fluttered out my window like a battle flag. We finally stopped at a tavern in East Dallas, a place where no one would possibly know us. Its lovely name—Ships—was spelled out in unlighted letters above the door. Inside, a dozen or so retirees and blue-collar types sat at the bar, drinking beer and listening to Patsy Cline on the jukebox.

"Ooh, I *love* this place," Sarah said. "I think we should come here every night, from now on!" She glanced at Jill and bit her lip. "Honey, I think you could use a little blush."

"I think I could too." As Jill tiptoed toward the back, Sarah grabbed our arms.

"Listen," she said. "Jill wants us all to have a four-way tonight, which is fine with me. The only thing is, John, she wants to be with *you.*"

It took a moment for this to sink in; by then Jill had returned, her cheeks stained a rosy red, her pupils dilated happily. She leaned against me, clasped my hand in hers, pushed her nose in my neck. "Whoa . . . I don't believe I really need another drink."

"All right," said Sarah. "We'll just do some shooters and go back to John's."

It seemed only moments later that we were strewn about John's floor, listening to a tape by Missing Persons. I watched in a kind of slowed-down time as Sarah raised her eyebrows at John and glanced at Jill. John seemed terribly uncomfortable. This was obviously a test of some kind, arranged and imposed by the love of his life. But what to do? If he spurned Jill's desire and failed to admit his own, she might call him chicken. He'd look hopelessly bourgeois, tied to the humdrum, afraid of new sensations. But on the other hand, making love to Jill could have even more dire consequences.

He turned to Jill as if to speak. She closed her eyes and kind of swooned against him, unbuttoning her blouse. Their faces brushed together; their lips met, touching, then nipping and gnawing. John pushed her shoulders back and buried his face in her breasts.

There was this little crash. Sarah had decided she wanted to smoke; instead of fishing around for a cigarette, she had turned her purse upside down and dumped its contents on the hardwood floor. I jumped two feet—John and Jill were arrested in mid-kiss.

Sarah stared forlornly at the floor, oblivious of the cigarette pack beside her foot. "Well!" I said. "How 'bout if we spin some more discs?" Perhaps that would get things back on track—we could always forget about this and go dancing. But I made a mistake by playing the record on the turntable. It was "Accidents Will Happen" by Elvis Costello—John and Sarah's song. She bolted up and strode to the bathroom, with me right behind her.

"I can't believe it, I can't believe it. And I've been so faithful to him," Sarah sobbed, lying so baldly I almost laughed. "Every man I know tells me he's in love with me. When I'm in New York or L.A., famous men—celebrated men!—tell me they want to make love with me, but I won't. Well, this is it. It's over."

"Come on, Sarah, you forced him into that. He thought you wanted him to act cool."

"Well, he certainly didn't have to. Listen, can we just go? I want to get out of here."

Back in the living room, John and Jill sat at opposite ends of his couch, their hands folded in their laps. "Um, can I have your keys?" I said to Jill. She handed them over. After a moment, Sarah walked out majestically, her head high, her gaze aimed at the front door.

She jumped up and down on the landing outside, squealing with delight. "Now we have the car, now we have the car! They're stranded! It's like they're on 'Gilligan's Island'!"

"They're Mr. and Mrs. Howell," I said, climbing in the Mercedes.

"No—they're the Professor and Mary Ann!"

I was just drunk and 'luded out enough for the $40,000 car to have little meaning. There was a steering wheel, a windshield, a road that shone in the headlights with perfect clarity, and a tongue in my ear, with a breathy voice saying, "Let's go to my office downtown. I want to check my messages." I knew this was a harrowing night for John, but I was happy. An amazing asterisk girl was beside me, primed for revenge. She wore a suede minidress, so skimpy that it kept riding up against the leather seat, so high I could see her lavender panties. Sarah followed my gaze and quickly skimmed them off her long brown legs, hanging them on the rearview mirror "for luck."

A guard unlocked the door of a fifty-story tower and pulled out a ledger for us to sign. "I know we may seem drunk," Sarah said, stumbling a bit in her stiletto heels. "But we're here on official business. You see, I desperately need my T-square." We rode an elevator up forty floors with the light flicked off, "so that minimum-wage jerk-off won't peep on the TV monitor," and Sarah nuzzled me in the corner.

I had a brief moral crisis. Maybe this was *wrong*. Sarah was my best friend's greatest love. She was obviously upset, not to mention looped, incapable of making rational choices. If I went further—if I followed her, as I found myself doing, out of the elevator, beyond a glass entryway, down a hall and into a darkened office, if I watched her, as I did, silhouetted before tall windows, with the American West spreading toward the horizon outside, beyond where she stood dropping her dress to the floor, if I bit into this proffered fruit, I might be destroying friendships, wrecking marriages, turning whole worlds upside down.

On the other hand, there were all those things John taught me. I closed my eyes and saw him wagging a finger at me, quoting

Immanuel Kant: "Dare to Know!" And William Blake: "The road of excess leads to the palace of wisdom!" Even Lipps, Inc.: "Do it/Do it/Do it 'til you're satisfied." When push came to shove, John's training took over, and passionately, almost instinctively, I dissolved under Sarah's caresses.

John didn't blame me, not much, not really. I went by his place with Jill's car around six the next morning, having deposited Sarah at the end of her driveway. I'd expected to find John still up, pacing about, calling the police, cursing himself. But his apartment was dark. I let myself in and found him in bed with Jill, curled up naked and innocent as babies. I didn't confess the whole story to him until a week or so later, when all was already lost. He took it calmly, especially when I pointed out that his theories were partly to blame.

"You know my favorite saying of all?" he said glumly.

"Sure—from *Animal House*. The statue in the college square, with the plaque that reads, 'Knowledge is Good.' "

"Yes. Well," he said sadly, "I guess there are times when knowledge is not so good."

We both nodded our heads and reached for our journals.

John Branch, in the darkest states of abject lovesickness, would deal with his pain by adopting "the karate attitude," a fatalistic acceptance, a sense of inner peace. It was amazing the number of influences John brought to bear on his life: a mood, an evening, a whole stage of his existence might be shaped by some nugget of Confucianism, a set of treatises dating to the Napoleonic Wars, or a few lines from a song by Bow Wow Wow. He could persevere over heartbreak; it could even strengthen him.

For a few weeks after he lost Sarah, John sat across from me at Piaf's, nursing a brandy, staring through a new crop of *ballet jeunes* as if they were but mist. Slowly but surely they began to take shape before his eyes—a lovely shape—and he was once again a man of action.

He no longer needed one, but a few weeks later a terrible distraction occurred. Duncan Becker, his old friend from high school, was murdered in Mexico, poisoned by his jealous lover. After the funeral, Duncan's father carried out a provision in the will by giving John a cardboard box filled with thousands of pages of typescript, scribblings, and tequila-stained notes: *The Scheherazade Incident* was Duncan's science-fiction masterwork, his life's dream. In the event of his death, he wanted John to edit the book and see that it was published.

The magnitude of Duncan's achievement, the discipline and vigor he must have applied to producing such a work, made John's newspaper clippings seem to him like so much wastepaper. I argued with him; I thought he was a superb critic, not simply because of his intelligence and insight, but because he supported the most mumbling actor, held out hope for the clumsiest modern dancer. Reading a John Branch review, you actually *learned* about the theatre, about music and dance. If his advice was taken to heart it could prop up a bungled production, add zest to uninspired direction. I tried to convince him that his criticism, especially in the *Observer,* was essential and needed. But still he doubted the value of his work.

"As Max Beerbohm said, 'We are not liked, we critics.' And as George Bernard Shaw said, 'I have never been able to see how the duties of a critic, which consist largely of making painful remarks in public about the most sensitive of his fellow creatures, can be reconciled with the manners of a gentleman.'

"What I need to do," he pronounced, "is write a play. Something big, something great—maybe another *Importance of Being Earnest,* updated to the '80s." We were both prone to procrastination, so to spur himself onward he wrote a note on a yellow piece of paper, WORK ON THAT PLAY TODAY!, and taped it to the bathroom mirror.

John really intended to work on his play every day. But who could blame him for neglecting it? Sarah gave way to Elizabeth, a jewelry designer from New Mexico. She was a slow burn, but within a month she showed great promise toward asterisk status. When Elizabeth made trips to Taos, John was with Anna, Margaret, or Adrienne, and then of course there were always journal entries to dash off. Between Filter Kools and cups of coffee he'd jot down tributes to some new darling he'd uncovered at an R&B bar, or an erotic coupling that had occurred so recently his hand trembled as he wrote. And even though the life of a critic had paled for him, there was still rent to pay, peanut butter to purchase, glasses of beer to be bought. So he sprang from ballet to play, symphony to opera, typewriter to typesetting machine. For two years there were stories and music and all the women in the world—with such pleasant obstacles, how could John find time to write a play?

By the fall of 1984 John had had a successive string of asterisk girls, sweet, startling affairs that burned with white-hot intensity and then crashed, or fizzled out like a wet sparkler. Once he was caught in flagrante delicto by a suspicious husband; he somehow pulled through that horror unscathed, though he developed a nervous facial tic that lasted two weeks. Other times his dream girls—a punk jazz dancer, a financial analyst, a gourmet chef— just seemed to flow out of his life as dreamily as they'd entered it. He would mourn them sweetly for a week or two, then set his jaw and struggle forward.

In all that time I'd had just one asterisk girl, a girl I loved. Her name was Hilary Hardcastle. We'd even teetered on the brink of getting married; late one night, happy and drunk but facing insurmountable odds (she was already engaged) we called long-distance information and tried to get numbers for the governors of surrounding states, to see if you had to wait for a blood test to get a marriage license. We woke up the next morning hung over and hopeless. By October, we seemed through for good. Hilary had moved to her family's inn on the coast of Maine, and I wandered around half-dazed, stung by lost love.

One night I was at On the Air, a dark little bar Hilary and I had practically lived in, leaning against the wall watching a New Order video, mourning Hilary in the privacy of my own vodka tonic. Then a girl appeared, weaving through the crowd with Mozartean grace, turning near the video screen to dance with another girl. She danced sexily, moving her limbs more slowly than the tempo demanded, staring into the other girl's eyes. She wore tight black leggings, a shirt that had been unbuttoned and tied, baring her midriff against the heat. Her hair was honey-colored and straight; it gave off a light of its own when she tossed it in the air.

As she was leaving I touched her arm and produced a card. I'd scribbled an embarrassing note on it in my slightly drunken state. She looked up at me, focused intensely, and left, my card clutched in her hand.

If English hadn't been her second language she might have tossed my note, or worse yet kept it around as a laugh for her friends. Instead it must have charmed her. A few days later, a strange, heavily accented voice appeared on my answering machine: "Hello, Davit? Greta is calling. I have your letter, from the bar for dancing. Please call me at . . ."

Greta was twenty-two; she'd arrived in the states only a few weeks before to work as an au pair for a wealthy Highland Park couple. They had a two-year-old son, and preferred keeping him home to day-care. Greta had to stay at the house each day until six, then be available for babysitting in the evenings. But her nights were her own, and she'd just begun to explore. I felt that exhilaration of discovery prospectors must have felt in the 1800s, scooping up a glittering panful of gold. There was something haunting about Greta. She had a curving, angular face, gem-like blue eyes, that oblique accent, and a way of looking at you that suggested she knew every secret you'd ever tried to hide. And she was full of secrets herself.

I wasn't up to her. My romance legs were wobbly, my lines tangled and forgotten. I took her to a Fassbinder film at the repertory cinema, then out for dinner, but we didn't click. My usual approach—a frontal assault of humor, conversation, and gazes meant to be soulful and earnest—she fended off with ease, blowing cigarette smoke and staring abstractly through the haze. She had that air of sophistication that Europeans seem to acquire at birth, while more and more, over the next few weeks, I felt almost midwestern, like an aw-shucks farm boy.

But at least I could show her off to John. He'd discovered so many incredible asterisk girls over the years I felt overshadowed. Maybe if he saw me conquer our first international asterisk, I'd measure up in his eyes.

They were introduced on Halloween, when Greta and I picked up John for a party. We'd had maybe six dates, each more strained and awkward than the last, and hadn't come close to being lovers. But as far as John knew, we were in the midst of a great romance.

"Guten abend," he said as he bounded into the back seat of my Dodge. I thought, Oh, great, the German routine.

"Ah, guten abend!" Greta said, then she rattled off a hundred words of German, to which John merely smiled and shrugged his shoulders in surrender. "I only know a little," he confessed. "Do you know Strauss's 'Four Last Songs'?"

An hour later at the party, I was blindfolded and led through a dark room, where strangers dunked my hands in jars of brains and alleged eyeballs. Unbeknownst to me, Greta took this opportunity to slide her hand in John's and squeeze it. He wasn't sure what this meant—maybe just a gesture of friendship. But later they were alone in the kitchen, and she suddenly put her arms around him and clutched him to her. He stood there clumsily, patting her shoulders, wondering if she might be about to cry. When I walked in she pulled away, leaving to get a drink.

"What was that all about?" I said.

"I don't know. She just came up and hugged me. I think she's sad."

"She's probably drunk," I said, feigning an intimate understanding. "She gets drunk on two drinks."

When we left, I opened the door for Greta and walked around the car. As I made my oblivious circuit, Greta turned toward the back seat and said to John, "I like you very much."

"I like you too."

I opened my door and climbed in. "Well, John, we'd better get you on home before your parents get worried!" I may even have whistled while I drove, my hand perched warily on Greta's knee. There was no music on the radio—it had been stolen—so to the accompaniment of my nervous whistling, John and Greta looked at pumpkins blazing in the dark, furtively holding hands and sharing a private reverie.

The day after Halloween, Greta called him to talk about their attraction. "Last night," she said in her slow, musical accent, "David was looking at me but I was looking at you." She couldn't understand my proprietary behavior; as far as she was concerned, we'd only gone out as friends a few times, and on Halloween we'd gone out with John.

"He feels like he discovered you," John said, "the way, when you discover a gold mine, you have a claim on it."

There was a pause on the line; John pressed the receiver against his ear, thinking they might have been cut off. Then, in a voice and cadence strikingly reminiscent of Greta Garbo, she said, *I am not a gold mine.*

When they met alone for the first time, they didn't make love. Their attraction was tense and electric, and they agreed to luxuriate in it. They'd talked about fiction that first night; now Greta pulled from her bag a gift, one of the *Schrödinger's Cat* books by Robert Anton Wilson. They moved about the city discussing plays, the German educational system, and the designer drug

Ecstasy, making stops anywhere they thought they wouldn't see me. They ended the night at 4 a.m. in a gay bar, and by then they already had a song. It was one by Jan Hammer that goes, "Don't you know that I love you? Don't you know that I care?"

Greta wanted to keep their affair a secret. She feared hurting me, mostly because of a very sad story I'd told her which was in fact patently untrue—I'd heard Garrison Keillor tell it on the "Prairie Home Companion" and thought it might come in handy. It was a bittersweet story about a Minnesota kid who rode a bus miles to school and was assigned a "storm home" in the event of blizzards. We were on the dance floor of the Starck Club when I told it, and by the end Greta was holding me in a comforting embrace. She whispered in my ear, "I think, dip inside you, in your heart you are still a storm child."

Once or twice a week, I took Greta on "dates." I couldn't make a move toward her—probably it was too soon after Hilary, but I felt like I was back in 1978, swooning over Cherry Blair from six pews away. Meanwhile, Greta and John were burning with passion. What made this all truly a comedy was my continued insistence to John—contrary to what he knew firsthand—that things were going swimmingly with Greta and me.

"Yes, yes," I'd tell him on the phone. "Greta is my dream, my ideal. I'm going to see her tonight." This would be startling news to John, since he was planning to see her that night and was, in fact, lying beside her at that very moment.

Years later, when I read all of John's secret journals, I discovered their quiet affair. It was difficult to believe, not because John was incapable of treachery (it wasn't treacherous, because I barely knew Greta, but he thought it was treacherous, because he believed I thought I did), but because John went through so much ecstasy and pain with her for so many months, it seems impossible he could have hidden it from me. For one thing, he was living in my place at the time. He was between moves from his old Argyle apartment to a larger one upstairs, spending a couple months at my duplex to save the cash. Those two months were hectic ones for John. When he talked to her on the phone, he had to make sure I was nowhere near the extension. When I walked in the house, he'd often slap his journal shut and pitch it under his mattress. He went to great lengths to coordinate their evenings—successfully—so that I would never run into them.

There were times, in the first weeks of their affair, when Greta would not be able to look at John. Sometimes it happened when they were making love, and she'd push the heels of her hands against his shoulders until he drew back and saw she was crying. I'd noticed this well of sadness too, and attributed it to homesickness. John sensed it was something much deeper, but she held it back even from him. "I have three locks on my heart," she told him one night, as they lay together in his brand-new apartment, long after he thought she was asleep. "I cannot dislock it, ever again."

He held her close and kissed her hair, wondering what to say but coming up with nothing. All he knew was he wanted to dislock it, oh he wanted to dislock it. He would try as hard as any man could to help her, to love her, to learn how.

Since neither John nor Greta owned a car, their courtship was conducted by buses, by the cars of friends (mainly mine; I was constantly handing John my old BMW keys, while I spent nights at home, still moping about Hilary), and, when the hours got very late and most everyone else in the city slept, on foot. They'd end up in the strip of gay bars and restaurants two blocks from the Argyle, strolling to John's in the early morning all sweaty from dancing. He lent her Norman Spinrad's *Agent of Chaos* because she seemed to like intellectual fiction; this casual loan from his sacred library was enough to convince me he loved her. She gave him a wondrous stack of surprises: washed-out photocopies of self-portraits she'd taken in Berlin. In the photos she was nude, her nipples painted with rouge, her face made up like an Indian princess. Her hair was windswept, and dozens of necklaces choked her neck, dripped from her hair and fists, dangled from her clinched teeth. John was impressed with how stylish and uninhibited they were. But even in the photos, even in the nude, she seemed to have secrets. Her eyes looked out at you, yet they were looking far away.

As Sarah had, Greta had other lovers, some of them women. But she didn't seek them out to hurt John or prove a point. She needed something—there was an air of desperation about her that was hard to ignore, so John was understanding. She always came back to him. One night, after he'd been out reviewing a play called *And Things That Go Bump in the Night,* he returned home to find Greta sitting against his door, smoking patiently. She'd had a bad experience at Starck.

"The American men, they say they love you so fast," she said, annoyed. "They meet me at a bar and they say they love me. How can they love me? They don't even know me." She looked so beautiful in her angered state, sitting just so under a low-hanging light, that John pulled out a camera to photograph her. He tugged at her hair to make it wild-looking, as it had in her photos. She tugged at his. He splashed her with Krizia perfume, she took it and splashed some on him. Then he pulled back and snapped her looking so intense and turned on her eyes seemed black as coals, obscured by a cloud from her cigarette. It would prove to be a haunting photo, full of haunting memories for John.

Their affair was revealed to me months after it began. It was, John said later, "a perfect transition. It couldn't have been better accomplished if we'd planned it."

The three of us had dinner together one night. I'd seen Greta less and less, once a week at the most, and wasn't dating anyone else. I could admit to John that I'd failed with her, but I didn't have to. She still wanted to see me now and then, so I figured I could maintain the fiction indefinitely. This night, the three of us dragged back to John's place about 1 a.m., tired from drinking too much too early. The plan was to rest a bit, get a second wind, and go dancing. Greta had an idea.

"Let's take a nap," she said. It seemed an innocuous proposal. John and I had both met her au-pair family, seen her two-year-old charge, and knew she existed in a world where naps were expected and welcome. But as we stretched out on John's bed, Greta between us, a Smiths album playing softly from the next room, the concept of naps changed wildly. Greta softly stroked my hair, giggled and whispered, "My storm child." Then her hand left me, and through the darkness, through a slight tremor in the bed, I realized she was caressing John as well. My head was spinning; this was the most intimate I'd ever been with Greta. And as far as I knew John was equally in awe, moving shyly against her touch. She leaned back and kissed my shoulder; I kissed her forehead. Then she moved back to John. Gradually her attentions shifted entirely to him, until she brushed against me in the dark and said, "David, we need another girl for this bed."

Reluctantly, against my will, I realized she wanted to make love to John alone. I'd always figured she'd be attracted to him sooner or later, but never thought the timing would be so frustra-

ting. It's not just that I wanted to make love with her; I was
starved for affection. After three months with a broken heart, it
had felt so soothing when Greta touched my hair and whispered
to me. But I did my duty as one of the guys. John, at least, could
be happy. I made up some story about going to look for an extra
girl and took my leave. I tried to collect my coat, my keys, and
shoes as fast as I could, but I was unable to make it out the door
before I heard her first cries and moans.

For a year, Greta was a feature of John's life. He saw few
others, could love no one else. He was romantic about her in a
way I'd never seen before. "I feel not lucky, but positively
blessed," he told me one night. "I feel loved in spite of myself,
though we've never used the word 'love.' I think it scares her."
I had a girlfriend in New York named Desi who was very much
like her; in a way our affairs were similar, though John and
Greta were much more erotic together, much more romantic.
But whenever she felt she was getting too close, Greta pulled
away. Once he didn't see her for three weeks, while she went off
to live with another girl. She lost her job as an au pair—too
undependable, too many late nights. Toward the end, she could
barely wake up in the morning to watch the kid.

She moved in with John in the fall of 1985, "just temporary,"
she said, "until I found a job." Those few months were a happy
time for John. She was mysterious and fun again; they took
exotic photographs of each other, went out nearly every night
(except the nights when Greta disappeared with others), and
talked endlessly in noisy bars. John had long before planned a
trip to Mexico with two friends, but when it loomed nearer he
hesitated. He was worried about Greta—she had been sinking
into a new blue phase—but she urged him to go. So he left her
his keys, his bike, his apartment, everything he owned in the
world.

When he returned to Texas a week later, there was a stack of
notes written on little squares of construction paper in the middle of his oak table. The top one had words that ran up and down
in curving lines. It read:

JOHN I HOPE YOU HAD A NICE TIME IN MEXICO.

He read that and smiled. But then he moved it aside and saw
the second note. It was written in measured lines, like a poem.
This is what it said:

I am not a person to be loved.
I am not a girl to kiss
There is nothing anymore in me
to give
No ground to grow love
The body is empty

He was afraid to look at the third note. He poured a drink, sipped it, wondered where she'd gone to. Her things were gone from his room. He looked at the note:

Love—ice
Ice—no love
No love—nothing

The last one seemed like a good-bye. When he read it, John started to cry:

Lieber John,
that I could be here.

It took him two days to track down Greta's latest girlfriend. When he found her, she confirmed his worst fears.

"She went back to Germany," she said. "Didn't she leave you a note? She told me she was going to leave you a note."

John had almost seemed to relish his earlier breakups with women: the ballerinas who would graduate from S.M.U. and move back to El Paso; the fashion writers who would leave the *News* or *Herald* for papers back east; and of course the calamitous denouement of his affair with Sarah. He came out of those with a delicious sense of sadness and longing, living, for a week or two, on a diet of brandy and sighs. But he'd quickly be out on the town once more, his nails buffed, his scarf thrown round his neck, his repartee ready to spring on whatever vixen caught his fancy.

But after Greta he was inconsolable. He spent those first weeks burning up the transatlantic cable, trying to get a number for Greta in Heidelberg. He felt he had failed her, and agonized constantly over having gone to Mexico.

"But you couldn't have known, John," I said. "It wasn't you, it wasn't her, it was just the visa. If she had to go, maybe she wanted it that way, without a lot of good-byes."

For the first time, I had trouble luring him out at night. He sat in his apartment, smoking and reading all his journal entries about Greta, looking through their pictures, walking from room to room through a haze of despair.

His moodiness was bound to affect other aspects of his life. One day he walked into the editor's office at the *Dallas Observer* and resigned. He'd never been an ambitious man; he didn't aspire to Pulitzers or wealth, didn't even care to own a car. But he felt an urge to shake up his life, to make more of a difference somehow. He had friends at Stage #1, one of the rare theatres in town that rose above the mediocre and produced thoughtful, sometimes daring plays, and they thought John could be an asset. He became an associate producer with a salary, business cards, an office, the works. We went out and celebrated with champagne (more $2.79 André; he hadn't got a paycheck yet, and besides, after that night with Sarah, this had become our favored method of impromptu toasting).

"There will be many actresses, great plays, works of art that shake the stage," John proclaimed, coming out of the despond he'd been in for months. We talked of opening nights, grande dames in lovely furs, catapults to Broadway. He'd scour the country for excellent scripts, interview playwrights in faraway bars.

"You'll have plenty of time to work on your play," I said. (He still shaved every morning looking at WORK ON THAT PLAY TODAY!) "Then your theatre can put it on, with John Malkovich and Madonna in the starring roles, and it'll hit New York and London, and you'll be richer and more famous than, than—"

"Than John Malkovich."

But within a month or two of work at the theatre, his dreams were dispelled. The job of associate producer was quickly reduced to fund-raising, annoying rich people at society parties, working the phones to drum up cash. It was frustrating and artless, and it had a curious side effect: John was constantly surrounded by the young, idle rich. Neither of us had ever been interested in drugs, but John was moving in circles where coke filled the air like the white smoke in music videos. He indulged, I think, out of boredom as much as anything else. Months had passed since Greta fled for the Continent, and he'd found no passion to replace her with. He didn't have a real problem with drugs—he wasn't an addict—but it seemed, in those early days of 1986, that it was one of the few things he cared about any-more.

Eventually John pursued other flames. There was an actress— a bright, funny girl named Gwen—who was performing in a Gilbert and Sullivan musical. John was impressed with her voice, and sent a note backstage asking her to join him for a drink. I ran into them that night at the Inwood Lounge and was struck by John's lack of formality. In the old days, he would have bolted up upon seeing me, his heels clicking together, and bow slightly, introducing his newfound amour as if she were a Russian princess. Then he would have ordered a round of champagne and raved about her flawless talents, all the while holding her delicate hands in his, never taking his eyes off her.

Tonight, he seemed to be moving through the motions of his classic seduction. He introduced us, gesturing casually as if we were already old friends, and allowed us to make our own conversation while he cupped his palms against his hot glass and stared into the steam of an Irish coffee. His heart just wasn't in it anymore.

I had moved to New York a few months before that night, and in some ways John was becoming a stranger to me. The politics and frustrations of working in business—even though it was the theatre business—drove him crazier than the *Observer* ever had. And the job's accompanying perks left him physically exhausted and overtaken by a growing decadence. There was little of the idealism and purity of high art John and I used to know so well: mainly, his theatrical career was marked by Mezcal shots and speed with dissolute actors at 5 a.m., white lines of Peruvian flake in fluorescent-lit bathrooms, unendurable board meetings, and sex without romance. On my visits to Dallas, I could almost see the joy and inspiration being knocked out of him, like the precious stuffing from a fragile rag doll.

That November, John didn't go to the S.M.U. Literary Festival. Only a few years before, he and I would have attended every reading, hung on every scrap of poetry and prose, collected maps to every post-reading party, where yet another generation of musky-smelling coeds from the dance and drama departments would be lined up like the ships at Pearl Harbor, awaiting our romantic assaults. But this year, John forgot the Literary Festival was even coming up. He spent those evenings at home, reading *BYTE* magazine and *PC World.* He was developing an interest in computers, considering a change in careers.

I was worried about John, but felt too estranged from him to know how to help. Luckily for John, help arrived not long after Christmas in the form of an old friend and standby, that angel of mercy—an asterisk girl. But this girl wasn't old. She was in high school.

"She's perfect, a dream, a wonder," John said, describing her in a rare call to New York. "She's everything I need. I met her last week at the Starck Club."

Julie was one of those girls who begin appearing at cool clubs when they're only juniors in high school, because they look sophisticated and twenty-one. John had lost what Fitzgerald called "romantic readiness," but he got it back with Julie. She revitalized him. She was eighteen, a little rich girl with a background of private schools, traveling, and rebelliousness. She was, John felt, his savior, an angel sent to rescue him.

She did him wonders. It was as if he had found himself again —she was the unformed mind, the young kid yearning for wisdom and true sophistication, that I had been nearly ten years before. For the first time in years, John lived the classical life. He played her nearly his entire library of albums, from Antheil to Weill, showing her how Chopin's études were mirrored in the rhythmic complexities of a Brahms concerto. He gave her books to read, wangled comp tickets to the symphony. (He couldn't afford tickets to the symphony, and this too was good—he had left his job at the theatre and was freelancing for the *Observer,* poor but pure.) They stayed up most nights until 5 a.m., reading Nabokov and Proust aloud, or just staring into each other's eyes. Then she'd race home to her parents' and jump in bed by dawn. John wrote me long, wonderful letters, the first he'd sent me in years, filled with Julie—his enchantress, his life. "Last night," he wrote, "we discussed Love and Rockets, Philip Glass, Catholicism and death, Stanley Kubrick's directing style, and Ionesco. Before she left she borrowed a Steve Reich record (didn't know his music) and three books: Peter Dickinson's *The Last House Party,* Ursula K. LeGuin's *The Lathe of Heaven,* and Stanislaw Lem's *Imaginary Magnitude.* It seems she's read a lot of Lem— amazing."

I flew to Texas that spring and met her; she was shy about meeting me, clung to John. They had a private language, communicating wordlessly on a wavelength all their own. I felt as if I had walked in on them making love, their feelings were so apparent and forceful.

Like all asterisk girls, Julie had a wild side. Her best friend Allie was nineteen and worked at a swank men's club as a topless dancer. They would drop by John's after Allie's shift and lounge about drinking Mexican beers, eventually pulling off their blouses because they were in a topless mood. John, ever the elegant host, would move about in a happy trance, handing them cold Coronas and sliding discs on the stereo. Once, on a dare, Julie even danced topless with Allie at her club (Julie! John's life and hope and heart!), and made $200 in tips.

When we were alone the next day, John astonished me.

"I want to marry her."

I spat a mouthful of iced tea, Danny Thomas–style. "You *what?*"

He looked at me earnestly. "I am totally lost inside this girl. We've already started talking about it. She's going to Stanford in the fall, and I'll follow her to California after she settles in. After the first semester we can live together. And we've already talked about getting married when she's through with school. I'll get a job at one of the computer companies nearby—it's right in the middle of Silicon Valley. And nights, at home, I'll write plays. She'll be my inspiration."

"Wait, whoa—a *computer* job? You're serious about that stuff?"

John's *New Yorker* subscription had been lapsed for two years. His apartment, when I'd gone by to meet Julie, was crowded with neat stacks of *BYTE, MacWorld,* and other computer magazines. He'd constructed his own primitive computer out of cheap accessories, but I still thought this was a sort of hobby. John always did have a scientific curiosity. He was the only person I've ever known who subscribed to *The Atomic Scientist.* (Julie impressed him even in this regard; he was delighted to learn she knew the magazine *Aviation Week and Space Technology.*) And he was, indeed, serious about it all: working in computers, moving to the coast, marrying against all the advice of William Blake, Oscar Wilde, et al.

"When I swore I'd die a bachelor," he said now, quoting Shakespeare from *Much Ado about Nothing,* "I never knew I'd live to be married."

"Does it worry you that she's so young?"

"No. In many ways, you know, she's much older than me. We even each other out."

I didn't hear much from John for the next few months. I'd call him now and then and he sounded great. Things were wonderful. The summer breezed by and Julie got a lovely dark tan. She had become very fond of Henry James, which John considered a personal triumph. She went to Stanford in September, and every day John walked to the mailbox in front of the Argyle, sending another letter to his love. He tinkered on his computer constantly, studied books and articles about mainframes, wrote letters of application to a dozen firms near Julie's school. To make ends meet, since his income from *Observer* stories was slight, he took in a roommate—Gwen, his Gilbert and Sullivan actress, who had long since become a casual friend.

I flew to Dallas that November for Thanksgiving at my parents' and dropped by John's as a surprise. I had idle fantasies that Julie would be visiting too, her friend Allie would be there, and that they'd be in another topless mood.

Instead, Gwen answered the door.

"Oh hi," she said. "I thought you weren't coming down for Thanksgiving."

"Well, I developed this sudden urge for Mom's turkey. Is John home?"

"No, you just missed him. He went to 7-Eleven for microwave food, but he'll be back."

"Well, I think I'll wait for him here. I need to look something up."

I was working on a story and needed to work in a line from one of John's books—an in-joke of ours from the first chapter of Kierkegaard's *Either/Or.* But as I scanned John's many bookshelves, I noticed something wrong.

"Say, Gwen," I called to the next room. "Has John been loaning out his books? He used to be so panicky about that, and Julie can't have carted off this much."

"No—he's been selling them."

I couldn't have heard her right. I asked her again and she walked into the room.

"He's been selling them. He's been real broke lately, so when he needs money he just boxes up a shelf and takes it to Half Price Books."

"But—but they'd only give him about fifty cents for each of these!"

She shrugged her shoulders. "Before, when he was planning to move out with Julie, he had to get rid of most of them anyway."

My mind was still wrestling with the image of John boxing up books when I caught that "before."

"What? John's changed his plans? He's not moving to California?"

"Why should he ask for more grief? He's depressed enough as it is."

I looked at her blankly.

"You mean he never told you? Two months ago, just after Julie got to Stanford, she dumped him for another guy. An eighteen-year-old kid she met at registration. She didn't even have the nerve to tell John—she had her dancer friend call him with the news."

I collapsed on the couch, stunned. After a while I thought of something and walked to the bathroom. WORK ON THAT PLAY TODAY! wasn't there. There wasn't even any residue from the strips of tape—John must have spent a long time scrubbing it away, removing every trace.

When John came back from the 7-Eleven, he looked frazzled. He clutched a paper bag with a heated burrito and a pack of cigarettes, but he made no move to eat. He slumped on the couch. My expression told him I already knew.

"I just hadn't got around to telling you yet," he said. "I haven't wanted to think about it."

"I'm sorry, John."

He had been up for three days. He'd been doing speed lately, and it bothered him to sleep because he always had dreams about her. He hadn't written for the *Observer* in months and was incredibly broke. "Yesterday, all I had to eat was a mustard sandwich," he said. "But with two kinds of mustard. I've been devoting all my time—up to sixteen hours a day—creating a new computer program."

He still planned to move to Silicon Valley and get a job in computers. He mentioned buffers, instruction-processing rates, pixel interpolation algorithms, and wanting to create a new kind of artificial intelligence.

"John," I said sadly, "that stuff isn't for you. You're a *writer*. You're an artist."

"You don't understand—there's art to this, too. It's beautiful." He crinkled up the top of the paper sack, tightening and loosening it. A true love had let him down once too often; he could never depend on journalism, on editors or actors or temperamental directors. Now, it seemed, he hardly cared about his writing anymore. The only thing he could depend on was science.

"The beauty of a computer," he said, "is its hardware, and it acts like it." He managed a smile, but he kept sitting limply on the couch, the burrito sack in his lap, the weight of the world on his fragile heart.

A few months later, I told John I wanted to write a story about him. He was very helpful. He even offered me the use of his journals—his private, precious journals. In all the years I'd known him, I'd only read a scrap here, a page there, when he felt like showing me something. Once or twice we'd compared things, as when we read our vastly differing accounts of the Night of the Great Calamity. But now I had a stack of two dozen spiral notebooks, two feet high. Our decade as friends stretched out before me in amazing detail, from our bounding days as young aesthetes to the latest accounts of his struggle to survive Julie. I realized suddenly that everything John had ever wanted to accomplish was right here, in these journals. There were a thousand stories, a dozen novels, plays, poems, anthems to romance. Someday, I hoped, he would transform them into works of art.

I'll always think it was a work of providence that I took John's journals to New York. A month later, after Gwen had already moved out, John was evicted for nonpayment of rent. Movers came when John wasn't home and put everything he owned out on the Argyle's manicured lawn. People stopped their cars to scavenge through his possessions—his records, his books, the stuff of a lifetime. By the time he got there it was a mess. He picked up the heavy, framed print of his picture of Greta. The glass was cracked; a clump of dirt and grass clung to a corner. That photograph was his most precious object; of everything that had happened, what hurt him most was that all he had left of his greatest love had been paraded and broken on a public lawn.

But his journals were safe with me. They are the sum of his romantic and literary life, a testament to something inside him that surely can't have died. Some people I know are worried about John, but I haven't lost faith in him. He's just in a rough spot now, adrift, failed by love. I believe he'll make it through somehow, make it back toward his dreams and his promise, to the magic of the written word. Someday he will be the way he was on July 18, 1983, when he sat in Piaf's writing in his journal about some new love: "This afternoon we went to the park again and drank wine and ate some hard rolls from La Madeleine. As the ripples in the water passed, the sun grew brighter, the berried bushes surrounded us, the ground softened beneath us—the world shrank into a small sphere around us, it became a bright goblet and we were brandy, swirled about gently and cupped by warmth. It was one of those occasions that abound in a simple joy and with traces of wonder here and there . . ." He will be happy again, because John always was happy when he was falling in love.

2

the shaggy club

june

It's 90 degrees in the offices of KNON, the Voice of the People. On a barstool outside the broadcast booth, a fifteen-year-old boy with a blond mohawk and a black leather jacket looks as if he might start crying any second. His parents don't understand him —they think that because he's a punk he must be on drugs, breaking the law, and maybe becoming suicidal like all those kids in Plano. Last week, as he stood in the hall outside his parents' room, he heard them talking about putting him away in some kind of hospital. So tonight, he has come to the ramshackle KNON studio just east of downtown Dallas to be near someone he knows will understand him: Shaggy. Shaggy is older—she's seventeen—and she picks up stray kids like him all the time. She's a disc jockey at the community-supported station; her show, "The Pajama Party," runs Saturday nights from midnight to 4 a.m., sending out new-wave and punk music to people who never hear it anywhere else. Right now Shaggy is on the air, and the kid with the mohawk is waiting to talk to her. So are three people blinking on hold, a couple of guys with the Tokyo Dogs in the broadcast booth, and three sweltering punks banging on the locked door downstairs. Midway through "The Pajama Party's" Uncool Hour, Shaggy punches line one.

"Hello, you're on the air," she says.

"Um, yeah," says a girl with a North Dallas "Val" twang. "I just wanted to say that I think it's *really* uncool for your mom to like make you change channels because Suicidal Tendencies is on."

"Whoa!" Shaggy says. "Somebody wouldn't let you watch a Suicidal Tendencies video, right?"

"Right."

"Whoa! *Un*cool! What could be so terrible about Suicidal Tendencies?"

"I know," the girl says. "I feel the same way. Totally."

"Hey, what does your mom think about the band U2?"

"She *hates* 'em."

"She hates U2. Hey, Charlie," Shaggy says to a guy who keeps track of her albums, "bring me those lyrics. Hey, go get your mom. I want her to hear this."

"Are you serious?"

"Yeah. Turn up the radio real loud, okay?"

"Okay."

"Hey, Mom, are you listening?"

"Yeah, she's listening."

"Okay. Mom, this is a quote from a band that was inspired by other European punk bands. This is evil punk rock we're talking about here. And this is a line from one of their songs: 'And it's true we are immune,/When fact is fiction and TV is reality,/And today the millions cry,/We eat and drink while tomorrow they die./The real battle just begun./To claim the victory Jesus won,/On a Sunday, bloody Sunday.' And that's one of these terrible bands, right? Seriously, that's something I'm kind of into, so if she has any more questions she can call me, and I'd be more than happy to talk to her."

"Oh, wow," the girl says. "*Coo*-ool!"

"Okay. And I'll play some Suicidal Tendencies for you sometime."

Shaggy's real name is Nancy Moore; her nickname comes from British slang, as in, "I'm all shagged out, tired, bummed out." She has been doing "The Pajama Party" on KNON since she volunteered to be a DJ at the station in January 1984, when she was only sixteen.

A year ago this month, just after her seventeenth birthday, Shaggy moved out of her parents' house in North Dallas, where she'd lived all her life, and into an old Oak Lawn rented house called the Bill House with a bunch of teenage punks. She was becoming a minicelebrity of sorts, but she had a lot in common with her roommates: an exotic, razor-clipped haircut (hers had a dyed-blonde mohawk streak down the middle), a passion for loud punk rock, and a thrilling sense of freedom at being on her own, in an all-night carnival where everyone around her was her dearest, closest friend. One of her roommates had moved from Wichita Falls, not known as a mecca for punks, and one was up from her wealthy parents' home in New Orleans, slumming for kicks, her Audi parked out front. Nearly all of them had had trouble with their parents.

In a way, Shaggy had started her move to the Bill House years before, when she became a punk at age fourteen. Those last three years had been terribly unhappy ones for her; she felt alienated and alone at school (she was one of only two punks at Hillcrest High), and things were worse at home. Her father had Alzheimer's disease and hadn't worked since Shaggy was thirteen; her mother suffered from high blood pressure and arthritis and also couldn't work. The family lived on Social Security and disability checks. Shaggy got her first job when she was just twelve, taking phone orders at a pizza parlor near her house. She'd worked ever since then and used her own money to buy whatever she needed. Hanging out with other punks—going to new-wave concerts, dancing in the parking lot of the Hot Klüb when she was too young to fake her way inside, feeling that she was around interesting people who accepted her—was about the only thing that kept her going during those years. Shaggy, the youngest of four children and the only girl (her brothers were all grown and gone), was growing up in a crumbling, unhappy house with parents who were both in their sixties and who didn't understand her, who misinterpreted her punk lifestyle as something dangerous and obscene. She had to get out or she'd explode. The month before she left, she was so nervous and tense from trouble at school and home and worrying about her parents that she had to go to a hospital for a stress-related nerve disorder. But once she was in the Bill House, carrying in her stuff and picking out her room, she felt safe. For the first time in years she was in a place that felt like home.

If you listened to "The Pajama Party," you'd learn a lot about Shaggy. For one thing, you'd know about something else that has kept her going—religion. She's not boringly, obnoxiously religious; she just believes in it and wears crucifix earrings not merely as jewelry, like a lot of punks do. Sometimes she reads Scripture from the Bible during her show to startle people, keep them awake, and maybe inspire somebody. But she sticks to the coolest chapters, like in Revelation.

You'll hear her do that if you're in Dallas on a Saturday night, tuning in the far left end of the FM dial, looking for something different. You'll hear the staticky murmur of a sweet, excited girl's voice: "You're tuned to ninety-point-nine KNON, the Voice of the People. I'm Shaggy, and this is 'The Pajama Party.' So listen up. Get a move on. Crawl out from under that rock! Now, only by request, here's Wall of Voodoo. Or is that *Doo* doo? Whoops! Sorry! *Voo* doo!"

Shaggy spins Wall of Voodoo, the Pretenders, the Cure, the Psychedelic Furs, Depeche Mode, Midnight Oil, Gang of Four— bands that have almost never been heard on Dallas radio. Between cuts, she interviews local punk bands ("Yeah, like, um, we were going to bring in a tape with some of our stuff on it, but Danny forgot it"), she reads public-service announcements that reflect her station's leftist sympathies ("We need whatever you can send to help those poor Nicaraguan children—blankets, toys, clothing, shoes, amplifiers, air-to-air missiles"), and she opens her mike to an assortment of oddball punks and misguided youths who happen by KNON on their way to the Twilite Room or On the Air.

If you listened to "The Pajama Party" all the time, you would swear that you almost knew her. While she was seventeen, Shaggy grew up in the world and on the air.

july

It's a hot Saturday morning a week after the troubled kid with the mohawk came to Shaggy for advice. It turns out he really was on drugs, and his parents really are sending him to a hospital someplace. So it goes. Shaggy is supposed to be ready for breakfast at 11 a.m., but the Bill House looks awfully quiet. A tire swing sways gently from an oak tree in the front yard, and Mexican-American children are playing soccer in the quiet distance behind the high school across the street.

Shaggy comes to the door, rubbing her eyes and squinting at the blazing sunlight shooting at her unmercifully through the glass. She holds a finger to her lips. She's had as many as seven roommates the past couple of months, but right now she has just three—and one of them, Jennifer, who has the Audi and the only checkbook in the house, is moving out. Royce, who Shaggy met at a Clash concert in Wichita Falls a year ago, and Diana, a friend of Shaggy's from Hillcrest, are asleep. So are four or five kids, the dregs of a punk band from out of town that played the Twilite Room last night. Punks can seem intimidating, but when they're asleep they can't scowl or pose; even with their leather wrist bands and spiky, razor-chopped haircuts, they look terribly innocent and undernourished, babies with made-up faces.

Shaggy steps quietly toward her room near the back of the house. The walls are covered with posters of British punk bands like The Clash and Gang of Four. The furniture is a mélange of whatever the roommates have been able to wrangle from garage sales or their parents: a scratched end table here, a turquoise vinyl dining room chair there. In Shaggy's room there are posters tacked on posters. Beside her bed is a nightstand bearing a Bible, pictures of her father and grandmother, and a photo of a punk band called Lords of the New Church. Shaggy has to be quiet even in her room because Royce sleeps in a big walk-in closet off the foot of her bed. He's always coming home a couple of hours after Shaggy goes to sleep, jumping up and down on her bed to wake her up, giving her the latest gossip about what's happening at the Twilite Room and on the street. Last night he came in, drunk, to relate his latest adventure. After a long night out, he and a Mesquite cowgirl punk named Daze robbed a flagpole and divided the booty: she got the Texas flag, he got the Stars and Stripes. He's sleeping underneath them now, while Shaggy pulls on a pair of hightop basketball shoes that were autographed by the UK Subs. They're men's size 10's. Shaggy has a trim figure, but she has enormous feet and stands nearly six feet tall. Her hair varies. It's usually dark blonde, and sometimes she makes it stand on end, as if by static electricity. Other times, she combs it neatly and flat to the side, like a boy's. Today it just looks slept on.

"Do you know why we named this the Bill House?" she half-whispers, sitting at her vanity to run a brush experimentally through her hair. "One day we were all sitting out on the front porch, which we do a lot because it's a nice porch to sit on, and someone said, 'This house needs a name!' And this boy named Ernie said, out of nowhere, 'Bill!' And it stuck." She stands up, ties a black bandanna around her ankle, and slaps the thighs of her jeans, as if she expects dust to fly from them. She has to be at work at Sound Warehouse Records and Video by twelve-thirty, so a quick decision is made about breakfast: Chinese.

"My home life was kind of difficult," she says a few minutes later, wrapping a spongy Chinese pancake around some *mooshi* pork at the New Big Wong. "More difficult than most people my age have to go through. My dad's disabled, you know, and so basically I'm more independent than most people. It just made more sense for me to go ahead and get out and get started early, because I'm going to have to do it anyway."

When Shaggy moved out of her parents' house in May, a drama played itself out on the front lawn. Tensions had been boiling between them for weeks; at one point her mother threatened to put her in a mental institution. As Shaggy carried arm-loads of her things out to Diana's yellow Datsun, her mother screamed, "You're not taking that out of this house!" And Shaggy screamed back, "Fine! I don't want any of it! I don't ever want to set foot in this house again! I hate you!" For her first two weeks in the Bill House, Shaggy slept on a lawn chair, until she saved enough money to buy a bed at a garage sale for $40.

Ever since Shaggy became a punk, her mother had worried that she was on drugs, getting in trouble, turning out bad. That worry turned into fear and then into anger. Over the next three years things got worse and worse between them. Shaggy had found something in the punk scene—a sense of camaraderie, of freedom, of belonging—that she had never felt before and desperately needed. When she was out till two in the morning with Diana or her friend Naneen, trying to get into the Hot Klüb, standing around with her friends all punked out and talking, she was happy. Her mother saw something else, though. To her the punk stuff seemed violent, jarring, and she imagined the worst about the world her daughter had embraced.

"All three of her sons hadn't turned out like, you know, perfect kids," Shaggy says. "I was her only hope at perfection, at the cheerleader and the straight-A student. But that just wasn't me."

Her parents' house was suffocating her. It had fallen into disrepair and neglect; the kitchen stove stopped working and never got fixed, so everybody ate fast food out. And the house was jammed with years' worth of stuff Shaggy's parents refused to throw away: newspapers, coupons, receipts, trash, clutter. Each room had paths you had to walk through. Shaggy's friends—the few she ever allowed to see the inside of her house—were appalled and couldn't believe she could live like that. One told her she would have given up if it had been her.

"My mother and I went up and down, back and forth, vicious, vicious, vicious," Shaggy says. "I tried to make her understand. I would literally sit down and say, 'Mother, I want to *talk* to you. I don't want to *fight* with you anymore. I want to tell you the absolute truth about where I'm coming from.' And she'd just be like, 'Nyah nyah nyah nyah nyah!'

"But this whole time, I never lost respect for my mother. I got angry with her. I thought I'd never be able to forgive her. But I did. I've always felt like she and I had a lot in common. She used to run around with musicians and stuff when she was young. I think that's what scared her most, is she saw that in me. She was just afraid for me. Things are a lot better now. She came to the Bill House one day, and she started bringing me things. She was the first parental unit out of all those people to come to the house. I think she started to miss me."

Talking about her parents so much is starting to depress her, so she moves on to other things, to Royce and Diana, her "absolute favorite people in the whole world," and to the different kinds of punks in Dallas. They have a whole breakdown of classes: the skate punks, who like hard-core punk music and skull tattoos and big, wide skateboards; the posers, kids who like the fashion and affect British accents but don't have a clue about anything; the new wavers, friendly kids who hang out at On the Air and are pretty cool but not really political; original punks, who were around when it all started in the '70s and should have outgrown it but haven't, even though some of them are in their thirties now; the peace punks, who, like Shaggy, listen to positive bands like U2 and the Alarm and try to get along with everybody; and then there's the Pinky's crowd. They're the punk equivalent of high-school socialites. They get their name from Pinky's, a ritzy, chic boutique across the street from On the Air that sells stylish new-wave designs at absurdly high prices. The Pinky's crowd shops there, whipping out their fathers' Visa cards whenever they see something in the window they like. "I definitely don't dig that kind of crowd," Shaggy says. Otherwise, Shaggy doesn't align herself with any one group; she wants to speak to them all. As she says that, she realizes she is almost late for work. There are people wandering the streets who need to buy some records.

august

The GOP convention is coming to Dallas in one week, and everybody's talking about it. During the Democratic one in San Francisco, police arrested scores of rampaging punks on TV every day, so the hard-core punks in Dallas feel almost obligated to cause trouble. They always think they're behind what's going on in the punk scenes out in California anyway. In 1984, being a punk against Reagan is extremely fashionable.

KNON, which is plastered with bumper stickers and posters that say things like REAGAN-BUSH '84, NUCLEAR-WAR '85, is coordinating communications for some of the protest groups banding together in the August heat, and meanwhile Shaggy has had the owner of the Twilite Room on "The Pajama Party," urging the Dallas punks not to get talked into doing anything dumb. A Rock Against Reagan punk concert is scheduled for next weekend; there's talk that the Dead Kennedys will be coming down from New York to do the show.

Things are happening at the Bill House, too. After Jennifer drove off for good, taking her Audi and her checkbook with her, a twenty-year-old skate punk named Jenny moved in to share a room with Diana. Jenny and Diana were like best friends at first, but that went downhill fast when it turned out that Jenny liked to live in a clean house. Diana isn't that concerned about housekeeping, and besides, she bridles at any form of discipline or authority. So since the morning when Jenny woke Diana up at eight demanding that she sweep the floor, roommate relations have soured. Shaggy and Jenny get along great, though. After so many scrungy, irresponsible roommates, it's nice to have one who enjoys a living room that's free of spilled beer. Shaggy is changing. She's not as tense and tough as she was when she moved in a few months ago, and she's looking a lot straighter too. She cooks meat loaf, she mops the floors, she shakes out the welcome mat. More and more, she's getting into turning the Bill House into a home.

On this particular Sunday night, though, Shaggy is tipsy. She's leaning against a pillar at the 8.0. Bar, after drinking exactly one and one-third Tom Collinses. Since she rarely drinks, the small amount of gin has a dramatic effect on her. Her eyes seem in soft focus, like the eyes of models in *Penthouse*. If you knew Shaggy only over the radio, you'd never guess this was her: she looks like a woman. Her short hair is neatly styled, brushed carefully to one side. Her lips have lipstick on them. She's wearing a conservatively cut, gray, knee-length dress, panty hose, and high heels. She looks more like twenty-five than seventeen, which is how she got in without being asked for her ID.

The 8.0. is crowded; it's Sunday Night A-Go-Go, and people are dancing to a band called the Fact. The lead singer, a thin, blond, brown-eyed guy named Steve Powell, is singing "A Hard Day's Night." Shaggy is in love with him. She decides that she always has, and always will, love him. As she decides that, she sways slightly. She leans against her pillar, points her index finger to her heart, and says, "Ouch," just like ET. The sad part is that Powell's girlfriend is only ten feet away, running the band's sound board. Shaggy thinks they may be getting married, which arouses in her a resigned, bittersweet melancholy, complicated by the fact that she has barely even met Steve Powell. He's her only real local-band crush. She gets hysterically melancholy when Mike Peters of the Alarm comes to Dallas, or Bono of U2.

A guy Shaggy knows weaves his way through the 8.0. crowd and stops by her side, relating his latest woes concerning his girlfriend. Shaggy, who has been drifting just a little, suddenly gets crystal clear.

"Don't give up!" she says passionately. "You never know. There was this guy that I thought I'd never see again—he stole my heart. And he stole my bass, too. No, really! He really stole my bass. We were going out, and he like gave me his class ring and everything, and then I heard he was seeing this girl. And after a while he had this girl, his new girlfriend, call me up and ask for the ring back. Can you believe the unbelievable gall? So that was it. I said I'm never seeing or talking to this jerko guy again."

As if troubled by the memory, she sips one of the remaining thirds of her Tom Collins through a skinny red straw and looks up to glance at the Fact.

"And anyway, one day, *out of the blue,* I called him. And I've talked to him since then, and today he came by Sound Warehouse and filled out an application, and now we might be working together. So you see? You never know."

Apparently convinced, her lovesick friend heads back to the bar. Steve Powell is singing, "There's nothing I wouldn't do for a girl like you."

"I've never really had a *real* boyfriend that really added up to anything," Shaggy says, filling in the details about the guy who broke her heart. He was a senior from Mesquite High School when she met him in line at the *Rocky Horror Picture Show;* she was a freshman at Hillcrest. Her parents wouldn't let her date back then, so all they managed in the two months they saw each other were some stolen kisses by the Asteroids machine at a Preston Royal video arcade. Since then, the closest thing she's had to a boyfriend is two sort-of dates with a British guitarist named Rob, who came through Dallas twice with a San Francisco band named Toxic Reasons. There are also a few guys who call her all the time at her show. One, an Italian kid named John Valenti, sent money off to someplace so a star could officially be named after Shaggy. So far, though, the Italian boy is just a voice on the phone.

"Sometimes I'll wonder, gaw, I've *never* really had like a *boy*-friend, and I wonder why," Shaggy says. "And then I remember, hey, I'm only seventeen."

An hour later she catches a ride back to the Bill House. As she gets out of the car, she's a little unsteady on her heels. It may be because of the Bill House spectacle. At 2:15 on a Monday morning, it's lit up like the World's Fair. Punk music is blaring from Shaggy's ancient component stereo, and the living room, which can be seen from the street, is a mass of gesturing, yelling punks. A skater, meanwhile, is riding up and down the sidewalk along the relative quiet of Cole Avenue, his tennis shoes flat against his oversized skateboard. He's one of the kids from the skate pad down the street. They keep to themselves a lot. Some skaters wear combat boots and shave their heads and read *Thrasher* magazine and climb on speakers at the Twilite Room so they can jump on the heads of unsuspecting, dancing Pinky's types. But you'd never suspect that of this kid. He surfs along above the concrete, gliding in and out of the shadows the trees throw against the ground and back into the electric-blue haze of the city streetlights. He looks spooky, thoughtful, phantomlike. Shaggy thinks his name is Ari.

Someone comes out of the Bill House and tells Shaggy about a controversy brewing inside. Ernie, a New Orleans kid who once actually lived in England, has painted a sign that reads NO SKATE PUNKS ALLOWED, and taped it to the Bill House door. He was mad because he went to a skater party last week and the skaters had hung up their own sign, which read something like NO NEW WAVERS or NO POSERS. Since the Bill House is over-whelmingly pro-skate, it's an argument between Ernie and everybody else. Everyone expects Shaggy to come in and referee.

Even though she's the youngest of the roommates, younger than almost everybody that hangs around, her stature as a radio star, along with her maturity and her solidity, has made her something of a den mother at the Bill House. She's not really in the mood to fulfill the role tonight, though; she's a little bit drunk, and she's still feeling deliciously tragic about the singer at the 8.0. She feels happy because things are going right for her.

For one, she's getting along better with her mother than she has in her whole life. They went out for barbecue at the Easy Way a couple of weeks ago and had a nice, long talk. They told each other they never meant those things they said last spring. It was a mother-to-daughter talk, but it also felt like they were both grownups. They talked about their problems, what they could do to help each other. The next time Shaggy's mother came over, she was carrying a sack of groceries. She also brought Shaggy a desk, even though she keeps trying to talk her into moving back home. But there's no way—Shaggy is having the best summer of her life. She never realized how miserable she was at home until she moved out.

Diana, who has been getting more and more hard-core these days and becoming more and more like the skaters, storms out of the house, furious. "I hate *everybody* in there, Nancy," she says to Shaggy. "Except you, and sometimes Royce." After a couple of fruitless protests, Shaggy agrees to go inside. But she's not happy about it. Shaggy loves Diana as a friend, but Diana is beginning to drive her nuts as a roommate. That wild, careless, impetuous streak that makes Diana so fun to hang out with can be a severe pain when it comes to cleaning up the kitchen. And besides, some of the skaters Diana has been bringing into the Bill House just don't get along well with people.

Almost as soon as Shaggy gets in the door, the noise level from the house goes down. It gets so calm, you can hear the sounds Ari's skateboard makes as he takes another pass down the sidewalk out front. He keeps his eyes on the sidewalk, watching the oncoming cracks, and the wheels of his skateboard go ka-chunk, ka-*chunk,* ka-CHUNK, ka-CHUNK, ka-*chunk,* ka-chunk.

september

Diana is unbelievable. Like a lot of hard-core Dallas skaters, she got herself arrested during the GOP convention. Fed up with four days of boredom in 109-degree heat, fenced off from the action hundreds of yards away, and with almost no attention from TV camera crews, the punks took a frolicking rampage through downtown the day before everything ended. Their chief offense: playing with people's food at a ritzy Plaza of the Americas restaurant.

During the protest, Diana met some peace punks from Austin. After she got out of the Lew Sterrett Justice Center, she decided Austin was the place for her, and she asked a friend to help her move down there so she could go to Austin Community College and be with her new friends. Just like that. Now she's living with about a dozen other punks in something called the Twelfth Street House, two hundred miles south of Bill.

While Diana was getting arrested, Shaggy was taking a different approach to protesting. She was standing on some steps outside the convention center, reading out loud from her Bible, mainly antimaterialistic verses from the New Testament. The Republicans were pretty cool about it; some of them even stopped and listened for a while. Shaggy and Diana had been growing apart practically from the day they moved in together. It was great early on; once, at the drop of a hat, they took a bus to Austin to see a show by the UK Subs. After four days of drinking beer and getting no sleep at all, they were driving back to Oak Cliff at dawn in Diana's Datsun on a Sunday morning, with the sun bright and yellow through the buildings downtown and not a living thing in sight. They looked awful, with makeup all over them, their eyes red and puffy, and yet it felt like a perfect moment in life. They agreed that it was the funnest thing they'd ever done and that they were each other's best friends in the whole world.

But more and more these days, Shaggy is cooling out, calming down from the days last spring when she had beat her fist against the lockers at Hillcrest if someone looked at her funny. Now that Diana is gone and Shaggy has started classes in the predominantly minority North Dallas High School across the street, the Bill House is running more smoothly. It may stay that way if Royce doesn't do the wrong thing. He's been thinking about moving into an apartment with Jennifer, the girl from New Orleans, so he can save some money. That would bum Shaggy out —just too many changes at once. Royce has been hanging out these days at the Starck Club downtown; it's an icy-cool disco with valet parking and a $10 cover, and it makes the Twilite Room look like a Texaco men's room. You can get in free if you know someone, and Royce is becoming the kind of person who knows someone in places like that.

Just after nine on a warm Saturday night in September, Shaggy calls me.

"What are you doing exactly right at this moment?" she demands. "What? A TV dinner? But I have baked chicken! I have baked potatoes! Open the oven, take it out, open your kitchen door, throw it on the lawn, and come over, okay?"

Twenty minutes later at the Bill House, there's a surprise on the living room floor. It's Diana, sorting through some record albums, looking for any that might be hers. She's up from Austin for a pretrial hearing about the protest and is staying in her old room with Jenny. Since she's been in Austin, she's gotten a radical haircut. Not one of those $50 cuts some Pinky's kids get at sleek Oak Lawn salons—hers looks like somebody did it with a crude pair of shears, in an alcoholic stupor. It's shaved so close to her skull on both sides and around the back that you can make out the marks of the teeth from the shears. "I think Nancy is in the kitchen," Diana says.

It's not Shaggy in the kitchen; it's Daze, the punk from Mesquite who helped Royce steal those flags. She's blonde, rather stoutly built, with a ragged, wide mohawk and a black leather jacket dripping chains and bright buttons slung over her shoulder. She's holding a can of Old Milwaukee in one hand and stirring a pot on the stove with the other.

"Hi," she says. "Want a taste? It's a Bill House feast. I came in, and Nancy just said, 'Daze, c'mere, make sure this doesn't burn while I go and take a shower.' " She goes back to her task, rolling the spoon around and around with what seems to be tremendous concentration. Daze is wearing a pair of painted Converse All Star tennis shoes; one of them has a spur attached. "I left the other one in a cowboy," she says.

Royce strolls in wearing a courageous mismatch of Salvation Army store plaids and polyesters. It's one of his looks. A twisted ribbon of blond hair sprays down into his face like freesia, but he makes no effort to brush it away.

"Hey, Royce," Daze says, "has the cat been fed?"

"The cat's dead," Royce says cryptically, seconds before a furry gray kitten skittles up and nuzzles innocently against his shoe.

Out in the living room, Jenny is looking through records and grinding her teeth at the prissy-pop Depeche Mode album someone has put on. She's pretty, with striking blue eyes and movie-star lips. When she walks into the kitchen, something more appropriately hard-core is blasting from the stereo. She pulls a fork from the drawer and, dodging Daze's proprietary spoon, spikes a chunk of potato. "Oh!" she yells, waving at her half-open mouth and rushing to check the oven. Two layers of an angel food cake are inside; it's for two friends of hers due in by car tonight from Meridian, Mississippi. Since Jenny works weekdays as a secretary, Saturdays are like holidays to her, and she's in a good mood. She's wearing a tight white tank top and faded-away jeans that are slit across the back of the left thigh. White cotton strings dangle from the split like angel hair, fluttering with every step she takes.

"Nancy, come eat your chicken!" Jenny yells down the hall. "We've already eaten your potatoes!"

The bathroom door down the hall opens, and Shaggy bounds out, wrapped in a beach towel. "Hi!" she says, slapping her forehead to say, yeah, I'm stupid, I'm late, I'm running behind, people are stealing my potatoes. She looks lanky and awkward, walking on the balls of her bare feet and pushing her wet hair back off her forehead. It doesn't help matters when Royce runs after her, whooping and nipping at her towel with his fingertips, chasing her into her bedroom. From the kitchen you can hear them laughing and screaming and then talking in their language, in which they drop their jaws, expose their bottom rows of teeth, and talk with a British accent, so that everything comes out like "finnah-finnah."

"You know what I love?" Diana is saying in the living room. "I love coming into town and taking the house over." She changes the record and puts on ultimate hard core by the Vandals—a punk version of the theme to *The Good, the Bad and the Ugly.* It's an instant hit. Everybody runs into the living room and starts slam-square dancing. Jenny's wearing a pair of bright red cowboy boots she bought this morning at a garage sale for $1.50, and she's stomping them joyfully on the hardwood floor, in time to the music.

After a while, when things calm down and a relatively sedate Meat Joy album is playing, everybody sits around listening to Diana talk about Austin. The punks are real divided there, she says, compared with the friendly partyers in Dallas. "Sometimes I'd rather be at a small scene," she says, "like in Dallas, where everybody has more fun." She tugs distractedly at her oversized T-shirt, which bears the warning CAUSE FOR ALARM.

Shaggy comes in from her room, wearing jeans and a T-shirt, her hair still wet and spiky. She switches the subject to something depressing: school. She's been going to North Dallas High right across the street for three weeks now, and though it's cooler in some ways than Hillcrest was, in others it's the same old boring waste of time. And now Shaggy can just sleep in if she feels like it on school mornings, since there's no mother around to kick her butt out of bed. She's been doing that a lot. She's also been asking people's advice about whether she should drop out, get a GED, and go to college later. With school, Sound Warehouse, and "The Pajama Party," she barely has time to eat anymore, and she's always run-down and tired.

A little while later, Shaggy sets up dinner for two on a round table out on the porch, under a bare hundred-watt bulb. There's a tablecloth, a fresh stick of butter on a dish, mismatched silverware, plastic Chanello's Pizza cups, and paper towels folded up carefully beneath the knives and spoons. It's an oddly domestic scene; the punks who skate by forty feet away regard it as if it's a mirage or some kind of elaborate joke. Shaggy sits down and tries to start eating but keeps getting interrupted by phone calls.

"That was Mr. John Spath," she says, rushing back to the table after her third call. "He's like a kid who brings me records to play on the show, and he's real cool, 'cause he's nothing but just a kid at heart."

She sits down, forks up a chunk of potato, and draws it toward her mouth. Before it gets there, Diana swoops out on the porch, stopping a few inches from Shaggy's raised fork. "Wait!" she screams. "What's that?"

"Potatoes."

Diana looks at the laden fork, her mouth open, and stares at the potatoes, willing them into her mouth. When Shaggy gives her the bite, she says, "Where's the chicken?"

"You want chicken?"

Diana nods, her mouth wide open.

"A simple 'Arf' will do," Shaggy says, sending the bite of chicken home.

"You're a *god,* Nancy," Diana says, bounding back inside.

There's a breeze on the porch, a yellow moon is coming up over the soccer field across the street, and the chicken and potatoes are delicious. Diana goes off on an errand, and Jenny strolls out to test her boots; they make gratifying *clunks* on the porch and look like bright red lipsticks against the weathered boards. "A lot has happened out here in front of the house," Shaggy says.

"One day," she recalls, thinking back on the blasé destructo attitude of past Bill House regulars, "I went out on the porch, and I saw that all of these glasses I had bought when we first moved in were all over the porch, and people were just sitting there looking at them, and they'd been there for like two days. And I go, 'You know, it would be really nice if, when everybody goes back inside, you would just pick up one glass and take it to the kitchen.' And they all looked at me like I was crazy. They had this impression that I was being their mother or something, scolding them, and I just got really fed up. And all of a sudden—the straw that broke the camel's back—I saw that one of my glasses had been tipped over and was *broken.* And I flew into a rage and started picking up glasses and throwing them on the sidewalk, going, 'Okay, we'll see how many glasses we can break. Let's break *all* of them, and then nobody can break anything.' And they were like, 'Nancy, what's your problem? If you wouldn't gripe at us so much about keeping the house clean, then maybe we'd do it.' And I'm like, 'Naaa, don't give me that.' And at that moment, I realized that this was like my subconscious saying all those things, and I was really saying them to my parents. Which is almost psychotic, you know?"

She sips her milk and gets quiet for a while, like she always does when she talks about her parents. Then she dabs at her lips with a paper towel and smiles. "It just goes to show," she says, "that no matter how bad things get, they can always get better."

Things don't stay quiet for long. People are starting to come by with records for "The Pajama Party." A party's going on at the skate pad down the street, and now and then it overflows and spills into the Bill House. In the kitchen Jenny is wailing with despair because her angel food cake looks like an old mattress. Shaggy gets keyed up and frantic, pitching albums into a white laundry basket, tossing boring 45s across the house as if they were Frisbees. In less than half an hour, Shaggy will be live.

october

Royce is gone. He moved into Jennifer's place, and it looks like they may be moving together to her old hometown, New Orleans. Royce is tired of his job driving a Slush Puppies truck and dreams of becoming a famous hairstylist on the Bayou. It didn't bother Shaggy too much when Diana moved away, but Royce is her last connection with the early days of the Bill House, with the best summer and happiest time of her life. And anyway, Royce has been running around with a real trendy crowd this last month or so, going to the Starck Club all the time. His new friends are the ultrahip, ultrafashion-conscious, recreational-drug-oriented crowd that Shaggy has never taken to, just a shade or two away from the unbearable, squealing Pinky's punks. Shaggy and Royce hardly ever go out like they used to, when they'd ramble around town from Tango to the Twilite Room, acting like outrageous twins.

Now Jenny and Shaggy have a new roommate, a girl who works at a vintage clothing store on Lower Greenville and has a pet rat that she dyed pink. She takes her rat everywhere, slipping it into her purse when she goes into clubs or goes to work. In the Bill House she walks around with the rat on her shoulder, following Shaggy and Diana from room to room, talking nonstop in a soft, distracted drone. She comes from a large family, and Shaggy thinks she has never gotten much attention. It's really kind of sad.

Tonight—the first cool Saturday of October—Shaggy is an hour into "The Pajama Party." Since she quit school last week—something she'd been leading up to for a long time—she has become a full-time music person. There's her job at Sound Warehouse, and there's the station. It's a couple of miles due east of downtown Dallas, behind a bunch of used-car lots on Ross Avenue *("¡Se Habla Español!")*. KNON shares a two-story clapboard house with Acorn, a left-leaning community activist group, in a neighborhood where the front lawns of apartment houses are dotted with pay phones and Coke machines. To get inside late at night, you have to push a button that makes a light blink in the broadcast booth upstairs. Then you hope the DJ notices it and sends someone down to let you in.

Elicia, one of Shaggy's informal assistants, unlocks the front door just after 1 a.m. Her job is answering the phone lines and, more important, letting as few people in as possible. She's a big blonde girl with wild, suggestive eyes and messy, spaghettilike stalks of hair. Elicia leads the way up a winding staircase, passing a sign that reads NO BEER BEYOND THIS POINT.—KNON BOARD. The walls of the studio are speckled with flyers and posters reflecting the station's mishmash of playlists—bluegrass, gospel, Latin, Celtic, American Indian, Cajun, Vietnamese, Indian, and punk. Leftist bumper stickers (NO EUROSHIMA: STOP THE MISSILES) fill in the blank spaces on the walls. Everywhere on the floor there are cardboard boxes jammed with record albums donated by KNON listeners.

"Here's something I haven't played in a long time," Shaggy is saying into her mike. She flicks a switch, and one of the two turntables to her right spins into "Doesn't Somebody Want To Be Wanted" by the Partridge Family. Instantly, the station's three phone lines light up. Elicia goes through them at her desk outside the booth, then sticks her head in the door.

"Negative calls on the Partridge Family, Shag," she says. "One guy said, 'Keep playing that and you'll go out of business,' and another one said, 'Maybe you should wait just as long to play it again.'"

"Well, too bad," Shaggy says, twirling around in an ancient office chair held together by duct tape. "It's on my promo, so I'll play it when I want." To get even, the next song she plays is by the Monkees.

The floor space in Shaggy's booth is about four by eight feet; her white basket of albums is in the middle, and a guy named Charlie is perched against the wall on a stool. He writes down every song Shaggy plays on a playlist stuck to a clipboard. John Spath, Shaggy's cool-kid friend, has brought records by once again. He has curly black hair, and an enormous black T-shirt hangs on his thin body. Almost every guy Shaggy knows looks like he could use a good, hot meal. John Spath is hanging around the studio with two other guys who play in his psychedelic band, the Mel Coolies ("You know, just like on 'Dick Van Dyke' ").

"Okay," Shaggy says, "the current cabin pressure is twenty-three point five and one-third percent per square inch." Her voice is in fine form tonight. Most of the time it sounds like it's about to break into laughter. She gives it her ultimate test, dropping into a deep, blaring FM style: "Coming up, a double shot of Psychedelic *Furs!* Only on Niiiinety Point Nine, the *rawwwwwk* of Dallas!" She settles back in her chair, opens up a notebook, and practices the promo she'll read on the air in a minute. The first one that interests her is about a shelter for battered women. "A woman is battered every eighteen seconds in America," she reads, "then fried." She is straying from the text. "Every eighteen seconds, a woman is battered and deep-fried to a crackly crunch. A special this week only at Long John Silver's: a battered women platter with shrimp and hush puppies. Only three ninety-nine!" When she reads the public service announcement on the air, she does it straight.

Elicia sticks her head in. " 'Kill the Poor' by the Dead Kennedys," she says. "A fifteen-year-old girl in North Dallas would *really* like to hear it." Before playing the Dead Kennedys, Shaggy interrupts the show for a sermonette.

"Earlier tonight," she says to Pajama Partygoers everywhere, "I was standing in line at Burger King, waiting to get a burger. It was taking a long time. And then I heard this man behind me talking about the ethnic qualities of the Burger King employees. And I thought, you know, how terrible! I am *so* sick of prejudice, but then it occurred to me that it's easy for us to say it's bad when other people are wrong. But when do we consider ourselves? And when do we think about the bad things *we* do? Think about it." She puts on a record and turns to face everybody in the booth. She's a little embarrassed. "Hey," she says, wiping her face clean of any expression and holding her hands up in peace signs. "Peace! Love!"

The Mel Coolies are having fun, which means they're causing trouble. They're all racing around Elicia's desk, answering the phones and saying dumb things, tapping on Shaggy's window and making faces through the glass while she's on the air.

"Could y'all shut that door, please?" Shaggy asks impatiently. The guys' voices keep carrying into her mike. Shaggy tries to pick up a call on hold, but there's just static on the line. "Elicia!" she screams, "will you *please* answer the phones?"

"That's what I'm trying to get them to let me do."

"Well, tell them to stop, okay?"

Elicia walks out to the guys and says, "You've been disbarred."

A few new stragglers are wandering around in the office when someone says a guy named Ward is on the line for Shaggy. "Oh, great!" she says. "Hey, everybody, *shh, shh,* okay? Really. I've got to have quiet." She picks up the phone, purses her lips, and says, "Ward? I'm worried about the Beaver."

Ward is a friend of hers. The last time they talked, Shaggy was kind of depressed. Since then, she has dropped out of school, which has chilled her out and calmed her down. "No, I gave up being grim," she tells him now. "I was grim for my whole life. Hold on—this record's freaking out. Shit! Okay. *What?* No! Of course not! Do you think I'd put *that* on the radio?" When they finish talking, Shaggy has agreed to play something else for him. "Okay, well, ten-four, Ward. Till then, may the Force be with you. And don't be grim, okay?"

Shaggy takes another call, leaning forward with her hand over her ear to hear better. After a long time, she hangs up. "She called me last week and was going, 'Oh, no, I think I'm pregnant,'" Shaggy explains. "And I basically gave her the scoop on what to do, gave her a little moral support, told her to get some professional advice. It turns out she wasn't, though, so I told her some things maybe to think about in the future." Sometimes Shaggy is a teen punk Ann Landers; last week a girl called who had taken some drugs and was freaking out. Shaggy talked to her, tried to calm her down, played a couple of songs for her. "I like it when they do that," she says. "Sometimes kids treat me like some kind of star, but I'd rather they treat me as just a friend."

One of the Mel Coolies nudges John Spath. "John Spath," he says, "we have to go. If there's a party to go back to."

People keep calling in with requests and calling back fifteen minutes later wanting to know what happened to them. "KNON," Shaggy says, when Elicia is busy with two other lines. "Yeah. Hi. Yeah, just keep it in your pants a minute, dude. Okay. Bye." She slams down the receiver. "That *guy* needs to calm *down!*"

At 3:16 in the morning, after a series of calamities involving skipping records, badly timed intros, and jerko callers, Shaggy sits back in her chair, pulls her knees up to her chin, and sighs. "Patheticness," she says.

After a while the light from downstairs blinks. It's close to four, the show is nearly over, and Brother Joe Norvell has already arrived in a blue suit, with a box of gospel records and what seems like the weight of the world on his shoulders. Elicia goes down to see who's at the door. It's Royce and his friend Keith. They're wearing their customary mismatched vintage plaids and polyesters, several shirttails out each. Shaggy is real glad to see Royce; she misses him, even though Jenny is furious that he hasn't squared his share of the bills yet. Jenny is another reason Shaggy doesn't see Royce so much these days. Here, away from the Bill House, they're back on neutral ground. Friendly ground.

Royce spots Shaggy's sermonette burger to the left of the controls. The ketchup on the wrapper has clotted to a deep, dark red. "Hey," he says, "are you going to eat the rest of that burger?"

"No," Shaggy says, "you can have it. Do you really want it?"

"Yes, I'm starving. So what are you doing after the show?"

Shaggy hands him the quarter-moon-shaped burger. "Well, raising hell, of course, with you."

december

Christmas is coming, the end of 1984. For the first time since she was fourteen and singing lead for the Spuratics—a group that split up after its third gig—Shaggy has a band. They don't have a name yet, but things are rolling. She's been practicing her bass a lot, and the Niteman, a DJ at KNON whose show runs just before Shaggy's, plays harmonica and guitar and does vocals.

He's a twenty-seven-year-old Harvard M.B.A. who got bored with business a year ago and showed up at KNON with a good record collection and an uncanny voice: he can imitate Bing Crosby one second and Joe Strummer of the Clash the next and have them both doing "White Christmas." He's also blond, blue-eyed, and smoothly handsome, nice assets for a lead singer. On lead guitar is a guy they call the Mighty Quinn; the Niteman met him while they were camping out for Bruce Springsteen tickets. Quinn is thirty-one, divorced, has a kid. Nowadays the three of them hang out together all the time. They jam old sixties rock-and-roll songs in the Niteman's Lower Greenville house, sometimes with a bunch of gawky Harvard M.B.A.'s hanging around wearing slacks and trying to seem loose. The Niteman's M.B.A. is behind him—now he wears leather jackets, black hightops, and pink-and-black bandanas. But he still has all these Ivy League pals. What he needs is a drummer.

Back at the Bill House—well, Royce moved to New Orleans. Jenny had to move back in with her parents so she could save money to go to the University of Texas. The roommate with the pink rat shaved her head almost completely bald and began telling everyone that Sid Vicious was actually Jesus Christ. She moved out in November for parts unknown. Shaggy's only room-mate now is a twenty-four-year-old drummer named Fish, who plays for Unterwasser and works as a manager at the 8.0. He and Shaggy have to split the Bill House's entire $475-a-month rent, plus bills.

After "The Pajama Party" tonight, Shaggy goes to the Lucas B&B, an all-night diner in Oak Lawn. A little before 5 a.m., she is jammed into a corner booth with Elicia, the Niteman, and four other guys, who all look pretty normal. The coming of cold weather has delighted Shaggy because it means she can wear her most prized possession: a weather-beaten white leather jacket with six-inch-long fringe spilling out from the sleeves and back. She bought it years ago on layaway at a vintage clothing store and loves to run down the street with her arms out to the side, like wings.

The only other customers at Lucas B&B are a smattering of gays fresh from the clubs on Cedar Springs, a couple of cops, and a few newspaper route drivers. On the air tonight, Shaggy said the apocalypse was coming because the earth is getting hotter every year. But now she's concerned only about her waffles. Lucas B&B is famous for its waffles, and Shaggy is starving.

"Hey," says the Niteman, slouching in the corner of the booth next to Shaggy, "how come you cats ain't got anything to munch on?"

"No money," says Jerry, a guy with a motorcycle cap near the end of the booth. "I've got five bucks to last me till Tuesday." Most of the others are similarly strapped, except for a scrawny kid who is almost getting squeezed out of the end of the booth; he has ordered a cheeseburger, a salad, and fries, which seems spectacularly extravagant at a time when all the others are feeling the Christmas budget crunch.

Shaggy is eating her waffles, and the Niteman entertains the table by doing imitations of Joe Strummer, who sings like he's got gravel in his mouth and isn't happy about it. The Niteman sucks in his cheeks, bulges out his eyes, and growls his way through "Silent Night" and "My Way."

"Next," says Jerry, "here's the new one by the Waffles." Everybody laughs. Jerry has given in to temptation and ordered some waffles with his remaining five bucks, and now everybody else is giving in too. Shaggy's disappearing order, swimming in butter and syrup, is impossible to resist.

"Here's the extended, remixed, EP dance mix of the Waffles' latest hit," says Shaggy, laughing.

"Boy, I'd like to make the Waffles video," Elicia says.

"Our children are growing up without valuable training as to how they can protect themselves against waffles," Shaggy intones in a Cockney-accented PSA voice. "Three thousand people die from waffles every day—that's nineteen thousand every year. These waffles are devastating our children. They eat them every night at 4:30 a.m. Ladies and gentlemen, it's not too late. Our children can be saved. Join Waffle Stompers of America."

The scrawny, starved-looking kid at the edge of the booth has finished his burger and fries. He's now unwrapping packages of Premium Saltines and eating them too.

When Shaggy gets home, it's nearly six in the morning. Sometimes, a long time ago, the Bill House would still be all lit up, and an Alarm album would be pumping from the stereo. But tonight the house is absolutely black and quiet—nobody is home. No music, not even a skate punk gliding by outside. Shaggy unlocks the door and walks inside. It's strange, like entering the house of a murder victim, looking for clues. On nights like this, when Fish doesn't come home, Shaggy can't sleep. She keeps a baseball bat in bed with her.

"It's so good to hear nothing," Shaggy says as she plugs in the blinking Christmas tree lights to give the place some life. "I go to work, and I listen to music all day. I get home, on goes the stereo. And at twelve o'clock, I go to KNON—more music."

In her new room, the one that used to be Jenny's and Diana's and a few other people's, Shaggy shows where she has put all her stuff. Her posters are more spread out on the walls, and her vanity has come out of the closet, just like Royce did when he inherited Jennifer's room last summer. On a cork bulletin board near her bed, Shaggy has found room to pin up more photographs. One is a picture of her dad holding her by her arms when she was just a baby, taking tiny, tentative steps across her parents' front lawn.

"You know, I look at that picture," Shaggy says, sitting on the edge of her bed, "and sometimes I think that my dad's really messed up a lot. He didn't save any money or buy much insurance, didn't plan in case something happened, and so he can't put me through college. But I look at that picture, and I know he taught me how to walk, you know? It means a lot to me."

She's coming down from the buzz of the show, from the buzz of the sugary waffles. It's her pattern on Sunday mornings. She'll be reeling off something amazingly important one second, talking about going somewhere and doing something, and the next second she'll just crash.

"Did I tell you yet," she says after a while, "that I've decided to move back and live with my parents again? Maybe as soon as New Year's. From day one, you know, my mother has wanted me to move back home. She'd be a lot cooler about things now— she'd have to be. I've proved that I can make it out on my own." She reaches down as if to untie her shoelaces, then realizes she's wearing her black boots. She's too tired to pull them off.

"I just realized I can't afford it here anymore," she says. "And I really need to save money and get a car and get some other things. Then I started thinking about their house, and how in a few years I may be inheriting it. There's so much that needs to be done first. My parents say that if I come home and take over the house payment, which is about a hundred and ten dollars, when the mortgage is paid off in a few years they'll put the house in my name. Just being back there will help a lot, making it so that my mother doesn't have to worry about how she's going to pay the bills and not have to worry about watching after my dad all the time. You just have to see it to understand. They've been miserable for a really long time. Just for the sake of ironing things out, I'd like to see my parents happy there, just once."

Shaggy pulls her legs and boots up onto her bed and talks about how much she misses Royce and Diana. She knows these are her last days in the Bill House, so when she walks through it she keeps bursting into tears: at the bathroom sink, where Diana did all her weird hair coloring; outside her closet, where Royce used to crash after waking her up with some wild tale; at the kitchen counter, where Jenny mourned over her mattress cake. She misses everybody who used to live here, who would be making noise and messes and trouble if this were a Saturday night in July.

"We used to do this thing with safety pins," she says out of the blue. "They were a real hoot back then. We'd rig it up to make it look like the safety pin was going through our cheeks. But I grew out of that. Not 'grow' in the sense of getting older, but 'grow' in the sense of finding yourself, knowing exactly what you want to do so you don't have to be anxious all the time. It's still fun—I still get in the mood to do that stuff once in a while. Like you're down at the Twilite Room and you just feel like being *tough* all of a sudden, so you're in the parking lot and you break a bottle or something, you know, to get that old feeling back."

She doesn't want to be alone yet, to go to sleep yet, even though she's tired. "I'm sleepy, but I'm restless," she says. "I feel like there's still something to do. You know, I can remember when I'd stay up forty-eight hours at a time. Now, I don't know, sometimes I feel really old. No, I don't. Not really. Even though I really do. As old as the hills."

3

cruising

It was 9:30 on a Friday night in November, and the stretch of Forest Lane between Cromwell and Rosser was ablaze with light: streetlights, headlights, taillights, Burger King lights, and the flashing red lights of Dallas Police Department patrol cars. It was one of those landmark Friday nights the cops on the Northwest Dallas beat always prepare for: the first Friday after the end of the regular high-school football season. The kids were on the streets with cash in their pockets, gas in their cars, and nothing to do, and most of them would end up cruising Forest sometime during the night, just as they had on the first Friday night of the school year and the Friday night after the homecoming football game, and as they would the Friday before the senior prom. The kids came from high schools all over Dallas—Woodrow Wilson, Bryan Adams, Skyline, Highland Park, but mainly Thomas Jefferson ("TJ") and W. T. White, two schools that lie a few miles apart to the north and south of Forest. And they came from suburban schools, from Plano and Richardson and Wylie and even from Fort Worth, more than thirty miles away—kids who had heard of the legendary cruising strip in North Dallas and wanted to get out on it.

Ever since the early '60s, high-school kids have been driving out to Forest Lane on weekend nights to cruise aimlessly up and down, drink beer, smoke joints, eat pizza, drag-race, throw things from car to car, and (the vast majority of them being boys) chase girls. No one knows for sure why they picked Forest Lane in the first place. It's in a dry part of Dallas, and it's certainly not a major entertainment strip like Lemmon Avenue or Greenville Avenue. It runs about fifteen miles across North Dallas, from Farmers Branch in the west to Garland in the east, through an almost exclusively residential belt of the city. The part of Forest where everyone cruises is exactly 1.2 miles long—the distance between the two legal U-turns. You can't see any houses along most of this part of Forest; over the years, the homeowners whose houses back up to the street have grown twelve-foot-tall hedges and erected fences and brick walls to barricade themselves against the adolescent weekend nights. Who can blame them? There are teenagers all over the world, but on Forest Lane the culture of high-school kids has for some reason found its Gilded Age. It is in full and unbridled flower here.

On this Friday night in November at the Jack-in-the-Box in the heart of the Forest Lane strip, a seventeen-year-old named Ken was leaning against his father's candy-apple-red '79 Firebird, his thumbs hooked in his pockets, watching the traffic shoot by a few feet away. Ken is a senior at Plano High School, the son of the president of a small computer company, and a lifelong resident of the northern suburbs of Dallas. He was cruising that night with his friend and classmate Jack. They were looking for girls. Early on in the evening, in fact, they had actually met girls—two pretty blondes cruising in a white Trans Am, but Ken and Jack had lost them in the traffic. They had cruised for another hour or so, and then they had repaired to a quiet residential street near TJ—a secret spot Ken had discovered in his junior year—to drink beer and talk about girls and cars. Ken's pride and joy, a "hopped-up, totally rod" '70 Mustang he'd bought the year before with money saved from years of throwing papers, cooking french fries, and selling slabs of Bermuda grass, was back home in Plano, safely parked in his parents' driveway. It's a "ticket car," one that looks so hot that it gets pulled over by the cops patrolling Forest as an hourly matter of principle, and he didn't want to bring it out to Forest anymore. Too many hassles.

They were back out on the strip now, leaning against the car at the Jack-in-the-Box, with a six-pack gone and a little buzz going. In the right lane of westbound Forest, cars honked, girls squealed, and one guy even mooned, but Ken didn't flinch. On Forest, the whole point of everything is staying cool. Not everyone is good at it—most of the kids breezing by Ken and his Firebird were borderline nerds, just cool enough to know Forest is the place to be on Friday night but not cool enough to know you don't go out on it in a Dodge Coronet. A year ago Ken probably wouldn't have been out on Forest, but during the summer his girlfriend moved to Houston, and ever since there hasn't been anything better to do. Ken is not a borderline nerd. He is compact and good-looking, with brown hair and dark eyes that seem to take things in without much surprise or interest. He is of the cool breed, the fast breed. He drinks, he drives a hot car, and he even races if the time and place are right. Jack is more boyish looking, less bold, less tough. But when Ken gets them in jams on Forest, Jack backs him up.

The wind was whipping now, cold, but a good crowd was sticking to Forest. Ken and Jack got in the Firebird and pushed a tape—Judas Priest, a heavy-metal group—into the dash. Ken pulled a tin of Copenhagen from the pocket of his Plano High School Marching Band jacket and stuck a healthy pinch of the stuff in his mouth. A Skoal spittoon on the Firebird's console was already sloshing with an hour's worth of rank, brown spit. "Here we go," he said.

They pulled out in front of a big pack of cars and slowed down to 25, so the cars behind would have to pass on the left and right. They let a Duster with a W. T. White sticker and two girls inside pass by—"Oh, my God! Ugly, ugly!"—and got in a fifty-yard-long line of cars to make a U-turn near Northtown Mall. On the pass back to the east, Ken spotted a Granada with a Berkner High sticker and two girls in front, two *great* girls. He pulled even with them, rolled down his window, and shouted out over the wind and the traffic noise, "Wanna get laid?"

The girl on the passenger side rolled down her window and said, "What?"

"What school do you go to?" Ken shouted.

"Berkner. In Richardson."

Going good, going good. Got 'em talking, and that's better than usual.

"So what are y'all doing?" Ken almost smacked into a pickup in the right lane. He slowed to 15 to match the girls' speed.

The girl in the passenger seat whispered to her friend and looked back, giggling. "Oh, nothing. Just cruising around."

"You know Chris Walker?" Ken yelled. "Goes to Berkner."

"Is he a senior?"

"Yeah."

"I don't know. I know who he is, maybe, but I don't know him."

"So, what's—" Crap. Two guys in a beat-up GTO had pulled up on the other side of the girls, and now the girls were talking to *them*. Jack leaned out his window and looked over the Granada at the guys in the GTO. "Hey," he yelled at the girls, "don't talk to them! They're nothing! Worthless!"

The girls didn't turn around.

Five circuits later, a huge old Cadillac with three girls in it, two brunettes in front and a blonde in the back, pulled up in the right lane beside the Firebird. The driver had her window down, and she actually talked *first*.

"Hey, guys, what school do y'all go to?"

"Plano," Jack said, and the girls exploded with laughter and variations on the word "gross." They said they went to Highland Park, Plano's archrival and nemesis on the football field. They all joked about it, and then the girls said, "Follow us." They pulled into the left-turn lane and parked in the empty lot of the Park Forest Shopping Center.

Ken and Jack wheeled in after them, of course. When they stepped out of the Firebird onto the asphalt, the ground felt almost magical beneath their feet. Girls—girls they had picked up on Forest—were walking toward them from just a few feet away. This was what they were out there for, after all. Every guy on Forest Lane, whether he's fifteen and driving his mother's Gremlin with a beginner's license or nineteen and looking back longingly on his high-school days, cruises Forest for only one reason: getting girls. Unfortunately, the girls are also on Forest for only one reason: to stick together while they flirt with the guys and then get home before their curfews. Therein lies the irony of Forest Lane. Every weekend for nearly two decades, some five hundred guys have cruised Forest looking to get girls.

That means that young men have driven up and down that strip more than half-a-million times with their eyes peeled for squad cars and their minds on just one thing, and it often seems that not once in any of those half-million attempts has one single kid ever succeeded in his quest. But they keep trying.

Jack and Ken fell instantly in love with the blonde, a seventeen-year-old senior. Her friends weren't bad either. The guys were getting somewhere talking to those girls in the Park Forest parking lot—really making it—when a dirty Pontiac LeMans pulled up. A spotlight shone in their eyes, and the cop behind the wheel said, "Y'all know you're trespassing?"

Of course they did.

"Well, yeah, okay," Jack muttered. "Guess we'll go."

The cop winked at them. He was stocky, about fifty, with a gray flattop and an enormous forearm that he hung out his open window. "Y'all have a good weekend, now."

As the cop pulled away, Ken spit Copenhagen juice and said, in a voice he thought was too soft for the cop to hear, "Aww, fuck you, you fuckin' pig." The LeMans's brake lights went on ten feet away, and then its reverse lights. The cop had heard.

Ken and Jack stood still, numb with terror, as the cop got out of his car in a rage. "I try to be nice to you punks, I could give you a two-hundred-dollar fine, even take you downtown, but I try to be nice and what do I get? You make me sick, with your dirty mouths. Give me some ID!" He looked over at the Highland Park girls, who were staring dumbly, as if they were bystanders at the scene of some hideous accident. "You girls best just ride on out of here," he said. The girls waved haltingly at Ken and Jack and drove away.

The cop took the guys' driver's licenses and flicked them angrily against his gun belt, over and over. "You boys know what I could do with you?"

"No, sir," they whispered in unison. That's all you say to cops on Forest, "Yes, sir" and "No, sir." "Fuckin' pig" is a serious mistake.

"I could take you downtown and put you both in jail right now," he said. "What would your mommies think about that? Would you like that?"

"No, sir."

The cop threw some more hell at them, then walked back to his unmarked car. "You stand there," he said, "while I go call these in." He drove out onto Forest and headed west. Ten minutes later, Jack and Ken were still standing there, freezing, wondering if they would ever see the cop or their driver's licenses again.

I went cruising on Forest with Ken and Jack to see if things had changed since I cruised on it as a senior at TJ back in '75. Those were different times, simpler times, I guess, for guys cruising Forest. The outcry from the residential community had yet to reach a crescendo, you could make U-turns just about anywhere if you saw girls driving by the other way, you didn't get in trouble for hanging around the fast-food restaurant parking lots, and the speed limit was 35 all along the strip instead of 30; in fact, you could hold it at 40 all night and get away with it. The CB craze was at its height then—it seemed like every kid at TJ got one for Christmas—and this made it tough as hell for cops trying to scratch out radar traps near Middlekauff Ford. Everybody always knew where they were.

But, God, if only I could have cruised in '72, the last year Forest Lane was wide open. Until '72, those huge shopping-center parking lots on the south side of Forest were always crowded with kids, hundreds of them, circling their cars together and hanging out. They'd gather in front of the FedMart and leave in their wake tons of beer bottles, cigarette butts, potato chip sacks, and burnt rubber. Then the FedMart threw its weight behind a keep-the-punks-off-the-lots campaign, and all the other stores signed petitions except for a gas station and a couple of quickie grocery stores that counted on the kids for business. "No Trespassing" signs went up, and things were never the same again.

Back then the TJ–W. T. White rivalry was at its peak; the W. T. White kids thought TJ was full of greasy, low-class trash, and the TJ kids, including me, thought W. T. White was full of money-coddled social climbers. The TJ–W. T. White homecoming game was an occasion for storied parking-lot fistfights at Loos Field, followed by especially fevered cruising on Forest; now the two schools are in different districts, and they don't play each other on homecoming weekend anymore. In the old days, the half-mile-long cinder-block wall that ran along the north side of Forest between Midway and Rosser was covered with graffiti on the order of TAMMY IS A DORK. But some art students at (where else?) W. T. White got the idea that it was an eyesore and could be covered over with colorful, life-affirming art. They spent months painting the entire wall with castles, clouds, and sunsets, and today their paintings are still there. Probably the only person who likes the wall in its present state is Tammy.

I used to cruise Forest with Charlie Stout and Jerry Shields, my best friends at TJ. I worked after school at the photo counter of a Skillern's drugstore, and every Friday night at ten, as soon as I got off, I'd meet Charlie and Jerry and we'd hit Forest. Jerry was an unsuccessful candidate for student council president that year, and Charlie was an ex-ROTC nerd who had seen the light, bought a Camaro Type LT, and transformed himself into a cool Forest Lane cruiser. We never actually got girls on Forest, but there was one legendary night when Charlie and Jerry came close. They persuaded two Ursuline Academy girls named Susan and Hope to actually get in Charlie's car and go to a Pizza Inn with them, and no doubt things would have gotten even wilder than that if Jerry hadn't called Hope "Faith" by mistake. Even on the night of our senior prom—a night on which we had *dates*— we heard Forest's siren call. The prom was at the Hilton downtown. We took the girls—in three separate cars in case one of us got lucky—to dinner at Ports o' Call atop the Southland Life building, danced the last dance (Chicago's "Color My World") at the prom, and then, in our tuxedoed finery, with a bottle of champagne stuck under the front seat of Jerry's Malibu, headed for the only logical place: Forest Lane, and a romantic nighttime breakfast at Kip's Big Boy.

We stopped cruising Forest the year after graduation. It's a funny thing, but when you're fourteen or fifteen you don't think about Forest; you don't even know about it. And when you're nineteen or twenty, you're caught up with college life or your job, and it seems way in the past, something you're supposed to leave behind. But for those three years in between, Forest Lane is everything. You go to school and work at your minimum-wage job just so you can drive out there at night to burn away from yellow lights and eat Super Tacos in parked cars, to feel like you're in control of part of your life at least, like you belong to something secret and cool and powerful. It's amazing how fast it slips away.

Jerry's married now, to a kindergarten teacher he met while they were both students at Baylor. They rent a house in the country outside Hallsville; Jerry works in Beaumont as an electronic data processing auditor for a division of Eastman Kodak. Charlie got married twenty days after Jerry—we had to rent tuxedos one more time—to an assistant manager of a telephone answering service, just as his four-year tour in the Air Force was ending. He lives with his wife in Lubbock, where he works nights as a computer operator for a bank and is studying to be an air traffic controller. I'm the last bachelor.

Ken and Jack had been standing in the freezing wind of the Park Forest Shopping Center parking lot for more than twenty minutes before the cop's dirty LeMans finally rolled back up. It stopped thirty feet away, its headlight beams hitting the boys' legs, and the cop spoke briefly with a motorcycle cop who had driven up beside him. The cop on the motorcycle drove off, causing Ken and Jack to sigh with relief. "Motor pigs" are the most feared cops on Forest; the cop in the car, they could take. He got out of his LeMans and walked up to them.

"You boys don't know how lucky you are," he said, in the voice of an executioner whose ax has been taken from his hands. "My sergeant is in a good mood tonight. If it was up to me, I'd take you downtown now and throw the both of you in a cell." He was yelling about five inches away from their faces, his eyes red with rage. "I'd give you both a two-hundred-dollar fine for trespassing, but then I'd've had to give one to those nice girls, too, and I didn't want to do that, not because of some punk with a dirty mouth."

He pushed the licenses into Ken's hand and jabbed a finger into his chest.

"I don't want to see you wrong up here again. You hear me?"

"Yes, sir," they said together.

"If I catch you wrong on Forest again, that's it, you're going downtown. You got that?"

"Yes, sir."

Back on Forest, Ken blew into his hand and sniffed. "I smell like beer?" he asked.

"Naw," Jack said.

"Hey, man, then we lucked out. I am *loaded!*"

They cruised around in silence for a while, coming down from the rush of their brush with the law. It was late, nearly 11:30, time to be thinking about heading north to beat their curfew. "God, I need a plug after that," Jack said, and he dipped a pinch of Copenhagen. Ken dipped one, too. Then, as if in a dream, as if prayers really do come true, as if to make up for the humiliation they had suffered at the hands of the cop, fate shone down upon them. The two blondes in the white Trans Am, the girls they had seen at eight and had spent the rest of the night looking for, were in the next lane, right beside them.

"Okay," Ken said, as Jack began rolling down his window. "Be cool. This could be it."

"Hey," Jack shouted, "what school do y'all go to?"

The blondes smiled. They were about the prettiest things Jack had ever seen, sixteen or so, with fresh faces, as clean and pure as baby powder. When the girl on the passenger side spoke, her sweet breath seemed to stir the white feathers dangling from the Trans Am's rearview mirror. These were the girls who got away, and the guys had been given another chance. Ken and Jack would be graduating soon. In a matter of months they'd be off at Texas A&M or someplace, studying environmental design or something. They had cruised Forest for two years and never gotten closer to paradise than they were at this moment. Two sixteen-year-old blondes in a creamy white Trans Am!

"Lake Highlands!" the girl on the passenger side said. "Y'all go to Plano, right?"

"Right! Right exactly!"

"See, we remembered from before."

"So," Jack said, trying not to say anything too risky, "what are y'all doin'?"

"Oh, just cruising." The girl on the passenger side leaned over her friend to get a better look at Jack. They were driving about 20 miles an hour now, going through the green light at Marsh Lane. "Do you know Lance Parsons?"

Jack, who until this moment had never heard of Lance Parsons, opened his eyes wide in astonishment. *"Lance Parsons?* Are you kidding? He's a great friend of mine!"

"Really?"

"Sure! Is he one of yours, too? Let's shake!"

They squirmed halfway out of the windows, the girl clutching her giggling, screaming friend, and extended their hands in the moving traffic. Their hands met, and clasped—nirvana! ecstasy! romance!—and then Ken slowed the Firebird down and drifted to the left.

"Hey!" Jack yelled.

But Ken was cutting over to the left lane, then into the left-turn lane, then shooting across the eastbound traffic and past Murray Savings, past everything.

"What are you *doing?*" Jack screamed at Ken. "Do you *realize* what those—oh. Oh, no wonder. Jesus."

Ken was retching silently into his Skoal spittoon. It wouldn't stop coming. He was getting it all over the seat, the console, the dash. Finally he pulled off onto a dark residential street and opened his door, finishing outside.

"You okay, man?" Jack asked him. "You need a beer?"

Ken managed a laugh but said nothing. He spit and wiped his mouth, then stood up shakily in the street. It was 40 degrees out and pitch-black. He pulled off his band jacket, unbuttoned his shirt, and rolled it up into a ball. He put the band jacket back on, fumbling with the snaps, and began wiping up the seat and console with his shirt. When he was finished, he threw the shirt in the street and collapsed in the back seat of the Firebird. "You'd better drive," he said. "Damn Burger King hamburger."

Jack drove slowly, going easy on the dips and bumps, and in a minute they were crossing Forest, past the lights and the noise and the action, and heading north on Marsh Lane toward LBJ Freeway. All in all, it had been a pretty good night.

One in the morning, after another Friday of cruising, and Ken was lying awake in his dark room, staring at the ceiling and waiting for his parents to go to sleep. He'd been out on Forest till his midnight curfew, and he was itching to get back out. Ken's father is precise about his curfew. Midnight is midnight, not 12:15 or 12:30.

When he was sure his parents were asleep, Ken got up, put on warm clothes and gloves, slipped down the hall, and went outside, feeling that tingling sensation of euphoria that teenagers feel when they go out into a forbidden night. He walked up to his Yamaha 400 Special—a beauty, shiny black with red flecks. He'd bought it brand-new for $1,500 cash in the fall of '79. For years he'd been cheap as hell, saving every nickel he made to buy the Yamaha, and later the Mustang. He put on his helmet—it matched the bike—and pushed the Yamaha soundlessly out of his parents' driveway. Up the street he kicked it to life and sped through Plano toward Dallas again. But not to Forest; it would be pretty much dead this time of night. The

real action, the fast action, moves to Emerald when kids' curfews clear the streets.

Emerald is a quiet, two-lane street in a warehouse district near
the west end of Forest, just off the Interstate-35 entrance ramp.
It's deserted at night, the perfect place to race without having to
worry about cops or having someone pull out in front of you.
Ken got there about 2 a.m. He pulled off his helmet, ran his hand
through his hair, and walked over to a bunch of guys standing
around a Trans Am. The driver was sitting on the hood, talking
the car up, saying how fast it was. Ken walked up to him, gave
him a long, level look, and then waved casually back to his bike.

"You wanna run 'em?" he asked. The kid did.

Ken sometimes makes money doing this, since guys who drive
Trans Ams and Corvettes are willing to bet that their rods are
unbeatable, especially by some little two-wheeled motor. But
they're wrong; the Yamaha has amazing off-the-line speed. Ken
lined up beside the Trans Am, someone flagged them off, and
they raced the length of an Emerald warehouse that's almost
exactly a quarter-mile long. Ken won by more than ten feet.

He should have gone home then, but something was driving
him that night. It was one of those nights when he gets moody
and very aware that this is his last year of high school, that very
soon he'll be far away from all of this. He felt a pang for his
girlfriend and wished for the thousandth time that she hadn't
moved to Houston. Were the letters he sent her every week keeping things going? He hoped so. He hoped she wouldn't do anything rash before the fall of '82, when he would join his big
brother at A&M and leave his parents in peace. A&M, Ken had
already calculated, is exactly 95 miles from his girlfriend's
house.

He decided to take a run into Richardson, a suburb north of
Dallas where he lived before his family moved to Plano in 1979.
It was getting very cold, and riding 60 on the bike up Central
Expressway made it seem even colder. He drove past his old
junior high, Richardson West, and finally stopped at a 7-Eleven
to get something to drink. Five guys were playing video games
inside; he recognized two of them from his seventh-grade class
at West. Small world. They all went out and looked at Ken's bike,
but there wasn't much to say.

When he cut off the engine back home in Plano, it was nearly
5 a.m. He had been up for twenty-two hours and had been cruis-

ing for more than nine of them. He pushed the bike up his driveway, went to the back of the house, and walked stealthily to his room, where he stripped off his clothes and climbed wearily into bed beneath a mass of sheets and blankets. Only one thing had gone wrong all night: he was to find out six hours later, after a rude awakening by his parents, that he hadn't been quite stealthy enough when he came home. As of this writing, Ken is grounded.

boys' night out

It used to be easy. I would be bored at ten or so on a Thursday night, and I'd call up Rich.

"Hey, guy," I'd say. "What are you doing?"

"Lying here with Anne," he'd whisper. "It's the anniversary of our first date. I met her after work with a dozen long-stemmed roses, then we had a wonderful dinner at Les Saisons and came home to pop some champagne. Now I'm cradling her in my arms on the couch, and we're listening to Keith Jarrett albums by candlelight."

"Great!" I'd say. "Sounds like it's time for another *boys' night out!*"

Twenty minutes later, Rich would be leaning on his horn outside my apartment.

We'd drive around and collect Lee and Jack, who'd stand in their doorways saying good-bye to their girlfriends, gesturing, shrugging their shoulders, finally walking out to the car saying, *"Women!"*

"Can't live with 'em," I'd say.

"Can't live without 'em," Rich would add. Then he'd pop the clutch and we'd head off toward guy world.

It felt good, being out. For a few brief hours, we were free, like kids playing hooky. We actually convinced ourselves we were getting away with something, and we'd laugh about it for hours. See, since most of us were in serious, meaningful, committed relationships with women, we had to be *nice* all the time. We had to dress up, be on time, meet our girlfriends' parents, and be faithful and pleasant. When we went out on our own, though, we had a rare chance to act the way guys are supposed to act: like jerks. Women don't really understand this, but it's tough these days for a guy to be himself. We're supposed to act like Alan Alda or—even worse—like Phil Donahue. Now women ask *us* out on dates. And they even aggressively initiate sex, sometimes while wearing wading boots. So when me and the guys would retreat to an old Ralph Kramden–Ed Norton ritual like boys' night out, it was about the only time we really felt like *guys*.

What did we actually do on boys' night out? Well, we didn't sit around doing what girls do—we didn't *talk* to each other. When women get together, I suppose, they can't help but get deep, serious and emotional, discussing their innermost secrets, new breakthroughs in feminine hygiene products, stuff like that. But boys' night out was never a time to get heavy. When I'm out with just one of the guys, me and him alone, and we're sitting at some bar tipping back Buds and mulling over old times, we may end up talking about our most intimate hopes and dreams—like wanting to ditch our girlfriends and impregnate Nastassja Kinski. But when we all went out together, we just liked to drink and bullshit around and tell dirty jokes. Historically, I think, men and women have been different that way: Girls have slumber parties. Boys raid them.

On the other hand, it wasn't all as macho and nasty as we'd make it out to be at 3 a.m., when we'd stumble home, trying to look anxious and guilty. Usually, we just drove around, howling out the windows, buying up six-packs at the Beer Barn drive-thru. Once I spent a whole boys' night out trying to talk the guys into going by Oriental Nude Models on Cedar Springs, just to see what it would be like inside. We compromised instead and ate sushi.

Most of the time, we looked at girls. For every one we talked to in a bar ("Hey there, darlin'! Oh—this is your boyfriend? Hi! How are you? Golly, you're a big fella, aren't you? Hey—how 'bout them Dallas Cowboys?"), there were a hundred others we merely gawked at or salivated over, while we compared their breasts to scoops of ice cream or national monuments. Our all-time favorite was a deliriously beautiful blonde in a silver fox coat, eating a corny dog on a stick at Fletcher's corny dog drive-thru at 1 a.m. We were parked next to her cream-colored Chrysler convertible.

"Look at her go at that thing," Rich said reverently.

"Wow!" I said, like a man just released from prison, gasping as she brought the corny dog to her lips, licked off a dab of mustard, and chomped down. For ten minutes our heads hit the roof of the car every time she dove down on that dog. It was one of our greatest boys' night out moments ever.

By the end of one of those nights we'd be tired, tanked up, and completely spent, as if we'd done a male version of the Jane Fonda workout. We'd feel blusterously macho, revitalized, like sailors after a long night's shore leave, and then we'd stumble drunkenly back to the brig. Were we in serious trouble? Were our girlfriends worried about us? Were they about to call the police? Who the hell cared? We were the guys, for Christ's sake.

That was all back in the old days—about a year ago, before Jack got married and had a baby girl, before Rich and Anne got real serious, before Lee got engaged and moved to New York. Back then, nobody could tell us what to do. Not even our girlfriends. Now Rich and Jack have to be home by midnight, and Lee might as well be on Neptune. To make matters worse, I'm always out of town working somewhere. Last month, after ten weeks away from Texas, I got to missing the guys. I was starved for such things as draw poker, male camaraderie, and pissing contests. As soon as I hit Dallas–Fort Worth Airport, I was on the phone.

"Hey," Rich said. "How ya doin'?"

"Great. And I'll be a lot greater in about six hours, in the middle of another famous boys' night out!"

"Can't tonight," Rich said. "I'm having dinner with Anne and some friends of hers from work. Maybe—uh—how 'bout Sunday?"

Sunday wasn't good for Jack; some relatives were flying in to see the baby. We finally got together on a Thursday night around ten. Whatever doubts I had were confirmed moments after Rich and I picked up Jack, whom we found on the sofa with his baby daughter Caroline cuddled on his chest. In the car, he actually started screaming about auto safety.

"Slow down, you jerk!" he yelled, as Rich whipped around a corner at 45 miles an hour. "Stop driving like an idiot!" Then, in a softer tone, "You know, only friends can talk to one another like that—you fucking jerk! You *moron!*"

But Jack really had a right to be worried. Rich was always getting involved in spectacular car wrecks that weren't his fault, and then tearing up streets for weeks with cars paid for by some insurance company. This month he was carving boulevards with a sporty Grand Am rental, and after a few minutes of yelling at him, Jack and I buckled up.

Rich seemed not to hear us. He just gunned the accelerator, pushed his glasses up on his nose, and fiddled with an unruly cowlick. "Do you think I need a haircut?" he asked, squinting in the rearview mirror. "It looks like I just took off a football helmet." I figured that Rich, more than any of us, needed this night out. He worked sixty hours a week getting a doctorate in psychology, specializing in marriage therapy, and then he did the graveyard shift in the Parkland Hospital emergency psych ward. He spent every other moment with Anne.

But it's not like Jack didn't have steam to blow off. A computer technician who played drums for a band called the Shitty Beatles, Jack had a brand-new baby who cried all night long and loaded its pants the rest of the time. Yup, the guys were tense, wound up, sapped of their precious bodily fluids.

Rich zoomed beneath a bridge at a calm 50, heading for downtown Dallas, where a string of hip new bars had just opened in the warehouse district. "Aw, look," he said, as we drove past a tiny toy store with rubber ducks and dolls in the window. "Look how sweet that is. It makes me want to punch out a little kid." A moment later, waiting at a light beside some empty skyscraper, we watched a limo pull up, disgorging a swank couple who walked into a gold-and-glass booth and dropped from sight into a fancy underground restaurant called Dakota. Both the guys turned to me.

"Hey," said Rich. "How come you're not treating us to dinner, too?" (I was picking up the tab for the evening—yet another inducement to get them out of the house.)

"It's because he's cheap," Jack said. "When Dave stops writing for tomorrow's fish wrapper, we can be eating buffalo steaks at Dakota!"

Ah, rowdiness, I thought. Things were definitely picking up. When a woman dripping furs stepped from a BMW half a block away, Jack rolled down his window and bellowed, "Hey! Is that *real* muskrat or *fake* muskrat?"

"Just what is this place we're going to?" I asked, looking back at the woman's frozen, horrified face.

"The Prophet Bar," Jack said. "I've been there, so it must be cool. What do you think that woman was doing? I bet she was going to get her squirrel wrapped, if you know what I mean."

The Prophet was dark and quiet, it being so early and all. In one room, a young man plucked torturously on a guitar beneath a spotlight, but nobody was there to watch him, including us. We slouched toward the bar area and quickly tanked up, figuring time was of the essence. Twenty minutes later, my arm was sore from whipping tens out of my wallet to buy us drinks.

Then I saw them. In a booth against the front window, two chicks. Mid-twenties. Sleek-looking, but casual. One had her foot up on the seat, her wrist poised on her knee, a long-neck beer bottle dangling from the tips of her fingers. Ordinarily, my heartstrings would've been trembling like wind chimes, but not tonight, and not for this young thing. She was one of the most dangerous hombres in all creation: *an ex-girlfriend.*

The guys went over to talk to them while I steeled myself with another shot at the bar.

"Hi, Dusty," I said when I finally joined the little group.

"Hi. I hear you're having a boys' night out."

"Right!" Rich chirped.

"Yeah! Yeah!" Jack said, punching the air with black-power salutes.

"Well, that's just incredible, because Cynthia and I are having a girls' night out."

A girl with a tray in her hand and an earring in her nose approached the table. "Hi, you work here?" Jack asked. "I'll have another Corona, and charge me double. Okay, Dave?"

"Wow, this is like the 'Twilight Zone,' " Rich said, as we sat across from the girls'-night-out girls. "You know, like the show where matter meets antimatter, and when they get too close—BOOM!"

"I think it's more like on the 'Flintstones,' " Jack said, "when Barney and Fred were mad at each other, and Wilma and Betty took sides, and they were all scrappin' and squabblin', and they couldn't even remember what they were mad about, and they all saw how selfish they were being."

Dusty's jaw hung open. "Why does this remind you of that?"

"Because I always look to the 'Flintstones' for an example," Jack said, slurping back half his Corona, "and that's the one I saw on Channel 11 today when I stayed home from work."

Dusty and Cynthia told us about their night so far. Rich gave their story such rapt attention that at one point, when he accidentally knocked his Scotch and soda all over the table, he barely paused to say, "Waitress! Another! Make it a double!" before looking into Cynthia's eyes and saying, "Yes? Please go on."

I could feel our momentum slowly dying. For one thing, chatting pleasantly with women is verboten on boys' night out. For another, I was thinking about how I was the only one of the guys who never had one particular girl to catch hell from after boys' night out, and wondered if I'd ever be like Rich and Jack, so urgently needed by someone at midnight every night. Dusty seemed to have someone like that now. Since the last time I'd been in Dallas, a ring had appeared on her finger.

"Wow," Rich said. "Look at that rock. Look at that ice."

Dusty began to talk about her wedding, and I suddenly began to feel faint. "You know, guys," I interrupted, "we really should go. I mean, this is *boys'* night out." I realized I sounded feeble, since there was an awkward pause, and I tried to make a joke out of it. "Come on, guys, really! We need to go look for some womans!"

"David doesn't *want* women," Dusty informed the group. "He just wants to pursue them."

By this time, I was gulping for air. I set my drink down on the last table before the door, and just barely made it outside. I strolled over behind Rich's car, kicking gravel with the toes of my boots. When the guys came out, I was leaning against the trunk, my arms crossed, looking up at the skyline towering above us in the west.

"What's Dave mopin' about?" Jack asked Rich. Then he slugged my shoulder. "Just because you spent twenty thousand dollars in there, it's no reason to act like the world has ended. C'mon. Let's go to the Video Bar."

I ducked my head, kicked at the gravel again.

"C'mon, let's go dance," Rich said. "Okay, wanna watch me and Jack dance?" They stood in front of me and did the hula.

"Ever seen a pelvis like this?" Jack crooned. "Hey! Can they show this on TV?"

I laughed. "Okay," I said. "Let's go."

Maybe they were trying to cheer me up, or maybe the Scotch and Coronas had taken their toll, but Jack and Rich were acting as crazy as they ever had in the old days. As we walked toward the Video Bar, we passed a building marked LONG MACHINE TOOL CO.

"Hey, I model there," Jack said, loud enough for people in the club's doorway to hear. "I do nude modeling there on Tuesdays and Thursdays."

The Video Bar was packed; it was hard to grab a waitress. "You haven't been waited on yet?" Jack said, strolling from the can, tucking his shirttail in. "Hell, pull your pants down or something." For a few shining moments, we caroused. We acted up. We gawked at girls and did stupid hula dances to a Grace Jones video. It really didn't matter that Dusty and Cynthia turned up a few minutes later; it was time for the guys to be getting home anyway. And it didn't matter that Jack stopped outside the club, got a piece of chalk, and scrawled I ♥ CAROLINE on the sidewalk. He was a father now; that was the way things were. It really *didn't* mean the end of the world, or even the end of the guys.

I thought about all this as we were driving home, just before midnight. Things change, I told myself. You get older, you slide through your twenties until you're just barely hanging onto them. People around you start settling down, getting married, buying washer-dryers. And with these things come maturity and responsibility. It's okay, I thought. So what if it's barely midnight? It was time to face facts: Things just weren't the way they were in the old days. It was just part of growing up.

Then I saw the flashing neon sign in a bar window a mile from Jack's: CERVEZA TECATE, it said. CERVEZA TECATE. CERVEZA TECATE . . .

I didn't need a Berlitz course in Spanish to figure that one out.

"Shee-it, boys," I cried. "Let's party!"

An hour or so later, a block from Jack's place, the Grand Am's headlights were shining on a plastic garbage can teetering on the edge of the curb. Rich's hands gripped the wheel; if he flicked it a bit to the right, we'd smack the can to kingdom come.

Jack put his hands on the dashboard. *"Punch it,* dude!" he screamed. *"Punch it!"*

Our tires skidded off the curb. The can went flying, careening end over end in the air, spewing out all kinds of bright-colored wrapping paper, probably the refuse from some kid's birthday party. Blue and pink bows and ribbon rained down on us as we fishtailed up to Jack's driveway. It was the kind of thing, like corny dogs and blondes and cream-colored convertibles, that we'll probably remember until the day we die.

5

modern girls

My girlfriend was very modern. She wore plastic jump suits and red Fiorucci boots, she went dancing every night till 2 a.m., she read *i-D Magazine* and listened to Orchestral Manoeuvres in the Dark, and she had no idea what she wanted to do with her life. When she began, through no fault of her own, to systematically smash my heart to bits last spring, I began hanging out every night at a place called On the Air. It was a little new-wave bar we used to go to together, full of sleek, heavily moussed modern girls who were becoming more and more of a mystery to me. They were all very '80s, cooler than Madonna, hipper than hip. I'd lean against a wooden rail and watch comforting U2 videos splash against the screen, drinking screwdrivers and trying to figure things out. Like, what do women want? How can we understand them? Is this my fourth or fifth screwdriver?

Luckily, I could always count on Justine and Suzi. They were roommates and waitresses at On the Air, and they took care of me, bringing me drinks and waving off my money and being careful not to ask me how things were going with my girlfriend. Justine and Suzi were nineteen and twenty-four and as ultrahip as girls can get. They were mini–new-wave celebrities on the Dallas scene, and sometimes they tried to explain to me what modern girls were all about. One evening, I asked them if they'd let me follow them around on a long Saturday night and write about what they said and did and danced to. I told them it might be helpful to many people and would place a grave responsibility on them, and they were both eager to do what they could.

"We'll take you to the Twilite Room and the Starck Club," Justine said. "We'll buy some Ecstasy and go shopping for toys at 4 a.m. We'll even tell you about orgasms!"

I said I couldn't wait.

Our Saturday night was balmy. Late April breezes were rustling up from the Gulf and swirling around in the curve of the U-shaped apartment building where Justine and Suzi lived. I knocked on their door. Loud music was coming from inside. I knocked harder.

The door flew open and Justine stood there, panting, in a camisole and a pair of French designer jeans. "Come on up!" she said, already running back up the stairs. "I'm on the phone, and Suzi's in the shower." I had to pause a minute, though, from the sheer spectacle of their apartment. Apparently, a burglary had taken place. There was almost no furniture and the carpet was covered with an amazing layer of tossed-aside things: clothes, newspapers, records, glasses with drops of wine in them, candy wrappers, Sweet 'N Low packets, lipsticks, and a plastic armadillo with a bikini bottom draped on its face. The kitchen appliances were covered with fabric-paint graffiti, and there were Magic Marker messages on the walls (FOR JENNIFER'S SHOWER MARCH 14—LINGERIE).

"Up here," Justine called. I bolted up the steps to her room, where the theme from downstairs continued on a grander scale. She had transformed her boudoir into a walk-in closet, with all her clothes scattered in mounds on the floor. She was sitting on a sort of precipice in the northeast corner, twisting a camouflage-colored bra in her fingertips, talking dramatically to some guy on the phone. "Well, honey, I *swear* ah just don't *know.*"

Justine and Suzi were in a transition period. Just a few days before, On the Air had been closed by its landlord for nonpayment of six months' rent. Accusations were flying—people were blaming the club's demise on everything from cocaine to comped drinks. But the saddest thing was that Justine and Suzi had lost their forum, their stage. In the dark, skintight recesses of On the Air, they had maneuvered nightly through cool crowds, with trays of drinks perched on their fingertips and tight black dresses hugging their hips. On the Air had been their element, and it was gone.

"I'm trying not to think about it," Justine said as she hung up and lit one of her trademark English cigarettes. "I'm *trying* to decide what to wear." She kicked at a pile of blouses and opened a door to reveal a stuffed closet. "I don't know if I should be innocent in white or deadly in black," she said. She picked up something from the floor of the closet, and as she did so, her breasts swelled against her camisole. "Hmmm—what do men like women to wear?"

As nonchalantly as possible, I suggested that what she had on looked just fine.

Justine just put her hands on her hips and laughed. "You child," she said. "You poor, sweet *child!*"

Suzi called out hello from her bedroom. She and Justine are nearly inseparable, but they're very different. Justine is wild, suggestive, nearly six feet tall, and she has the careless, outrageous aggressiveness that comes with being both cool and nineteen. Suzi is soft-spoken, fragile; strikingly beautiful but in a calm, gentle way. It's as if her face were sculpted and the artist had put something sad in her blue eyes.

"Suzi just got back from Oklahoma," Justine said. "She was visiting her parents. Don't I look like a queen in my room?" She sank back down onto the thronelike mound of clothes, running her hand through skirts and lingerie as if she were testing the waters of a pool. "Dirty underwear. It's my life."

"Justine!" Suzi called from her room. "Could you open my door a second, please?" Justine went out into the hall, and I heard Suzi say, "Is this too sleazy without a slip?"

"No, you look beautiful. You make me sick."

"It's not too sleazy?"

"No. You look like an angel."

Justine came back in, dialed the phone. She had directed me to a safe spot on her bed where I could sit without messing up anything. "Hi, Mom, how are you?" she said. "Remember how I told you I was going out with David and Suzi tonight? Well, what do you think I should wear?" She took a drag off her cigarette, listened and waved her hand impatiently. "Well, that's *you*. You went to Smith. You're *sensible*. What color should I wear, white or black? Yes, Mother, I'll wear something flattering."

She hung up, decided to wear something deadly in black, and fished a bottle of Soave Bolla out of a corner. It had been propped against the wall, and a cork was bobbing around inside it. Justine had taken a few swigs when she noticed me watching the cork. "You want some? Suzi! Do you want some wine?"

She found three plastic cups on the edge of the bathtub and rinsed them out in the bathroom sink, but by the time she measured the wine into the bottoms of the cups, it hardly seemed worth the effort. "I know," she said, brightening. "Go buy us some champagne. We'll be all ready to go when you get back."

When I returned with two cold bottles, the girls were putting on makeup. Justine, in a scooped-out black dress, was painting her nails with pink Wet & Wild, her stereo blasting out "Seventeen Seconds," by the Cure. Ten feet away, in Suzi's room, a stereo was playing, less loudly, "Love Song," by Simple Minds. Suzi was in a lotus position on the floor, facing a big round mirror leaning against the wall. She closed her eyes, brushed makeup across her face in delicate strokes, surveyed the results.

"It's so weird to be back from my parents'," she said. "It was so quiet there, in a clean house." Her prim, angelic outfit turned out to be a long white-cotton '20s dress. Suzi's room was neater than Justine's but not by much. Fashion magazines were spread out all over, imported British monthlies that, when you opened them and turned a few pages, had photographs of girls who looked just like Suzi. The only orderly thing in the entire apartment was Suzi's suitcase, which lay open on her bed. Inside it, her clothes were neatly folded, her socks carefully rolled into identically sized balls.

"I hate that mushy song," Justine said, walking in and scowling at the Simple Minds album. "It's so stupid, like, 'I want to trust you, I want to be close to you.' "

"It's nice," Suzi protested. "It's romantic. You don't like it because it's not sleazy enough for you."

"I'm sorry, but romance is dead in the '80s," Justine said, gulping some champagne. "That's why men suck now, because they forgot what roses mean. It's just 'Hey, baby, wanna fuck?'"

"You'll like this song by Depeche Mode," Suzi said to me. "It's called "Somebody," and a cute guy with blond hair sings it. It's pretty."

Justine made a face. "It's sappy, it's mushy, it sounds like shit! It's too desperate, too gross. It's like Norman Rockwell." Then she ran into her room and turned her Cure tape full blast.

While Suzi painted her eyelids with a tiny brush, Justine showed me a list of contenders for her "royal throne." On a wall between the bathroom and the bedrooms, in purple and red Magic Marker, were lists of dozens of names of men Justine and Suzi wanted to sleep with and/or marry. Most were celebrities, such as Mike Peters of The Alarm and Mick MacNeil of Simple Minds. Others were famous only around Lower Greenville, the funky Dallas neighborhood the girls lived in. All the names had little boxes beside them, and some of the boxes were notched with check marks. A scoreboard by Justine's door awarded 50 points for celebrities, 5 points for "gay boys."

"I'll tell you about modern girls," Justine said, twirling her empty cup around so I'd pour more champagne into it. "The only thing they want to have in life is fun. They live in dives, work yucky jobs, nothing glamorous, but it pays bills, and they have money for drugs, money for clothes, money to buy the Pill each month, 'cause naturally fun equals sex, sex, sex. Modern girls are liberated; that's the key. I mean, we shave our armpits, but that's about it. No more of this tradition. And modern girls are good in bed; right, Suzi? And they're not hung up about anything. They get bummed with men occasionally, but their overall attitude is 'Fuck 'em if they can't take a joke.'"

"I think they're more open during sex," Suzi said, sitting on the carpet in her doorway, taking little sips of champagne. "It's more mutual fulfillment. Before, the guys were like, *errrrrr*"—she jerked her hands up in the air and scrunched up her face. "They were just all out for what they wanted, and you could lie there like a dead dog and they probably wouldn't care."

"But now we gotta get something out of it, too," said Justine. "Like, we'll get on top, we'll do positions we like, we'll find out ways—I don't care if it's in the shower or on a rug with cat fur, we do what we wanna do. Also, girls will buy guys flowers, too."

"What about modern guys?" I asked. "What are they like?"

"Usually, they're artistically inclined," said Suzi. "They run a wild art shop or a wild clothing store or a video bar, or they're video jocks or they work for the arts, and their hair is like—it's never parted in the middle or to the side, it's kind of disheveled. And I love baggy boxer shorts on guys. I like baggy pants and suspenders and rolled-up T-shirts, or else the James Dean kind of rebel look." She slipped a single black O-ring onto her right wrist, then twisted a string of tiny fake pearls around it.

"So what if you met this perfect guy—what would you do?"

"For me, the ideal date would be sitting outside at a French restaurant," said Justine, "wearing my Korean Ray-Bans, drinking wine and having a cigarette in my left hand, talking to an ideal guy. He's got a suntan and disheveled hair and a cigarette and a goofy leather jacket, with nice Italian shoes with nice white socks. He'll talk about Camus or some great artist and talk about silly things, like what your roommate did to you when you were asleep. Then he'll take the half-wilted carnation out of the vase and give it to you."

"In a way, I'm so traditional," Suzi said. "To me, an ideal date would be to go on a picnic and have a basket with fruit and cheese and a bottle of wine. Just sit around and talk and relax and enjoy each other's company. Just to be with somebody."

The champagne was all gone. "Do you think we should go out somewhere?" Justine said. "It's only eleven."

I'd borrowed my best friend's 1966 turquoise Tempest. It moves around corners like the Love Boat and roars like a Greyhound bus, but it has nice lines and a tape deck. We drove it to the Inwood Lounge, a sleek, high-tech bar with soundproof windows through which you can see foreign films playing at the movie-house next door. There was running water along the walls, a revolving hologram of Marcello Mastroianni smoking a cigarette, and a center table where Justine and Suzi sat drinking Bailey's on the rocks. They had said their hellos to half a dozen people on the way in, including a razor-thin bartender with a curly spit of black hair dangling down his forehead.

"That's Tony," Justine said. "He programs all the music they play here." Above the hum of the crowd and the rush of nearby water, a song by Bronski Beat was playing. Modern music.

Justine was running our table, switching topics of conversation every ninety seconds. ("David, did you know I've had three Greek guys in a row? It's incredible. Suzi's been a vegetarian for six years; me, six months. I'm moving to England and getting married this year. Just wait.") Then she froze, looked sideways, and made a face.

"A guy just walked by who always bothered me," she said. "He always came into On the Air and tried some line on me. He's the kind of guy who wears skinny ties and goes, 'I'm *new wave!*' All I could do was laugh at him." She took a drag off her cigarette and glanced at her roommate. "You're talking a lot, Suzi."

"I'm sorry." Suzi sipped at her Bailey's, looking over toward Justine's inept suitor. She'd been staring for a long time in the direction of Mastroianni's holographic image, seemingly in another world.

When she got up to go to the bathroom, Justine leaned over and whispered, "Suzi's depressed."

"What about?"

"I don't know. Probably this guy Bud. You know, that blond-haired guy who looks sorta like a British rock star? She's been going out with him for a few months, and he's a real jerk. I don't like him. You can't joke with him, and Suzi and I joke so much. And besides, he's fucking around."

We decided that just wouldn't do. We were getting drunk, and we wanted to be happily drunk. We wanted Suzi to be happily drunk. Justine stabbed her straw into her drink. "Our mission: Cheer up Suzi."

The lounge was fully stocked with upscale new wavers. Models with electrified hair stood under neon lights and posed like friezes, clutching napkin-wrapped drinks. As Suzi maneuvered her way back to our table, the neon seemed to spotlight her face and her long white dress, which swayed gently with each step.

"Doesn't Suzi look pretty tonight?" Justine asked.

"Yes," I said.

"Hey, Suzi, tell David which one of us is sexier."

Suzi sat down and smiled, rolling her eyes. "Justine will tell you she's 10 points sexier and I'm 4 points bitchier."

"It's true! The *Cosmo* quiz told us! I'd used every position, so I'm 10 points over you."

"But you're five years younger than Suzi. How could you be so far ahead?"

"I've learned enough between eighteen and nineteen to last a lifetime," Justine said. "At fourteen, I learned that men sucked; at fifteen, men sucked; at sixteen, men sucked *dicks;* at seventeen, I found out all men were gay; at eighteen, men sucked; and at nineteen, men are all getting married."

"I'm going to make a call," Suzi said. "This is too depressing."

"Depressing? Everybody falls in love with you! It's always 'Where's Suzi?' I can't even have a boyfriend without him falling in love with Suzi!"

We watched Suzi walk off toward the phone. "She's probably going to call Bud," Justine said, shrugging her shoulders. Then she pouted and looked provocatively toward the bar so our waiter would come ask what she wanted.

By 12:30, we'd gravitated downtown to the Twilite Room, the only hard-core punk club in Dallas. It shared a block with a bail bonds place and a porno moviehouse, and it was crowded with a mix of scuzzed-out young punks with violent haircuts and crucifix jewelry, drunken, aging punks left over from 1978, and S.M.U. frat rats shooting pool. Justine introduced me to a blonde in her late twenties. "This is Terri," she said. "She used to run that vintage clothing store Shady Lady. Now she's teaching me to be one."

We decided we were getting too buzzed; we needed something refreshing, like a few bottles of cold Mexican beer. A sexy bartender in a black prom dress pulled the tops off a few Coronas, and I took them back to where the girls stood lounging by the jukebox. Justine asked for a quarter to play "The Day the World Turned Day-Glo," by X-Ray Specs, and we leaned against the wall, sipping our beers. Our attempt to cheer up Suzi had backfired, and now all three of us were feeling pretty bummed. Maybe it was from drinking wine and champagne so early. It was stuffy and loud, so we retreated to a quiet spot, a fire escape that looked down on the grimy eastern edge of downtown. We sat down, clinking our bottles on the wrought iron, and Justine and Suzi talked about men. It wasn't like earlier in the night, though, when they had seemed like '80s versions of Ann-Margret in *Kitten with a Whip.* Now they weren't joking around.

"It's weird how I met Bud," Suzi said. "We were giving away albums at On the Air, and I was throwing them down from the VJ's window, and I hit Bud on the head." She looked tired. She pulled her knees up to her chin and looked down at some Mexicans pulling up to the bail bonds place. "I told myself when I started dating him, 'Don't fall in love with him, because that's the only way you can have a happy relationship with him.' I mean, he's a nice guy, but he has a lot of problems, and until he works them out, he won't be a good boyfriend—you know, someone who's able to give in a relationship. But *noooo,* what do I do?"

"Does he know you love him?"

"No, I've never told him that. See, what's so stupid is I have a hard time admitting my feelings, because I don't trust men. Because I've been hurt so much."

"Why do we get stuck with all these bum guys?" Justine yelled. "We deserve so much better. I think that Suzi and I are two of the nicest, most ideal people to go out with, 'cause we're honest when we want to be. And we respect guys more than anyone I know."

"Like, with Bud," Suzi said, "it's how he treats me. A lot of the time, it isn't the way you'd treat somebody you really cared about. It's like I have a really bad self-image at times, or else why would I put up with that?"

I was astonished. "But there must be millions of guys asking you out all the time! Nice guys, great guys."

"It seems like nobody ever asks me out," she said. "I've been stood up more than any girl I know."

"I don't understand why you'd go out with someone who makes you feel that way."

"It's because," Justine said, "there's no one else special to go out with who makes her feel important, and she's too good a person to feel lonely all the time."

The problem, the girls agreed, was just what Justine had figured out at fourteen: Men suck. They chanted it together, like a mantra, so loud that a couple of punks looked up at us from the sidewalk below.

"That says it right there," Suzi said. "I really respect men who are intelligent, who aren't into themselves or how they look. But every guy I've gone out with who was smart has been dry and boring, and then the ones I'm attracted to who are rebellious and fun, like Bud, are always promiscuous and not willing to have a relationship. It's, like, I give up, I really do. If somebody were to come along who was really caring, it would be 'Bye, Bud.' But right now, I'm just kind of waiting in there."

We talked a long time, about how Suzi didn't meet her first boyfriend until she was a shy sorority girl at Oklahoma State, and then, after two years, when they'd made plans to get married, she found out he was gay. And how none of the guys took Justine seriously, since she was only nineteen. And how they both loved to buy *Brides* magazine so they could look at the bridal gowns, and how they sometimes stayed up late at night talking about what they wanted to name their kids.

"I want to get married within a year," Justine said. "Preferably to Mick MacNeil of Simple Minds."

"I don't think I'm ever going to get married," Suzi said, touching her Corona bottle with her fingertips. "I've always wanted to, but I don't think I ever will."

It was approaching 2 a.m. when we climbed into the Tempest and drove across downtown to the Starck Club, the chicest, coolest club in Dallas. Created by the French designer Philippe Starck, it's the kind of place where Grace Jones gets flown in to perform for the city's slumming café élite and the top crop of new wavers who used to go to On the Air. A line of BMW's and Porsches ringed the place; we had to wait awhile before a valet took the keys to the Tempest, and then the girls strode quickly up the Starck steps, slipped past three dozen people teeming against a velvet rope and swept inside with me in their wake, never slowing down as an alert doorman recognized them and whipped up the last rope between us and Starck's pulsing interior.

It was all smooth gray cement and cloudlike couches and curtains, packed with a writhing ant farm of night people.

"You know what we need?" Justine said.

"Ecstasy."

We'd discussed this on the drive over from the Twilite Room. Since it was too late to get a drink, taking Ecstasy was our only hope of slipping out of our gloomy moods into something more, um, comfortable. This was April, back in the good old days, when 3,4-methylenedioxymethamphetamine wasn't yet illegal. We knew it was supposed to mess up your blood pressure and destroy brain cells, but this was Saturday and that was a price we were willing to pay.

Justine went off into the crowd, looking for some, while Suzi and I made our way to the bar. Amazingly, there were still a few seconds left to get a drink. We got four kamikazes for the girls, a double screwdriver for me.

Justine reappeared with two tanned, smiling guys who could have walked out of an episode of "Miami Vice." "These guys will go get us some X, but they want to see your money," she whispered to me.

I slipped some twenties out of my jacket pocket and one of them said, "A-OK!"

Justine's trip alone through Starck seemed to have revitalized her. She shot down her kamikazes and waved at people and kissed an enormous but infinitely graceful black guy who was wearing a tux and waiting tables. His name was Michael. He bussed Suzi, too, and gripped my elbow with his free hand as we were introduced, then went back into the breach to pick up glasses. It was nice meeting someone friendly there—sometimes, places like Starck can be just too cool to take. The "Miami Vice" guys came back with the X, three flat white tablets wrapped in a single piece of toilet tissue. I gave them three twenties and we took the X as casually as if it were aspirin.

Justine had barely swallowed hers when she yelled, "Yoo-hoo! Bart!" and ran over to retrieve Bart Weiss, the former video program director at On the Air. She gripped the arm of his black-leather jacket and said, "You've got to dance with me. But wait here a minute." Suzi and Bart and I stood around talking for a while. A song by the Thompson Twins pumped from the dance floor, which was in a big pit in the middle of the place, and I found myself thinking about my girlfriend.

"It's *really great* being around people in such *very good* moods," Bart said. He had his own reasons to be bummed—On the Air was closed, and he was going through some rocky times with a woman he'd been dating for years. He was at Starck to have fun, to drink and dance with someone like Justine, but the sight of him made Suzi and me mope even more.

Justine came back, stripped off Bart's jacket, draped it on Suzi's narrow shoulders, and turned him out toward the dance pit. "Well," she said, turning back to me, "I've conquered one man tonight."

Suzi and I leaned over a rail and watched them dance in the throbbing recesses beneath us. Justine swirled around so her black skirt would revolve, and her cigarette orbited around her, like a tracer bullet in the dark. After a while, we wandered back to the spotlighted stage and sat down on the steps, our chins in our hands. Every now and then, someone would come up and say to Suzi, "Excuse me, but I just wanted to tell you you look absolutely beautiful," and she'd smile politely and say, "Thank you."

I found a napkin and wrote Suzi a note: "So . . . is your life going the way you want it to?"

She read it, gestured for my pen above the noise of a New Order song, and wrote back, "No—not at all." When I wrote back asking her to tell me her troubles, she wrote, "I can't—I wish that I could, but I'm sworn to secrecy."

Time passed. The X was kicking in big time. But instead of brightening our nights to the 120th power, it just seemed to make things more bleak. "I don't think we're in party mode," I wrote to Suzi, "and we're certainly not in Depeche Mode."

"I think," she wrote back, "we're in bummed mode."

Suddenly, with a calm, romantic detachment, I wondered whether or not I was in love with Suzi. I knew the X was part of it—you can fall in love with bright, shiny objects when you're on X—but I'd wondered about this before, without it, during those long, late nights at On the Air. I'd always dismissed it in the bright, sober light of the mornings after. I knew I was too straight, and maybe too plain, for her. The guys I always saw her with wore complicated leather jackets, tied bandannas around the calves of their boots, and never seemed to smile. Their jaws were always dusted by a three-day growth of beard, and they regarded the world around them—or at least On the Air—with boredom and purposelessness. They made me feel too grounded, too true to life, almost like Ward Cleaver.

And yet, I'd always sensed in Suzi something deeper, more yearning, than the cool posing of the people she hung out with. She sometimes seemed bored by the whole scene, or at least resigned to it. Sitting on those steps, I remembered another explanation Justine had offered one night. "Sometimes," she'd said, "Suzi just doesn't like herself very much. It's something that happens with people who are perfect. They're real hard on themselves, and then they can't be happy. And that makes them not be perfect anymore."

I was in the middle of writing Suzi a long, important note when she suddenly stood up, dropped Bart's leather jacket to the floor beside me, and walked away without a word. I watched as she stepped through clouds of cigarette smoke lit by bright spots of light, between people who had already paid tribute to her and up to a guy with disheveled blond hair, a guy who looked like a British rock star. Oh, yeah, Bud. I looked down at my napkin—the ink from my long, complicated note had seeped through it. She couldn't have read it, anyway.

When I caught up with Justine, it was after 4 a.m. and she was still dancing, this time with three gay guys. One of her partners was wearing an ascot and a black-linen suit; he held out his white hands like fans in the air while he danced. Justine was a little drunk. She fell down once while I watched them slink around to Tears for Fears, and later she knocked over a chair on her way to the bar. "That guy's name is Travis," she said, dabbing her forehead with ice water and pointing to a guy who'd said hello to her. "I met him at some frat party at S.M.U. I had a whole bottle of champagne to myself, and he wanted some."

Justine waved to someone else, showing all her teeth as she smiled. She seemed to have limitless energy, but I was fading fast. I'd been foraging through Starck, looking for Suzi, for what seemed like forever, and I'd promised myself once again that this was the last time I'd ever do X.

"Have you seen Suzi?" I said.

"She went off to have breakfast with Bud," Justine said, making a face.

"Oh."

She led me back to the bathroom marked *Femmes,* a needless distinction, since half the people inside were *hommes.* It was a huge room, all mirrors and stainless steel, with a cloudlike couch in the middle and stalls behind swinging doors. A refugee from El Salvador handed cotton towels to people who barely acknowledged her—they were too busy gaping at their frightful 4 a.m. reflections in the fluorescent light.

"I'm so bored," Justine said, pursing her lips before the mirror, "and my hair looks like rat fuck." Then she straightened and put her long gold necklace between her teeth, like a bit.

I had dreamed of walking out of Starck and having the Tempest brought up so I could stroll outside with these two incredible modern girls on either arm, climbing into that turquoise cavern to the oohs and aahs of an adoring crowd. But when Justine and I got outside and stood together on the steps, waiting in line for a valet, I just felt like I'd been in a war or something. I saw someone I knew, and he asked me how things were going.

Instead of saying, "I may feel worse than I've ever felt in my life," I shook his hand and said, "Oh, I can't complain."

Justine decided she wanted to go to Denny's for an egg and some hot tea. When we got there, the hostess and waiter did a *Hello, Dolly!* routine with her and gave her her usual corner table. On a whim, I ordered a Grand Slam Breakfast—I thought it might be what I needed. While we picked at our food, Justine talked about how "Heroes," by David Bowie, was the most important song in the world. She talked about her plans to write a book called *Justalonia's Guide to Sex.* She talked about how she wanted to be "Andy Warhol famous" and how she thought men should wear skirts to night clubs. "It's the newest thing," she said. "It's the androgynous look of the '80s."

By the time I drove her home and saw her to the door, it was getting close to dawn. A train was going by a long way away, a pickup loaded with Sunday papers pulled up to the curb, and Justine kissed me good night on the cheek. I went back to the Tempest and steered it west. I was in something my grandmother used to call a "state." As far as I knew, I hadn't learned anything that could help me understand my girlfriend, that could help me understand women or anything at all. All I knew for sure was that I wanted to get home, fall onto my bed, and go to sleep for a long, long time.

6

too cool to get married

When my girlfriend told me she was getting married, I tried to keep things light. "Does this mean we can't go to see Pee Wee Herman at the Majestic Friday night?" I asked.

She looked at me with the most terrible sadness over her chicken *fajitas*.

"I don't know what we're going to do."

It was even more sudden than it sounds. Hilary and I had gone out for a year and a half, enduring more breakups and catastrophes and separations than some couples experience in a lifetime. A year before, I'd lost count of the times I had pledged to my closest, disbelieving friends, "I'm never going out with Hilary Hardcastle again." And her exasperation with me had known no bounds. We were different in so many ways. Yet here we were, a year and a half later, eating a midnight dinner in our favorite bar and grill, totally at ease and in love.

So why was she marrying someone else? That night I thought I understood. They had gone out for years in college, and he was my polar opposite: responsible, mature, a day person, a hard worker. He was in computers, he would probably make lots of money, and he took things seriously. But I was just like Hilary. We were both twenty-seven, and though we'd had various romantic entanglements in our lives, neither of us had been tied down for long. We liked to play. We would go out every night till 3 a.m. and sleep every day till noon. We'd arranged our lives to make that possible. I wrote free-lance articles for everyone from the *Dallas Observer* to *USA Today,* and since I write fast, I rarely worked more than twenty hours a week. Hilary, who had a degree in speech and theatre from Austin College in Sherman, was a cocktail waitress at the Melrose Hotel and something of a new-wave personality around town. Everywhere we went, people knew her—we'd go drinking and dancing at the Twilite Room, at Tango, at On the Air, eating a late breakfast before we called it a night. We regarded each other's frequent flirtations with casual bemusement and never planned anything more than a day in advance. She let me borrow her punk-rock T-shirts.

The trouble with all that was that it made Hilary happy. Then, the next day, when she woke up in her dazzling wreck of a room, she would worry that she wasn't getting anywhere, that she had been doing this same thing for too long and needed to settle down. It appalled her that she was twenty-seven. She began thinking about babies. She was the oldest child in a large, wealthy Highland Park family, and although she had been on her own in some ways since she was fifteen, in other ways she had always been taken care of. She had been searching for something for a dozen years, and that night, over *fajitas* at the Prospect Grill, she told me she didn't think it was us.

She wasn't sure it was her fiancé, either, but she believed it was what he offered her: stability, security, a home, a family. Her vision of marriage and parenthood was a lot like mine: romantic, magical, mysterious. She really thought that being married would solve all her problems, that it would force her to change the things in herself she wanted to change, that she would be able to be serious, to handle things.

She told me all that, saying "I'm so sorry, David" every few sentences, and I never interrupted her. Most of the time, I wasn't looking at her either. I was examining the contents of my vodka tonic. Finally there came a pause I had to fill. I drained my glass and said something I really believed at that moment: "I understand. If I was going to get married and have kids, I'd have to marry someone like him too."

We left a good tip for Ruth, our waitress. She had waited on us through other serious, emotional talks and she knew when to leave us alone and when we desperately needed another drink. We walked by On the Air next door, but I didn't feel like dancing. "Are you sure?" Hilary said. Hilary thinks dancing can cure anything. We stopped on the sidewalk and she looked up at me, and she knew I was sure.

Like a lot of our friends—most of them single and in their late twenties—Hilary and I had always known we were different from our parents. Hilary was born when her mother was only nineteen years old, and within eight years she had a brother and three sisters. Now she was "almost thirty," as she always put it, and not only childless but husbandless as well. Yes, she loved me, she'd say, but love wasn't enough. Yes, I could buy just the right birthday present: shiny red plastic Fiorucci boots. Yes, I could glance at her across a crowded room and tell if she was happy or sad or bored or tired. Yes, she liked the way I lifted her into the air and swung her around in circles across the bohemian, two-lane climes of Lower Greenville, long after the bars had closed. But she had been having fun all her life. Now she felt that it was time to do something she *should* do—find the father of her children.

I met Hilary in January 1983, after I tried to pick her mother up at a party. It was a Christmas party at the home of an ex-girlfriend of mine, and Mrs. Hardcastle was the most interesting female there. I attempted to flirt with her by discussing G. K. Chesterton, a writer she seemed to hold in great esteem. That was difficult, since I had never heard of the guy, but she thought I was cute, nonetheless. "You should meet my daughter Hilary," she said. "She just broke up with her boyfriend, and I think you two would have a lot in common."

So I called the kid up. What a mismatch we were! Hilary had a brilliant, analytical mind, was very well read and educated, and though she had a well-developed wild streak, she was incredibly conservative politically. As for me, I had only two years of junior college, I leaned to the left politically if I bothered to lean at all, and though I had something of a reputation to the contrary, compared with Hilary I was incredibly straight.

And yet we liked each other. I thought she was striking. She was tall, rail-thin, with a short, uncontrollable shock of walnut-colored hair, big slate-gray eyes, and a wide mouth that spread into the nicest smile. We talked and talked. Breaking the pattern of most of my relationships, I didn't fall in love in an hour. I *liked* her. We were friends, and something more. We went to old movies at the Granada Theatre, swam laps underwater in swimming pools at night, and made hot chocolate and tea in her mother's antique kitchen at 4 a.m. Sometimes her mother would come downstairs in a white cotton gown, find us talking about science fiction or El Salvador at her Shaker table, and join us. They looked beautiful to me, mother and daughter, and they spoke with such reverence and enthusiasm about everything, from their inn on the coast of Maine to *THX–1138*, that I could only marvel and throw in a comment here and there. I felt lucky to know them.

Then Hilary would disappear. She would drive off to Sherman or Austin or Houston, and I wouldn't hear from her for weeks.

In the meantime, I would be busy looking for the love of my life. I'd never been married, never even hung up shirts in a woman's closet. I had thought I'd found the one for me a year before. We fell in love in an hour, and that set off a series of disasters we scarcely noticed. We planned out our whole lifetime together, and after four months we broke up. It was like one of those windup toys that run like crazy after you first let them go, then slow down, then stop. I'd been repeating this routine for years. I would be absolutely sure I was in love, that this girl, or this woman, was for me. But then we'd be in a restaurant, sticking our forks into our spinach salads, and I would find myself looking around at the women at other tables, wondering what they were saying, what they could tell me about life, what they looked like in a Danskin.

There was a barely married blonde I'd met at an S.M.U. Literary Festival party—I knew it wasn't true love, but she had beautiful hair. There was the sister of a friend of a friend, a University of Texas junior with an all-over tan and a vivid imagination. That lasted two weeks. There was an actress—two actresses. One I had absolutely nothing in common with, almost. The other moved to New York the morning after a discussion I'll never forget:

"David," she reasoned with me as we sprawled, tear-stained, in the privacy of her own room, "love does not conquer all."

I bolted up and paced the floor, gesturing wildly.

"But of course it does! *Of course* love conquers all! That's why they have that saying—you know, 'love conquers all'?"

She moved to New York anyway.

There was a slinky paralegal who worshiped my writing even more than I did, which made me nervous. There was a ballet instructor who was just too Eastern—she meditated in the nude by candlelight an hour and a half every night, which was fine by me, but she also railed on and on about my being a Capricorn, and her refrigerator never had anything in it but yogurt and boiled chicken.

And then there was Hilary. She would reappear as quickly as she had left, as if nothing had happened and no time had passed. One morning I came out of the shower and found her taping a sandwich bag full of chocolate chip cookies and a note to the window in my front door. A minute ago I dug around in my desk drawer and found the bag. A fine, bone-colored dust is all that remains of the cookies. This is what the note says:

> David!
> Hello—I did manage to both find your door & forget the nuts—yet, you are not here to appreciate the results. I hate writing w/ pencils. Mama Mía will surely die if she does not get her books back soon! Especially one by Wilfred Shytes?—something like that.
> P.S. I graduated. Am now formally adult.
> See you later, H. H.

We went for breakfast and marveled at how we could have gone so long without talking. I liked the way she ate fried eggs and how she was nice to the ancient waitress in the hairnet and support hose whose vocabulary consisted of the words "M'elp you?" The squeaky, cartoon cadence of Hilary's voice and laugh gave me a thrill, and I realized how much I'd missed her. I guess she disappeared all the time because of this guy; I never really asked her to explain, and she never volunteered to talk about it.

We became closer, actually explored romance. But it never seemed to work in that direction. We weren't "just friends," but we weren't passionate lovers either. There was a kink in the works somewhere that I didn't understand. Now I think it was probably her old college boyfriend and fiancé-to-be that was on her mind. Anyway, that is one of the things I've always liked about Hilary—there's so much about her that escapes me.

We danced. She would call me at midnight, when I had just gotten home from an early date, and say, "Hi, David Seeley. Aren't you restless?" I'd pull on my white Pro Champ tennis shoes and a black T-shirt, race to her rented condo in my Dodge, and sit around for an hour while she decided what to wear. We'd get to Tango in time for after-hours dancing and see a dozen people we knew. She'd wear, oh, red Fiorucci Safety Jeans, a huge, tattered Psychedelic Furs T-shirt, startling earrings, layers of undershirts and camisoles, slick shades, and dancing shoes. Her hair would be sculpted with French mousse, and we'd dance until we were soaking wet and the lights went up and we were forced from the floor. We'd get a sackful of doughnuts at Lone Star Donuts, and sometimes the next day's *Morning News,* and go wind down at her place. Sometimes we'd talk till dawn to the accompaniment of albums by the Psychedelic Furs and the Cure —about Kierkegaard (I'd listen), Thomas Disch, Frank Herbert, Ray Bradbury, William F. Buckley (she converted me to his prose if not his politics), Fitzgerald and Hemingway, Tom Wolfe, what we should name her Siberian husky's puppies, and how B&B and coffee was the greatest.

Then she would disappear again. And one or two times, so did I. That winter her break with her old boyfriend seemed complete, and Hilary and I were getting very serious. But the timing was bad for me. I was involved with an elementary school-teacher; when I got over that, Hilary had retreated again.

One day she began to talk about babies. She wanted one. She had been drinking and dancing and staying up all night for twelve years, and she felt like it was time to change her life. Maybe move out to the country with her husband—she glanced at me—and weave rugs on her loom as she raised a family in fresh air and sunshine.

We'd talk about marriage and babies in unlikely places, say, ten feet away from a raging Billy Idol video at On the Air. The idea appealed to me in an abstract, romantic way, but—now? in 1984? I'd get nervous and try to talk sense to her.

"Hilary," I would shout into her ear over a video by Frankie Goes to Hollywood, "so we have a kid, right? Okay. Now, every day from now on, 365 days a year, for twenty years, at 6 p.m., we'll have to have dinner on the table for the kid. Two vegetables, meat, bread, and milk. Then we have to make sure the kid eats it. You can't drag in at 9:30 and say, 'Oh, yeah, dinner.' You can't grab a burger at Snuffer's at eleven when you realize you're hungry, or have a midnight After the Show Special at Lucas B and B. Six p.m. For *twenty years.*"

I'd sit back, and we'd both feel a sobering rush of adrenaline at the thought of such shocking responsibility.

But she wouldn't be dissuaded. "The country?" I'd say. "There's all the crickets, and the moths beating against the porch screens, and no place to dance or see movies or eat."

"But I like the country," she'd say. Slowly and surely her old boyfriend came back into her life. He could offer her all that stuff she wanted so much. He was responsible and serious. He would know what to do. He loved her, and she trusted him. In many ways he was like our parents, whereas we were just like us. And anyway, Hilary had been thinking about marrying him for a long time.

The day before Hilary dropped the bombshell over our *fajitas,* he flew her to Sherman in a Cessna—he had just gotten his pilot's license—and proposed. Now she was officially thinking it over.

Hilary hates to hurt people, so after a few days I pretended everything was okay with me. Young people today, I read in *Newsweek,* breakdance and experiment sexually in spite of the looming threat of nuclear war. Well, if my own apocalypse was to be Hilary's marriage to someone else, I'd just have as much fun as I could until the day it happened.

We went out every night while she thought it over—I have no idea where *he* was—and for a couple of weeks Hilary and I were closer and happier together than we had ever been before. We were always staring into each other's eyes and intertwining limbs just off the dance floor and taking forever to say good night. We both knew that any night might be our last together.

She told him yes, and then told me, but we still went out. We saw a press screening of *The Bounty* and raced to Mistral to use my press comps to see Huey Lewis and the News. Nothing seemed to change between us, and I wasn't about to suggest that it should.

I never asked Hilary about her fiancé, because I didn't want to know. I suspected that her love for him was the real thing. It had

substance and commitment, things we didn't always have. Sometimes our nights together were like an escape from reality. They
let Hilary elude the pressures and responsibilities of accepting a
serious lifetime choice, and they let me indulge my own yearning for romance and drama, for theater. I'm not saying our
feelings for each other weren't genuine—they were. But we were
younger than we should have been, and that youth often showed
up in our lives as carelessness and immaturity. It often got the
better of both of us.

One night, a couple of weeks after Hilary got engaged, I did an
amazing thing, something I had never done before. Of course, we
were at On the Air. The level of my screwdriver was perilously
low, the Thompson Twins were blaring, Hilary was putting her
Glenlivet and water to her forehead to cool off, and I said,
"Maybe we should get married."

Hilary looked at me for a long time. "You're just saying that
for the shock value."

"No," I shouted into her ear. "If I was, I'd have said, '*Will* you
marry me?' "

"Well, we can't talk about it here."

Pinky's, a hip boutique across the street, was where we always
parked our cars. We strolled across Lower Greenville, which was
quiet at 1 a.m., and looked in the windows at a pair of shoes we
always lusted after but never bought. They were khaki WilliWear
high-top tennis shoes. We dreamed about them.

"I've thought things over," I began, "and I think I've worked
out some problems."

I was about to reveal to her the McDonald's solution, which
had actually been authored by Monika Maeckle the night before.
Monika, who was three months pregnant, was an old girlfriend
of mine who lived and worked in El Salvador with her husband,
Bob Rivard, the *Newsweek* correspondent there. I had told
Monika about the six o'clock dinner horror and how for that
reason I could never have kids, and she dismissed it with a wave
of her hand. "Listen," she said, forever altering my notion about
how children can be raised, "all you have to do is take the kids
to McDonald's."

"See," I told Hilary excitedly, "it takes all the pressure off.
It would work. The kids would love McDonald's—all those
Mcshakes and Mcfries, the playground in front. And we could
take them to the Highland Park Cafeteria for good vegetables

and have Chinese on Fridays. See? Breakfast is easy—Pop-Tarts and Malt-O-Meal. And they'd eat plate lunches at school."

Hilary smiled at this perfect plan, focusing not on me or the WilliWears but on something else. The future? Our future? Did we have one? Then she laughed her squeaky laugh and made me admit that I hadn't thought up the McDonald's solution by myself.

Was my pseudoproposal just a shock tactic? Maybe, in a way. I felt that Hilary didn't know what to do, that she was torn, grasping at things, putting a lot of pressure on herself. "If I don't get married now," she would say seriously, "it may never happen. I'm almost twenty-eight! I just know I *have* to do this, that's all. I love him. He wants to marry me and have kids with me. I *know* he wants to."

I would say something like, "Okay." And I'd think, "Well, Dave, maybe you should do it. Pull out the big guns. Say, 'Damn the torpedoes!' "

I would take it from the fifth pocket of my Levi's 501's, hold it up in the dim light at On the Air, and say, "Hilary." She'd look down and see the ring, and all I would say would be, "This was my mother's."

Other times, the idea of doing that terrified me. Her urge—and my growing urge—to settle down and get married glimmered out of some beacon from within. But on the surface, where we led our lives, it all seemed impossible if we spent a few minutes thinking it over. My deepest doubts came not during discussions with Hilary but during talks with friends who were in almost the same boat. Like the time I had drinks with a writer friend of mine who helped me understand what Hilary was going through. The friend was twenty-eight and successful in everything but her personal life.

"I don't know how many lovers I've had," she said, sipping her drink and talking low. "I used to know, but I stopped counting. Around thirty, maybe thirty-five. I'm not ashamed of that—it doesn't seem to me out of line. And yet, I think the more lovers you have, the more difficult it is to choose one you'd be willing to put up with for five years, not to even think of twenty-five years. And forever seems out of the question because of the pattern of failure we've all built up. You get to the point where you look at the person you're with and say, 'I love you. So what?'

You just aren't willing to make a commitment. You don't know *how* to make a commitment, since you've never made one.

"My friends are the same way. We feel like already a marriage wouldn't last, so why have kids, because they'd be a product of a broken home. And we're saying these things even before we get married."

Then she told me something that she admitted embarrassed her. "There's something that I do," she said. "I ride my bike from my apartment building to this comfortable middle-class neighborhood, and I see kids helping their fathers wash the car in the driveway, and mothers through the kitchen window doing dishes or making dinner, and I feel it's my rightful place, but for some reason fate hasn't granted it to me, hasn't granted it to a lot of us. I feel like I belong there, but as close as I get to it is riding my bike down that street. Then I go back to my apartment, and I'm alone."

For a day or two, the doubts and fears of my friends would stick with me. I couldn't see how Hilary and I could get married. We were so screwed up. And there were so many women out there, so many things worth doing late at night, when babies need to be changed and fed. I would pick up magazines like *Time* and *Esquire* and read harrowing stories about the new monogamy and the end of the sexual revolution. Everyone but us, it seemed, was getting married and having kids. I'd wonder: How? Where are the instructions?

But then I'd get a call from Hilary, and we would meet at some candlelit table. Her lips would taste of B&B, and all logic would go out the window. No matter what it took, I wasn't going to let her go.

In desperation, I was convincing. All the big decisions in my life have been forced on me—they just happened—and maybe that was the way I'd get married too, because if I didn't, I wouldn't get to go dancing with Hilary anymore. For a week I barraged her with stories, examples, and solutions that showed how irresponsible children like us could raise their own kids. She could work in a job she liked, and I could stay home with the kids and write. Or we'd make enough money to hire a Finn to stay with the kids from 8 a.m. to 6 p.m. weekdays. "Oh," Hilary said, "that would be great!" We would raise our daughter, Katie (we had decided we'd have a daughter, and we had already given her a name), on a home diet consisting entirely of Franco-American UFOs. As soon as our kids could talk, we would teach them to tell long, involved jokes. We'd have a happy house.

I developed more solutions to satisfy my own fears and anxieties. There was the "All Things Considered" solution.

"See," I told Hilary, "if I write a screenplay and make $125,000, and we do buy a house in the country, say, 50 miles west of Austin, I can listen to 'ATC' every day and feel like I'm still living in the world. And I can watch the "CBS Evening News' too."

More than ever I felt I couldn't lose Hilary. She had become too much a part of me. I embroidered loving stories of our life and our child, stories so detailed and heart-wrenching she couldn't possibly keep them from coming true. She would be getting dressed, sitting on the edge of a bed covered by dozens of dresses, camisoles, and pants. I'd kneel down on the floor in front of her, place my hand on her flat belly, and rest my face placidly on her knee. "Someday," I'd say, "you'll be getting dressed to go to St. Paul Hospital, and your belly will be like a weather balloon, and I'll be frantic and worried and I'll love you so much, just like I love you now."

She'd get sad. "David, I'm *engaged,*" she'd say. "You can't say things like that."

"And later," I'd keep going, sitting on the bed beside her and holding her hands in mine, "Katie will be two, and she'll try to be like Daddy in every way because he's so hip and cool. I'll say, 'Katie, want to go out and eat, or do you want Mommy and Daddy to slave over a stove with UFOs?" and she'll say, 'Prospect Grill, of course!' I'll kiss her and say, 'Let's go tell Mommy,' and we'll tell you, and then I'll say, 'Okay, Katie, what do we do now?' 'Wait for Mommy to get dressed!' 'And how long will that take?' 'A *cen*tury!' "

By now Hilary would be covering her ears with her hands and shaking her head no.

Hilary was moved by those stories, but deep down, just like me, she wondered if I would pursue them in reality as passionately as I created them in the safety of my imagination. She didn't trust me—she doubted whether I could handle being a husband and father at this time in my life. She didn't have those doubts about her fiancé, who went to bed early and got up early, who didn't like to go out much, who would have a top obstetrician lined up, would be insured a dozen ways, and would do things like build a second nursery on the back of the house, whereas I'd be pacing nervously in the hallway saying, "Another baby? Oh, my. Oh, dear. Oh, Lord. Whoa. Gosh. Huh."

Still, Hilary hadn't been able to bring herself to say, "David, get lost." The almost certain inevitability of a breakup neither of us wanted gave our meetings a deliciously painful, romantic glow.

One Tuesday night I stopped by the hotel where Hilary worked. I was in a suit; I had just been to a wedding. "David," Hilary said briskly, a bit officious in her makeup and high heels and white silk blouse, "I don't think we can see each other anymore. It's causing problems between me and . . ."

"Okay."

"Do you want a screwdriver?"

"Okay."

"I'm serious, David."

"I know."

She brought the drink. I was sitting in a fine leather wingback chair, paralyzed. She set the drink on the table. "I'm sorry, David." She looked around at her other tables—it was a busy night.

"But I know you love me," I said softly, after a long time. "And you know I love you. How . . . how can . . ."

She fled to the back room. When she came out, I don't know how much later, the drink was there but I was gone. I called her at home late that night. "You know what this means," I said. "We can't ever see each other again. It will be like we died in a plane crash and life suddenly had to start all over."

"Why does it have to be that way?" she said. "Can't we still be friends?" It went on like that, and it was awful. And then we were just making each other miserable, getting too upset, and our ears were hurting because we'd been on the phone too long, listening too closely for each other's words. So we said good-bye.

That next week was . . . you know how it is when your heart is broken. You think you'll never be happy again. You can't listen to the radio, because you suddenly realize that every song is terribly sad—and applicable. Your friends can only say the wrong things ("It's probably for the best"). You forget to shave.

So I decided to fall in love. Boom. Like that. I wouldn't let myself think about Hilary or I'd go crazy. There was this magazine editor I knew, a woman in the Midwest. We began burning up her Sprint line for hours each night, and I'd say, "So, are we in love yet?" I ran into an intelligent-looking redhead while I was shopping for a Mother's Day card, and I made a public plea for her to call me in a column I wrote for the *Dallas Morning News*. (It was called "Ask a Single Guy.") I even looked up the Eastern ballet instructor, who said that all my problems would be solved if I took lots of lecithin.

I was cracking up.

The next Tuesday morning, a week after Hilary and I had ended it forever, my phone rang and woke me up. It was Hilary.

"I'm calling," she said, her voice still scratchy from sleep, "because my horoscope this morning says, 'Make contact with old friends.' "

We went back to the Prospect Grill that night. "I've really missed you," she said as I walked up to the booth where she sat waiting for me.

"I've missed you too. This much." I held my hands about two and a half feet apart, and she laughed her squeaky laugh again. Ruth brought us drinks, gauged our mood, and stayed way over by the bar while we talked.

"I don't know what I'm going to do," Hilary said. "I have to marry him. I know it's just something I've got to do."

"Angel said you've been depressed all week. Like me."

"Yeah."

"I've got an idea," I said, sitting up straight and making a face.

"What?"

"Let's not talk about this. You know, it gets boring! Let's eat for instant energy and then go dance till three."

"What a great idea, David Seeley!" We looked over at the bar at the same time, and Ruth went back to order our *fajitas*.

It was sweltering inside On the Air that night, but there was a good crowd. A fifteen-year-old girl with a severe punk cut danced with us; she was a friend of ours. She looked about twenty-one and always reminded Hilary of the fifteen-year-old she used to be. The girl was also the best dancer in the place. We were moving around the floor, cool and new wave, to "Power and the Passion" by Midnight Oil, and I grabbed Hilary and shouted to our friend, "Aren't we a cute couple?" She nodded. "Don't you think we should get married?" She gave me a funny look, laughed, and shrugged her shoulders. I guess she just didn't understand the older generation.

We got too hot, so we went outside. A front was coming in

from the north; the breeze that rustled down Greenville was delightfully cool and scented with far-off rains. We crossed the street and found something astounding in Pinky's window—a new shipment of WilliWear high-top tennis shoes in all different colors: pink, red, white, gray, and assorted two-tone permutations that far eclipsed the khaki pair we'd grown attached to. "Oh, they're wonderful!" Hilary said. "I want those and those and those." We marveled at the limitless possibilities life can offer, and we took off our shoes and socks and stockings and sat on the curb, spreading our hot toes to the breeze. A Volkswagen Beetle roared down the street; the woman behind the wheel was waving to us.

"Look, it's Ruth!" I said. I wondered what she thought about us, shoeless and intertwined in the lights of Pinky's window. I hoped she thought we were happy. It was one of those nights when you feel like everything might work out after all.

That was all months ago. Something has happened to Hilary and me since—her engagement now seems irrevocably broken, but that has only torn us farther apart. In many ways, she is inconsolable in her realization that had things worked out differently, she would be married today, putting up a Christmas tree in her new home, and biding her time until babies arrived. But she's lost all that, and I've lost something too. Unprepared for this sudden, cold reality, we can't seem to connect anymore. We talk sometimes about meeting again when we're forty and finally able to settle down. We assume we'll have grown up by then and figured things out. But these days, when that future seems impossibly distant, when I'm feeling inconsolable myself, I remember that night on the curb outside Pinky's. It was a cool night, a good night, and Hilary was in my arms.

desi

As far as I know, the first time I saw Desi was on the morning of January 1, 1982. The first sunlight of the new year was slanting into my room, and Desi—or rather, an amazing creature I had no memory of—was asleep in my arms. Her skin was bare and warm against mine, and we were burrowed under a pile of blankets, curved together like two spoons.

I was afraid to move, even though my arm was tingling, caught in the lovely trap of her shoulders and her thicket of strawberry-colored hair. Maybe if I awakened her, she'd disappear, *poof*, like a dream or a ghost. More likely, she'd start screaming and the cops would burst in. So I held my breath and scanned back on the night before. One by one, the parties took shape through the haze. The early ones seemed sharp and vivid. I could recall addresses, see Michelle greeting guests at her door, remember jokes told by a drunken dance critic. Above all, I could remember the delicate stems of Michelle's fluted glasses, how light they were, how airy; the only weight came from the champagne, and it kept disappearing.

After 1 or 2 a.m., things faded in and out. My friend's car

nudging against an oak tree outside some party; the sharp, un-
welcome light of too-white bathrooms; the pumping din of Orchestral Manoeuvres in the Dark. There were girls, but there sure
wasn't *this* girl. How could I possibly have captured her? Did I
jot down the line that won her heart?

She stirred. Her hand skidded up my chest, cupped my shoulder. Instinctively—there must have been tenderness, caresses—
I touched it, turned her palm outward, opened her fingers like
the petals of a flower. She smiled sleepily through that lovely veil
of hair, and spoke. "Are we still the same person?"

Her voice was breathy, light, almost a Marilyn Monroe whisper. But her hand was the only thing that sparked a memory.
Somewhere, somehow, deep in the night or early morning, I
could see her telling my future, reading my palm. "I've seen this
hand before," she'd said. And she opened her hand beside mine,
skinning our palms together, showing our lifelines and love-
lines, pink mirrors, as alike as twins. I remembered her skimming her palm back and forth against mine, warming our skins,
staring quizzically into my eyes. "Maybe you're my long-lost
brother."

"Oh, I hope not."

But that's all I could ever remember.

Only rarely in my life have I gotten so sloshed that I forgot
what happened. On the other occasions, there wasn't much
worth remembering. I might have sat down in funny places, or
smoked clove cigarettes on the hood of a car, or fallen hopelessly
in love with girls in a music video. On the mornings after, I
wouldn't rack my brain trying to fill in the blanks. I'd just eat
aspirin and pancakes and try not to move my head much. But
there are times when I would give anything to know what went
on that New Year's Eve, how I managed to fall into Desi's hands,
what it was that drew us together. I was unaccustomed to luring
girls home from parties. Even at the peak of form, my mind clear
of drink and repartee sparkling from my lips, I couldn't imagine
wooing a girl like Desi. More than likely I'd probably stammer,
pop out a contact lens, lose my footing on some spilled beer. And
yet, here she was. Nearly unconscious on Moet & Chandon, I had
made a romantic coup.

I was afraid to ask her name. What if I had whispered it all
night against her ear, like a poem or a prayer? We lay languid
in the sunlight for hours, waiting for our temples to cease pound-

ing. Finally she stretched, kitten-like, and smacked her lips. "We need to show in-*it*iative," she said. "Don't you think we should take a hot, hot bath?"

"Yes. But there's only a shower."

"Hmmm." She scrinched her eyebrows in concentration. "Well, let's give it a try."

As the hot water splashed on us, she leaned against the wall of the shower, feeling the cool tile on her shoulder blades, and spread her hands across her face. "Mmm . . . this is just what I needed. Isn't it wonderful when you get just what you needed? Listen—I'm real embarrassed about something. I can't seem to remember your name, exactly."

We both laughed, and shook hands formally as we introduced ourselves beneath the hot spray.

"My name's Desi," she said.

"Desi? Desi like Desi Arnaz? Desi as in 'Babaloo'?"

She nodded, scooting around me for her turn in the water. "*Exactly* like Desi Arnaz. My father was Cuban, my mother was French. He was a tremendous fan, back in the '50s. They were going to name their first son Desi. Instead, I came along, and they gave it to me anyway."

A few minutes later, I found her naked and dripping on the kitchen floor, inspecting the open fridge. "Listen, I don't suppose you have anything for a girl to drink."

"Well, there's frozen orange juice. And milk—well, fresh out of milk."

"I was thinking of something more along the lines of a nice liqueur."

"There's vodka."

Her eyes lit up. "Ooo, now we *are* talking."

Over a peach and a glass of cold Absolut, Desi filled in some details she might have told me the night before. She'd grown up in New York and France, and had spent the last few years in Paris, painting and working as an artists' model. She'd moved to New York only a few weeks before and had flown to Texas on a sudden whim. "A girlfriend of mine was coming down here for that party," she said, "so at the airport, I just decided to zoom off with her. I was in sort of a jam and needed to fly the coop, anyway. Two weeks in a place and already in a catastrophe— that's a record, even for me."

Desi spent a week holed up with me, sipping champagne glasses of Absolut from breakfast till midnight, staying in a tipsy swoon as she weaved stories about her past.

In Paris, artists were always falling in love with her. She had been modeling there since she was seventeen, and had put together a rich mosaic of love affairs, some chaste and romantic, some violent and sexual. By the end of every spring, her hunger for romance and sex would be so sated, she would flee to an island off the coast of Crete. A rich man in his fifties owned the island and lived there in virtual isolation; he had met Desi once in Rome, and been so charmed that she had an open invitation. For the last three summers she had stayed with him there, rarely talking or making love, just painting canvases with blue skies and seas, and swimming off the end of a narrow pier.

"Someday if I'm ever rich, I want to live like that," she said. "And I'll have a sailboat, and I'll spend half my time on the sea, swimming and swimming, brown as a coconut."

"What will you do if you see sharks?"

She smiled a funny smile. "I'll swim into their mouths."

One night she asked me if I believed in past lives.

"I do," she said fervently. "I absolutely know I've lived before. Once I met this gypsy woman on a road, and she looked into my eyes and just seared me. She began to tell me all these things about myself, about this boy I loved, about my little brother who died. She made me some tea and said she had an interest in me. I felt faint, like I was hypnotized. She told me that years and years ago, during the war, I had been a courier for the Resistance. I was captured by the Germans on a train and taken right to a death camp, where they fed me to an oven while I was still alive. She described it to me—it was an oven the size you'd cook a pizza in. Then I remembered something strange—when I was a little girl, maybe five or six, my mother and I were traveling and we stopped to visit a concentration camp. They're like shrines to Jews, and she thought it was important that she pay homage. But I wouldn't go in. As we walked toward the gates, I started screaming. I grabbed hold of the wire and wouldn't let her take me in. I never knew why that happened, until this woman told me."

I asked her why she had left Paris for New York.

"Oh, it was time to go. I kind of wore out my welcome in Paris. It seems like I just cause trouble if I stay in one place too long."

When we went out on the town, Desi wore a black minidress so tight it was like the wrapper on a piece of candy—it was the only outfit she'd brought to Texas—and a twenty-pound leather jacket that dwarfed her. It drizzled zippers and belts, it was skinned in spots "from the Autobahn," and it was Desi's prize possession. When she was angry she'd reach back and flick up the collar, which she did nightly at 2 a.m., when the bars closed. "What do people do for fun in Texas?" she'd say. "It's hardly even dinnertime!"

Though she had just the one black dress, somehow the contents of her purse enabled her to vary her outfit from night to night: snips of black cotton to tie in her hair, bits of chain and dried flowers to pin near her breasts, an endless supply of earrings. She drank constantly, from the first light of day to the last moments before sleep, leaning over to scoot her glass on the nightstand and blow out candles. "I'm in training," she said, when I raised my eyebrows at her once. "And I'm on vacation. And it's okay, really." Everything I learned about her came in the form of stories; she was careful not to give away too much or to be specific about dates and names. It didn't do to be direct with her, to ask probing questions. A query like, "So, what do you actually do for a living?" would elicit a puzzled, uncomprehending gaze, as if you were speaking in Portuguese. Not asking questions, one quickly learned, was the way to Desi's heart. She wasn't being cold or rude—she merely had a shell she was quick to crawl inside. When she saw she was safe from grilling, that she was no longer taken for an ordinary girl, she would smile happily, beam as if bright TV lights had been removed from her eyes. Her lightning-bolt earrings would flash around dizzily, and she'd say, "Let's go someplace!"

I was surprised, as those few nights passed, that her attentions didn't stray toward some frazzled Oak Cliff artist, or to a coked-up bass player from Lower Greenville. In our nights together, I could affect a persona that attracted her: soulful, silent, staring, smoothed by Absolut, reading scraps of Victorian poetry to her, drunk, on the fire escape of a punk-rock bar. I could dance with her, kiss her roughly, and maybe even seem cool. But Desi's wild nights lasted twenty-four hours a day, and we quickly discovered we weren't the same person at all. Compared to her I was unbelievably straight. In the daytime I read the *New York Times*, drove to Sears to charge up the car battery, paid bills, shot baskets. But that didn't seem to bother Desi. She seemed drawn to my straight side. Perhaps she needed an anchor, a point of reference to keep for the years ahead. She once told me I was the only "nice person" she knew in the world. We may have had just a glancing romantic blow, followed by a painless parting, but when I drove her to the airport for her flight to New York, we were both pensive and sad. We weren't romantic exactly—we certainly hadn't fallen in love. But something had drawn us together. As we stood at the gate waiting for her flight to be called, Desi bit her lip, as if she were hesitating to tell me something. Then she looked up at me.

"Listen . . . do you know why I came up to you at that party? Do you know why I went off with you?"

"No."

"You reminded me of someone. A boy I knew in Paris. We were living together, there at the end."

"Was he the bad thing that happened to you, that made you go to New York?"

Desi brushed her hair from her face. Then she said, in that soft voice, "No, he could never be anything bad. He was so naïve. He acted like I was the only one in the world he could ever love. He clung to me like *this*, you know? Like a child clings to its mother. He smothered me, followed me everywhere. Finally I just had to go away. I went to London and saw my parents, stayed with friends a few weeks. When I got back to Paris, I found out Marcel —that was his name—I found out he'd killed himself. He went down in the Metro, and, you know. . . . It was just too, too awful." She brushed her hand against the shoulder of my coat. I didn't know what to say.

"When I saw you at the party, at first I thought you were Marcel. Then I read your palm, and it was spooky. I thought you were a ghost. And you were quiet, just like him, and you looked at me with those eyes, like you knew me. I was just lost. I had to stay with you."

They called her flight.

"Well, I must go. Ciao!" She kissed my cheeks. "Good luck! See you! Ciao!"

She left for New York, and after that for London or Paris—she wasn't sure which. I checked the mail for postcards every day, but when months passed without one, I wasn't too surprised. I was barely twenty-five, and there were plenty of nice Texas girls to go out with. In time, that week with Desi began to seem like a dream, a delicious romantic episode. I really thought I'd never hear from her again.

If we hadn't met on New Year's Eve, I sometimes think, Desi would never have remembered me. But she had a thing for anniversaries. It reassured her to hold a page full of numbered days, and know that each box represented something she could count on, like a birthday or a Psychedelic Furs concert. So at Christmastime, one year later, Desi's voice appeared on my answering machine, a tiny whisper from a long way away. She was flying to Dallas with her girlfriend again, to come to another party. Could we maybe get together for a cocktail?

She arrived at my place in an ancient, borrowed VW Beetle. "It feels so funny to drive," she said. "I think I may have bumped something." She looked striking. Her hair was dyed a deep auburn and coaxed into tiny wavy curls, and she wore all black beneath a U.S. Marines greatcoat.

"What happened to your great leather jacket?"

She looked at me, processing the question, repeating the words with her lips. "Oh—this guy has it. It's a long story." She said the jet lag was getting to her, but I imagined it was all the little Smirnoff bottles on the plane. Also, Dallas was a shock after what she'd been used to.

"I've been in New York like this whole year," she explained. "Everything's so hard and tough there, so, just, *grrrrrr*. It's like a daily fight just to walk down the street, and you get used to it. You develop a rhythm."

I brought her a drink. "Oo, this will help steel my nerves. Thanks. Going to a place like this, I just freak out. There's just *nobody* on the street, you know? And nobody honks. And everyone's so nice. And nobody yells." She shivered at the thought, like a kitten trapped in a box, devoid of sensations.

"Well, I'll take you someplace noisy," I said.

The Twilite Room was absolutely suitable. It was the only hard-core punk club in town, and they had four terrible, loud bands that night. We toasted our anniversary with red wine in little plastic cups, and listened to the crashing repertoire of a band from El Paso. Some skinheads in jackboots jumped up and down from the stage, banging together. Beer was getting splashed on everyone like perfume. Desi and I were sweating inside our sweaters and could hardly hear each other speak. She found the whole experience soothing. After a while the band took a break, so we sat in a corner to talk about New York. Desi had stories to tell, but her voice was so soft, and the Dead Kennedys were pumping so loudly from the jukebox, I had to press my ear against her lips to hear her.

She said she lived in the East Village of Manhattan, a strange neighborhood peopled by junkies, hookers, hard-core punks, and old Polish immigrants. She'd found a tiny studio five floors above Avenue B, in a graffiti-spattered building that was half burned out. When the landlord first showed her the apartment, she looked out at the building next door and saw six pale men sitting around a table. One was slumped over, possibly dead. She worried this was a bad sign, but the landlord explained that the men were papier-mâché and told her not to worry because the sculptor was about to move them out and begin making an Easter Island head.

Right after she moved in, Desi made friends with Babette, a dominatrix prostitute who lived across the hall. "She's very nice," she said, "but she makes a lot of noise. One time I woke up and there were these really awful, unbelievable screams coming from her place, even worse than usual. And then they stopped, and someone knocked on my door. I never look through the peephole, because I'm afraid there'll be an eye looking at me on the other side. So I said, 'Who is it?' And she said, 'It's me, Babette. Let me in, okay?' I opened the door and she came in, all covered with blood. She had on a black latex thing, a garter belt, high heels, and lots of chains. And she had this bloody machete. So then she said, 'Do you mind if I use your phone?' The cops came, with all these sirens, and they pounded on everyone's door, but I didn't want to get involved. And Babette just talked away about the weather and stuff. And hours later, the guy she'd slashed came back from the hospital and started banging on my door, going, 'Babette, come out. I love you. I know you're in there. Babette, Babette, Babette . . .'"

Things like that happened to Desi a lot. One night she was at Danceteria, and a guy she was dancing with suddenly put his hands on her throat and began strangling her. They were knocking over speakers, falling over people, and bouncers were beating his head in with flashlights. When they finally pulled him off her, one of the bouncers said, "Sorry, but that guy's crazy. He's always doing that." Another night she came home to find a Puerto Rican lying on her stoop with a bullet hole in his forehead. A week later, she was walking to her job at a movie-theatre box office when a high-speed cop chase erupted on the block; the car the cops were chasing catapulted over a cab and landed about six feet from Desi's tiny, shaking feet. Her only romantic interest in those early days was a guy who claimed to have been in the Sex Pistols, but she ditched him because he shot his dope up under his tongue.

As she told me her stories, she drank her vodkas like ice water. She didn't really get drunk; after six vodkas, she just seemed to calm down. Her stories took on more detail, were populated by more numerous and more vibrant characters. The current leading man turned out to be someone she'd met in Greece a year before, a heroin addict named Michael—the guy who had commandeered her prized leather jacket. He'd appeared in Manhattan and crashed at her apartment two months before, and that very night he was still in her place, 1,600 miles away.

"He's interesting," Desi said, sounding a bit sleepy. "He's very thin and very, very handsome. But he doesn't work or anything —I pay all the rent. Sometimes people come to our place, celebrities even. They give him money to buy dope, because he's not afraid of going down in the holes to get it."

The Twilite's bouncer put us out at 2 a.m., with a few bruised punk stragglers. Desi's Beetle was alone on a long, dark street— the only sounds we could hear were a ringing in our ears from the turned-off amps, and the whistling wind. "Wow, this is creepy," Desi said. "Is the whole town like this? Isn't there anywhere riveting we could go?"

I thought of a place. Desi drove a few blocks, following my nervous directions, but after she scraped up against a parking meter, we switched drivers. Minutes later we were at the Argyle, a seven-story, red brick apartment building that had been an elegant hotel in the '20s. "This is where we find Club 242," I said.

"It looks great." Desi stepped out, clicking her heels on the quiet street, and we pushed my friend John Branch's buzzer.

It was 2:30 on a Thursday morning, so I knew we'd find John up and around and ready for anything. He'd been sitting at his dining table, smoking cigarettes and writing in his journal, and when he came to the door he was pleased.

"Ah, the nightly girl delivery! How charming! How called for! Your coats? You know, this beautiful girl delivery business is such an extraordinary enterprise!"

John and Desi hit it off right away. The three of us sat up till dawn, playing Bauhaus tapes, scanning John's massive library, which covered the walls of every room including the bathroom, and indulging in various exotic refreshments. When the sun came up, Desi yawned, moved her chair next to mine, and burrowed her face against my shoulder. In the car on the way home, I looked down in my arms and found her sleeping. Her face looked untroubled, innocent. I couldn't reconcile that face with those ugly scenes in New York. Earlier that night, I had already made the decision—or maybe the discovery—that we would no longer be lovers. I thought she needed something else from me; there was a dark undercurrent to those stories. I felt that many of her misadventures involved sex, and that it was often just another bad thing that happened to her. At the Twilite, I'd noticed a bad bruise on her shoulder blade, and asked her what had happened. "Oh, it was just a present from a friend. An ex-friend. An ex-, ex-, ex-friend." If she needed me as a kind of haven from all that, an oasis of "niceness," then that's what I'd try to be for her. She was a little tense until she realized I understood this, and then she squeezed my hand, kissed my cheek. Now she lay cradled against me, dozing and content. She finally felt comfortable in Dallas.

The night before she left for New York, Desi asked me for a favor. Would it be okay if, on nights when Michael wasn't around, she called me sometimes?

"Of course."

"See, a lot of the time, I end up sleeping alone. And sometimes I have the most horrible dreams. I mean, you can't imagine the kind of dreams I have. They're just gruesome. And I wake up so, so scared, and I can't go back to sleep. I just sit up and stare all night, watching the windows."

"Well, the next time that happens, just call me. I'll try to calm you down."

"Sometimes it's real late."

"It's all right. I'm always up late anyway. Just call, okay?"

Through the telephone lines, Texas became more than an annual refuge for Desi. As the weeks passed, we kept in touch mainly because of her dreams. Once she was a princess in France, centuries ago, the captive of an evil, filthy black knight. They were traveling on foot and they came to a stream that was swollen from heavy rains. "We'll have to cross," the knight said. He took out a dagger and slashed it across Desi's throat, spilling blood all over her gown. It hardly hurt at all. With the slice in her throat, she was able to glide through the water, to swim, to fly. When they got to a village beyond the opposite bank, the knight made her peel down her blouse, exposing her wound and her breasts, so that all the village could see her pain. She was white, drained of blood, but she held her head high as she walked, strangely proud of her shame.

Her dreams were always like that—violent, mystical, tinged with madness. Telling them seemed to comfort her; they became stories she wove over the phone, instead of stark realities that pierced the darkness of her room. Sometimes I called her in the middle of the day, so she wouldn't associate me only with foreboding nightmares and 4 a.m.

Late at night on Valentine's Day, she called not with a dream but a tipsy plea. She had gotten no Valentines—"absolutely zero" —and she wanted to know if I'd give her one over the phone. I told her to hold on, gripped the receiver in my fists, and said, *"Shit!"* I'd forgotten to send her one. I'd forgotten to send anybody one—I'd already gotten in trouble for this with other women that day. I went over to my bookcase, scanned it, and got back in bed.

"Have you ever read *The Great Gatsby?*"

"No," she said. "Michael's not here. I haven't seen him in three days. You know, when he first moved in here, he got mad all the time. He'd yell at me because I forgot to do stuff. But pretty soon I was getting mad all the time too, even louder, and we started having all these huge, huge fights. Everything in our apartment is broken. My doors are all in pieces. One night we were so loud, Babette even called the police. Which is really weird, after all the stuff we've heard from her place. They got here and I just went berserk. They almost arrested me."

I read her the scene where Daisy meets Jay Gatsby at Nick Carraway's place.

"That's nice. That's so romantic. I'm just scared sometimes, you know? I'm sorry I called so late. Were you sleeping? I thought I heard someone breaking into the apartment, on the fire escape. I tried to hide behind a door, but all the doors are broken down."

I read her a sentence that I thought was the most romantic I'd ever read: *"Daisy put her face in her hands, as if to feel its lovely shape."*

"It's beautiful," Desi said. "It's like poetry, isn't it? I may go out later, to the Continental Club. It's way over on the west side, on like Tenth Avenue, in this big warehouse. It's only open from 2 a.m. to noon. I know a German girl at the bar—she gives me free drinks. I just need to chill. I've had to take sleeping pills every night since Michael's been gone. Actually, I have to take them every night anyway."

She asked me to read about how Gatsby and Daisy met again, but instead I read the scene where Daisy is about to marry Tom Buchanan, and she's drunk in a bathtub, clutching Gatsby's letter, squeezing it until it rolls into a ball and begins to come apart like snow.

"Read me the ending," Desi said. "I'll probably never get around to reading it anyway. Does it have a happy ending?"

"Well—not really."

"Oh, then don't read it. Don't, don't, don't read it. Please just don't, don't read it."

"Okay."

"Do you promise? Do you promise me you won't read it?"

"Of course."

"Let's just not talk, okay? Can we just hold on, so I'll feel like someone's here? Is that okay?"

I held on. It was a balmy night in Dallas—the window was open at the foot of my bed. I knew it was freezing cold in New York, because I'd looked at the temperature readings in the paper that day. I did this often; it made me feel closer to Desi. But never as close as I did that night, clutching the phone against my pillow, listening as her whispers calmed down to a steady, even breath. It was as if Desi was falling asleep in my arms.

Michael's absence turned into a banishment. Desi decided that when he came back, she was going to set all his stuff out in the hall and ask for her keys. "I'll be very calm about it. That will impress him." She surveyed her apartment, saw the pockmarked walls, the busted doors, the hole in a cupboard exactly the size of Michael's fist, and decided she'd had enough. "We're through, finished, kaput," she said over the phone.

"That's good. He seems like kind of a bad influence."

"Oh, well, he's not really. I'm just as bad an influence on him. That's why we attract each other. It's like magnets—we're both drawn to disaster. But I'm changing my electrons, I really am. Only nice boys like you from now on." She giggled. She'd been drinking more than usual, or using something stronger.

"I think you miss him."

"Who?"

"Michael."

"Oh, I guess I am used to him. But I'm trying to build up an immunity."

She gave a rundown of all that was wonderful without Michael. Her apartment, which had been an absolute wreck, was clean and neat. Her cat Alexis and all its babies were much calmer. She often got to sleep sometimes before 2 a.m., a New York record for her. Above all, her place was peaceful. There were still the background sounds of gunshots and sirens, and high-pitched shrieks from Babette's place, but these only made her studio seem more calm. There was a hollowness in her praise of all this tranquility; I remembered how the peace and quiet of Dallas had put her in a shaky, paranoid stupor.

"Just be careful," I said. "If Michael comes back, stick to your guns."

"I will, like glue. Like absolute, total glue."

With Michael gone, Desi had a run of good luck. She and Babette met a rich Mexican at a party, and he flew them both down for a free weekend in Acapulco, just to stand around and look beautiful at the opening of his new nightclub. She sent me a postcard from the beach ("Iguanas everywhere. The sun is out. I forgot what it was like to feel good.") Back in New York, she met a photographer who said he was doing a book of lingerie photos. He gave her a suite in the Plaza Hotel and photographed her for two days, half-clothed in silk and satin. She could order anything she wanted from room service. "I'm living on champagne and caviar," she told me during a string of long-distance calls. She kept sniffling, and I knew champagne and caviar wasn't all she was living on. "Do I sound excited?" she said. "Do I sound energetic? Do I sound pretty?"

She even had a chance for a role in an Off-Off Broadway play. "It's about this man and woman in a tiny apartment who have real dull jobs, and they're going out of their minds. They come home one night, get on the telephone, and just go crazy. It's a real phone, and we'd call up and order all these things, *expensive* things, Chinese food, groceries, theatre tickets. We'd call the stock market and transfer a bunch of money to South America. Then we'd just wait for all these delivery boys to arrive, and see what happens."

"It could be a big hit," I said. "You could become a famous star. It might run for years and years, like *Cats* or *Oh, Calcutta!*"

"I don't know," Desi said seriously. "I think we'd only be able to do it twice."

Weeks passed with no sign of Michael, and Desi started hitting the skids. She'd been working as a receptionist at a hair salon, but she got fired for not showing up. She began a series of affairs, some lasting only hours, with a parade of shady characters she met in East Village bars, on the street, or in the hallway outside Babette's. One night I told her I was worried about her, especially her drinking. And I knew she was doing a lot of drugs.

"I know, I know," she said. "I've been trying really hard to straighten out, believe me. Lately I've been trying the hardest. But you know, I have to drink a certain amount, and take some Valium or something, just to get through the day. Just to be like a normal person. It's just chemicals. I sound okay, don't I? I just sort of got screwed by this guy recently. Maybe I get too emotional, too carried away with other people's trips. I'm always plugging into the disaster zone."

She got the part in that fledgling play, so she and Babette and a young skater punk who lived in the building went out to celebrate. They were having an actual dinner at an actual restaurant off First Avenue when Michael walked in. He'd seen Desi through the window. He came up and said a few words, while Babette and the skate punk seethed. They both hated him. Michael had some really good dope, and some works and everything. Desi thought about it for two seconds and went off with him.

"I was crazy," she told me the next day, calling from a pay

phone near Tompkins Square Park. "I don't know why I went with him. We just did it right out on the street, and I got a huge bruise from it, because he banged me up and it's always bad when someone else does it. It hurt so much later, I was worried there was quinine in it, 'cause that can kill you. It was just out of control, the whole situation. I maybe, like, ask for trouble sometimes, but I'd never ask for *that*. It just scares me sometimes."

"And he's back with you now."

"Yes . . . he's back with me now. You know, sometimes he can be evil. I mean really, really evil. But he's only bad for me sometimes. He helps, though, too. At least when he's here, I'm not restless all the time. I can chill, you know? It's good to have conclusive evidence that there's someone even more fucked up than I am."

They got along for a good while; she didn't call me at night for a month, which seemed a good sign.

"We're living as man and wife," she joked. "We're like the mom and dad on 'Leave It to Beaver.'" But sooner or later, there was always a catastrophe. Michael would get beaten up over a bungled drug deal, and Desi would have to nurse him. "His lips are like two big apples," she told me once. "I can't even see his eyes. What's that stuff that's supposed to be good for swelling?"

"A hospital."

"Oh, he won't go to one of those. Believe me. Anyway, I'm afraid of hospitals."

Another time they were robbed, but the burglar was just looking for dope. Probably a friend of Michael's. He just smashed up the place and stole Desi's radio.

I asked Desi if they still had terrible fights, if she was scared of him.

"No, I do all the hitting. But I always just graze him. When I get that mad, I shake too much to be effective. Do you think I should take boxing lessons, or maybe ju-jitsu? Then even when I'm out of it, maybe the training would just take over."

Back in Dallas, I was having romantic battles of my own. I had begun a two-year love affair with a quizzical, sexy, dancing Reaganite named Hilary Hardcastle. For differing reasons, Hilary and I were as off-and-on as Desi and Michael. In our varying moments of freedom, Desi and I stayed in touch, keeping abreast of each other's chaotic love life, offering advice and counsel. Desi tried to leave Michael again and again, but it would never quite take. She was just stuck on him. Now when he disappeared for days or weeks, she no longer had periods of tranquility. Without him she would sink more deeply into drugs, fall into dangerous situations, and come close to losing it.

One day she called in a state of panic, trying to say a dozen words at once. I calmed her down as best I could, and asked what had happened.

"An hour ago I got in, I came in, I got home," she said. "I was lugging this big box, and I smelled a fire in the building. I climbed all the stairs and it kept getting stronger. I opened the door and the doorknob was hot, and it was my place that had the fire. The fire was in *my* stove. Alexis was meowing and meowing. She hit me in the face. There was kitty litter all over the floor. All my plants are dead, the fish are dead, everything is *dead!*"

"Jesus—did you call the fire department?"

"No, see, see, see—there was smoke everywhere but no fire. How does that happen? I didn't know what to do, so I just took a shower and a couple of Valiums. This whole day has been a complete disaster. On top of everything, my radiator is leaking so much it's popping up the hardwood floor. If you step on the tile, water shoots up in the room. For the whole past week I've been really on edge. Like last night—I went to dinner with this guy named Philip, and the very first thing, he orders a plate of mussels and goes to the bathroom. He's like in there forever, right? And in the meantime, the waitress comes over with this *whole plate of mussels,* and sets it down right across from me. So it's just me and these mussels. I mean, can you imagine? So I'm looking at them, and like, they just start *yakking.* They're all yakking like crazy! When Philip walked up, I said, 'Get rid of those things! They're yakking at me! They're driving me crazy!' He was real good about it. He dumped the plate on the floor and stomped on them. I need to calm down. Maybe I should take a Darvon and cool out. But if I start taking those again . . ." She picked up her cat. "Poor Alex. Poor, poor Alex. Do you hear her purring? Talk, baby. She's happy because I'm holding her so tight."

"Listen," I said, shushing her, "what do you think about having me up for a visit?" I'd been thinking about it anyway; I'd sold a story the week before; a check had arrived that very day. It had to be spent on someone, and it couldn't be Hilary—we had split up not long before, maybe for good this time. Michael was gone, Desi was hysterical, and New York was the greatest city in the world. It all added up.

"That would be great," she said. "Can you afford it? Can you come tomorrow? Let me tell you all about everything. First, don't let the cab driver screw you. Just say 'I'm going into the city,'' give him my address, and act real bored. Then, let's see . . ."

It was late January when I landed at LaGuardia Airport, and the *Daily News* at the newsstand had a banner headline:

—2°: THE BIG CHILL

After a careening ride in a barely heated cab, I stepped out on Avenue B just after midnight. All those nervous visions of Desi's block hadn't included icicles on street signs and Christmas trees on curbs. The icy weather provided a softened introduction to the neighborhood; even the corner drug dealers found it too cold to be out that evening. Desi's building, too, appeared less ominous and looming than it had in my imagination. It was an old building, but ornate and interesting. The graffiti on the stoop seemed almost decorative. Two years of mythology were waved away by the bracing wind—this was merely Desi's block, Desi's house and, five flights up, after an unseen kachunking of a half-dozen locks, there was Desi herself, kissing both my frozen cheeks and ushering me inside.

"Was your flight nice? How much was the cab fare? Sometimes it's only $11. You look *tanned.* Do you want something to drink? A vodka? Some cocoa?" It hardly seemed possible, but Desi looked even thinner than she had the last two New Year's. Every time I saw her, there was less of her. But still she was extraordinarily pretty—I was struck, every time I saw her, by just how pretty—and she seemed alert and well. Her light blue eyes sparkled. Following my glances, she waved her arms about and said, "Well, home sweet home!"

By Texas standards, her apartment was ridiculously small. It really was bottle-shaped. The "bottom," where you'd slap a label, was set off by a screen whose fabric fluttered here and there, battle scars from the Desi-Michael wars. Behind the screen, a futon sat plopped on the hardwood floor. Alexis and her six new kittens burrowed around in the sheets. There was also a chair and several of Desi's paintings.

"Do you do any painting these days?" I asked.

"Oh, gosh, never. Not since I moved here, really. I mean, some-times I'll do little drawings, on napkins and stuff. Usually when Michael's not around. But I always just crumple them up." She showed me some paintings she'd done in Greece, really her last work. They were all in the palest blue. Desi was shy about them. "Oh look, isn't this typical? I think this was about the last one I did."

It was a man sitting in a chair, shirtless, with suspenders against his brown skin, shadows on his face. He stared coolly outward; it was a cold painting. "Michael," Desi said simply. "It was right after I met him, on Mykonos."

We stared at him dumbly for a few minutes, and then Desi said, "Well," and finished the tiny tour, walking past the screen to a loveseat and table, where a goldfish named Sunny swam in a glass bowl, and toward the neck of the bottle, where a skinny kitchen and bathroom were jammed.

"It gets pretty small with all the babies these days," Desi said in her hushed Monroe whisper, "but it's easy to clean." I noticed in surprise that her refrigerator was papered with Marilyn's face, photos clipped from magazines and newspapers. I'd never known Desi was a fan. "I love her," she explained. "She was really, really great, you know? I wish I could be just like her."

We passed those first few days in serene domesticity. We'd wake around ten, and Desi would send me out in the snow for some juice at the Korean market, or a jar of plum butter at the Polish grocery. Back in the apartment, Desi would be wrestling with eggs and muffins. She was a spectacularly ineffectual cook, and I urged her not to worry about dinners. Off First Avenue, there was a string of Indian restaurants, and one night we had sandwiches and beer at a dive around the corner. When Friday was upon us, though, I decreed that we were having a "big date." Desi seemed a little uncertain about this. "Maybe we should stay in and watch TV. It's so cold out." We'd done just that for three nights, except for one movie in the Village. I'd been amazed and pleased by how tranquil her life seemed. Twice she'd gone to work at her gallery, and I'd spent the afternoons sight-seeing or looking up friends. The rest of the time, we took bundled-up walks or read or played with Alexis's kittens. All the wild stories I'd heard for so long seemed to have happened in some other world, not this one. We were in a spell, and perhaps Desi was hesitant to have it broken. But she relented, and after she spent two-and-a-half hours deciding what to wear, we were on the street, hailing a cab.

We had dinner at the Odeon, at a table right next to Andy Warhol and six of his hangers-on. This detail pleased me immensely, but Desi was unmoved. ("He's always everywhere.") She chirped up brightly, though, when we were served a bottle of Dom Perignon—a nice little chunk of my Desi savings. We had a great meal and another, cheaper bottle of bubbly. A bit dazed and happy, we headed back uptown for the Danceteria, the site of Desi's near-extinction while dancing the year before.

It was around midnight, and the club was jammed. I carried Desi's enormous fake-fur coat down to the basement, checked it, and spent half an hour looking for her on the club's four floors. I found her sipping a martini and watching a monitor in the video room. "Hi!" she said. "Try this. It's delicious." As we watched videos and danced, Desi drained a few martinis, and her face began to change. First there was a slackness in her expression, then a drowsiness in her eyes, and finally, a firm set to her jaw. By 3 a.m., she was having trouble standing, but she wouldn't leave the dance floor.

"Let's dance," she said forcefully. "Come on." Then she'd lean into my body, and I'd have to prop her up against a column.

"Let's go, Desi."

"No! I'm having *fun!*" She'd swivel unsteadily on her heels a few minutes, then collapse in my arms again. Finally I leaned her against a wall and held her face in my hands.

"Desi. *Desi!*"

Her eyelids fluttered. "What?"

"Stay here. I'm getting our coats. Stay right here."

I wanted to take her with me, but the crowd around the coat check area was unbelievable. Maybe sixty people were jammed in the little basement area, pushing to get to the window. It was like the Who concert in Cincinnati—you could feel the breath being squeezed out of you. I grabbed our coats more than half an hour later, and somehow waded back up the stairs.

Of course, Desi hadn't stayed right there. She was nowhere to be seen. Christ, what had happened to her? Abducted by skinheads? Crushed beneath a knot of people? Out wandering in the street? I went up and down all four floors, again and again, but it was no use. Desi had disappeared.

Someone tapped me on my shoulder. A guy with spiky black hair grinned at me. "Hey, isn't she with you?" He pointed at the dance floor. Desi was dancing sluggishly in the middle of the crowd, her shoulders dipping from the weight of her arms, her eyes looking straight down at the floor. I went over and grabbed her.

"No!" she yelled. "You just don't want me to have any fun! I never get to have *any* fun! *I want to dance!*" I didn't wait to discuss things with her partner. I swooped her up in my arms and carried her downstairs. A bouncer at the entrance, who already knew about my frantic search, saw us, laughed, and pulled up a rope that held back about fifty people who still wanted inside. Desi was kicking and screaming for this captive audience. I practically threw her into the first of a line of cabs, and gave the driver her address. She was furious, but halfway home she was sound asleep. I had to carry her up the five flights to her apartment, and when I finally staggered inside with my lovely burden, I was so exhausted I collapsed us both on the futon, and conked out myself. This was the Desi I'd heard about in her stories, the Desi who broke apart doors, who shot up on the street, who had fights so violent her dominatrix neighbor called 911.

The next day, Desi apologized for her "behavior of last evening." She couldn't remember much of it, but she knew she'd been a bother.

"I've tried to be *so, so* good this week," she said. "I didn't want to screw up your trip. And, like, I've done no drugs at all, just Valiums. Usually I at least take Elavil and Atavans and sometimes the really strong ones Babette gets from her methadone program. The need for those is almost as strong as the need you have for heroin."

"Then why take them?"

"Because they're the ones Babette gets. And they *do* something."

I asked Desi to be straight with me, not to hold anything back. I was worried about her. She didn't have to act like a Southern Baptist just because I had once been one. I wasn't going to run out of her life if I knew what it was really like. Then she told me many things. Yes, she'd shot heroin sometimes, but only rarely. Mainly she just shot up coke. Yes, she knew she drank much too much, and she figured she'd have to go into a treatment program for it sometime. But it had been real hard lately.

"There was this guy, Will. We were only together a week, and he wanted to live with me. He thought we could help each other. But his ex-girlfriend is a dominatrix, and he needs someone to be like that. I'm just the opposite. I'm not gonna go around and act like a bitch, just to make someone feel better. I could very possibly *turn into* someone like that, if things keep going the way they're going—I could turn into an hysterical bitch like I did with Michael. Will is a really great guy—he hasn't touched heroin for seven years. He's real stable in that respect. He goes to school, works in a studio, he's unbelievable. But he has these quirks."

He pestered her so much that she went to spend a few days with Tamara, a Russian girl she'd met at Downtown Beirut. While she was at Tamara's, Will threatened to cut his wrists. He didn't do it, but still, considering what had happened to her old boyfriend in Paris, it jarred her. "I thought maybe I should be with him, take care of him. But another thing is, he walks too fast for me. And he's too together. He'd wake up in the morning and shake me, and say, 'Desi! It's time to get go to work! You've got to get up!' It was like having a nursemaid. And if we go out, he can't drink really hard alcohol, because it would kill the methadone. Really, he's just too straight for me."

"Is he okay?"

"Oh, I know he's fine now. He got pulled together last week. I told him it's a good thing to be alone and cool out and chill out. We parted on real good terms. You know, both of you amaze me, because you're so good and talented and creative and on the ball, and it's too much for me! It just *amazes* me! I gravitate too much to the loony bins."

Will wasn't the only friend of Desi's to be visited by misfortune. Babette had been moved—forcibly—from her place across the hall and into a little cell on Riker's Island, for maybe as long as five years. She'd fallen in with a rather rough character who devised a foolproof scheme that would make them quick cash. He rented a sleazy hotel room in Times Square, took a tire iron out of his shoulder bag, and sent Babette out on 43rd Street to get dates. When she brought a john into the hotel room, her boyfriend would spring at them and slap the tire iron upside the man's head. Then he'd steal his cash and credit cards and kick him out in the hall. It sounded like a reasonable plan to Babette, and things went swimmingly until her seventh date in two hours had the nerve to call the police. Two cops kicked in the door just as Babette was helping to count the loot, and the john fingered both of them. He went all the way, too—swore out a warrant, showed up at the trial, pointed unwaveringly at Babette when directed to do so—and she got two-to-five for her part in the robbery.

"She'd have got probation, if it weren't for her record," Desi said. "I'm really worried about her in there. She was so brave at the trial—she wore these dark glasses and a leopard-print jumpsuit. Her lawyer wanted her to dress up as a schoolgirl or something, but she said, 'Desi, it's just not my *look.*' But she's really, really addicted to dope, even more than Michael, and I can't imagine her in a little hole for years and years. I don't see how she can survive it."

On my last night in New York, we decided to stay at home and drink like fish. "Just like Sunny," Desi said. "We'll watch him for tips." Since Desi drank like a fish from breakfast to bedtime anyway, this wasn't a big deal for her. But I decided to experiment, just once, with trying to keep up with her. When we were very tipsy, she had a sudden urge to sketch me. She got a grocery sack from under the sink and sat across from me, drawing with a charcoal pencil. "You know, I haven't drawn anything for more than a year," she said. "Maybe two years." She bit her tongue, looking from me to the sack, and suddenly burst into tears. She began to tear up the sack, in lengthwise strips, and then into smaller pieces, and rolled it all up in a ball. "It's no good. It's just no, no good." She was drunk and angry and brushing away her tears.

I kneeled down beside her and touched her face. "I wish I could make you happy," I said. "I wish I knew a way to help you."

"Maybe you'll move here sometime," she said, sniffing. "I think I need you."

We'd talked about this before. I actually had been thinking of moving to New York. In a romantic, vodka-assisted rush, we planned out my life in Manhattan: I could move into the studio with her, and Michael would be banished for good. I'd work at the little table, have free lunches with women's magazine editors, and bring home the leftovers for our fridge. Desi would work at the gallery and come home and paint. She'd become a famous artist and eventually buy us a wonderful loft in Soho.

"And we can buy an island off the coast of Greece, near my friend's, and I'll go swimming every, every day," Desi said.

"There may be sharks," I said, hiccuping. "What if you run into sharks?"

"We can *both* swim into their mouths."

We were being silly and our moods had swung sky-high. Then Desi had a pang of fear.

"You wouldn't ever try to send me to Bellevue, would you?"

"Of course not."

"And what if I go crazy sometimes? What if I hit you? You'll have to have a lot of stamina and guts to put up with me."

"Don't worry about it."

"So you want to take the chance?" She looked at me seriously. I told her sure.

"*Bon d'accord.*" She kissed both my cheeks gravely. The next morning, I sat in a window seat of a 727, shielding my bloodshot eyes from the sun, gulping aspirin against the ball-peen hammers bopping my head. Everything looked much more difficult than it had the night before. For one thing, Desi's phone had rung incessantly at five in the morning, and she refused to answer it. "I know it's Michael," she said. She wouldn't even let me get up and take the receiver off the hook. "He'd know. He'd hear you. He'd come banging on the door." So we lay with the covers at our chins, our toes peeking from the blanket, listening to the dark forces of her other life screaming in the gloom.

I moved to New York a few months later. Lee Hunt, an old friend of mine from Dallas, was moving there to work for a cable TV network, so we decided to get a place together in Greenwich Village. Moving in with Desi was no longer possible—Michael kept drifting in and out of her life like a bad tide, and besides, Desi decided that if we went through with our plan, she'd drive me crazy in two weeks and I'd never want to see her again.

Lee and I shelled out $6,000—picture us stunned, senseless, handing over cash like robots—for the assorted deposits and broker's fees on a $1,600 two-bedroom on Greenwich Avenue. We had to eat macaroni and cheese for months, but it was worth it to be in that apartment. It had windows on three sides and views of two gardens. Trees swayed outside the back windows, and the Jefferson Market clock tower loomed above their branches. If we wanted espresso or some pasta, we could walk downstairs to the Florentine coffee house below us. The sun shone on the wood floors all day long.

I made a date with Desi the very first day. Tired from unloading the truck, I took a cab across town to Avenue B. I paid the driver and turned to face Desi's building, and there was Michael. He was leaning against the stoop, his hands in his pockets, waiting for something. I recognized his face from the painting, and he was wearing the big leather jacket he'd grabbed off Desi two years before. It looked even more beat-up than before; there were new scratches and scrapes and what looked like a knife slash on the right shoulder.

Michael grinned at me flatly. He had messy black hair, lines in his forehead, a dust of black sandpaper on his jaws. There were clunky boots on his feet, one with a hole in the toe. Maybe he saw me eyeing the jacket; maybe he just had me pegged for a tourist in the neighborhood. But he knew who I was. I took the first step past him.

"You from Texas?"

I stopped, turned. "Yep." Time for a nice drawl—at least I had that advantage.

"You going up to 51?"

"I reckon I am."

We just looked at each other.

"Well, have a nice time, cowboy." He walked off down the sidewalk, laughing.

I cursed myself all the way up the stairs. *Jesus!* What an idiot. I thought up many comebacks on the five flights of stairs, lines that bristled with irony, but it was too late to use them now. I looked down at my chinos, my white sneakers, my big old watch. *Jesus!* Even if I'd fired a retort at him, I'd have looked stupid. Satire can't conquer everything. Crazy thoughts zoomed through my head: *I've gotta get some motorcycle boots, maybe a pair of leather pants. Boy, that'd sure show him! Then I'd get some respect!* By the time I reached Desi's door, I was out of breath and furious with myself.

"Hi," Desi said. "You're here! I can't believe it! Is the movie about to start already? I was just getting into the shower."

We ended up going to a midnight movie. "Don't worry about Michael," she said later. "He would never bug you or anything.

I think he just wanted to see you. He's known about you a long time, that you lived in Texas and I'd come see you and everything. It's like, he thinks it's funny."

Michael's tolerance of me was galling. I didn't want him to fly into a jealous rage and stick switchblades through my ribs, but it was unseemly that I merely amused him.

"You have to understand," Desi said. "He's seen me with so much worse. He doesn't mind when I'm with other guys—it gets me out of his hair. If I was with him too much, he'd just go nuts. And see, he knows you're so nice."

"Jesus, am I really so goddamn nice?"

She looked at me, surprised. "Of course you are. You're the nicest person in the whole world."

I wanted to save Desi—it was one of my big plans for my year in New York. But with Michael around, my plans were reduced to a hundred tiny rescues. I'd take Alexis to the vet when she got sick, because Desi couldn't stand to see her get shots. I'd zip over to the East Village as often as I could to take Desi out to dinner —worried that she never ate anything, I'd make her clean her plate. Now and then I'd loan her $20 to take care of some minor catastrophe, usually involving Michael and a pawn shop. But other times Desi could be so adorable, and such a case, that I couldn't help but fall for her.

Once she called late on a Monday night, nervous and scared. "I think there's someone on my fire escape. Will you come over? It's probably nothing, but . . ."

I pulled on some jeans and a T-shirt and made the trip over. When I buzzed her, she didn't answer for so long I really started to worry. But finally she buzzed me in, and after I climbed the stairs and heard her unlatch all the locks, I was greeted by a startling sight: a naked, soaking-wet Desi.

"Excuse my undress, okay?" she said. "I was just taking a bath."

I followed her back in the bathroom. "No prowlers? No burglars? No monsters on the fire escape?"

She sank into a tub full of bubbles, and gave it some thought. "I think there must be a tree branch scraping against something out there. It's real suspicious. Say, could you do something? Would you shampoo my hair? I love for someone to shampoo my hair."

That week it was thick, choked with mousse, wound together in raggedy dreadlocks. But as she squirted out gobs of cream and helped me squeeze the suds through her hair, it softened, smoothed, became lustrous and straight. "That feels nice," she said. "My mother used to shampoo me like this when I was a little girl. She'd sing little songs in French, and I'd just lean my head against her hands. Sometimes I'd fall right to sleep, and I was small, you know—my feet would only reach halfway across the tub—so I'd start to slide, slide, slide into the water. But she would always catch me and dry me off and put me to bed."

After a while, Desi stopped talking and closed her eyes, humming a song to herself. She was not a little girl. Her legs were long and lovely; her knees poked out above the islands of suds. When she began to fall asleep, resting the weight of her head against my hands, I rinsed her hair, drained the tub, patted her dry, and tucked her into bed. "Would you tell me a story?" she whispered. "Tell me one of those wonderful, wonderful stories you used to tell me." But before I could remember one, she was already dozing. It was good to see her sleep, all safe and clean and warm. All she wore to bed was lipstick—it was a habit of hers—and I remembered from the days when we were first together that when she woke up in the morning, her pillow would be covered with kisses.

Now, instead of calling late at night, Desi would sometimes just drop by. One freezing December night she buzzed from downstairs. "I just had the most terrific urge to come see you," she said. She unwrapped a long red scarf from around her neck, and did what she usually did when she came to my place. She strolled through the rooms, gaping with awe at their size. They seemed normal to me, but to Desi they were auditoriums, convention centers, exact-size copies of Madison Square Garden. Her tour of the apartment was accompanied by a distant wail from the street outside, the sound of an angry man honking.

"Oh, I almost forgot," Desi said. "I came over in a cab, but then I found out I only had a subway token. See, the pocket of my coat has this hole in it."

I bounded downstairs and pushed the door open. A cab was pulled to the curb; the driver took his hands off the horn and began screaming at me in a sing-song African dialect. I handed him a five, and he screamed some more, so I handed him a couple of ones and he peeled off toward Seventh Avenue. When I got back upstairs, Desi was in the kitchen, standing before the open refrigerator. "So much food," she said. "So many things.

Oh! A cucumber! This is truly, truly perfect!" She pulled open drawers until she found a knife, and began cutting the cucumber into slices. "I'm going to teach you something," she said.

We lay down on the living room floor. Desi had scattered some candles about, and we'd turned off all the lights. "Now," she said. "Lie down beside me, and close your eyes. Now put these right on your eyelids."

"You're kidding."

"No, really, you'll see. Now. See? We're lying here, it's quiet, there's only candlelight, and we have cucumber slices on our eyelids."

"I hope Lee doesn't walk in."

"Shhh . . . can you feel it? It just *drains* away all the poisons." She sighed. I felt her hand search out mine. After a while, it actually did begin to make sense. Desi moved her hand around until it was beneath mine, her palm facing up, skimming softly back and forth. I felt the strongest pang of true sadness. It had been four years since I first felt her hand against mine. Back then, Desi had seemed like some amazing new-wave angel, full of delicious secrets and unbelievable stories. We were both so much younger then. Times like this had become so rare, times when I remembered how she used to enchant me, how I used to dream of her. There were so many bad things in her life, and even though I was her ally and friend, I was powerless to help her ward them off, to make her happy.

"You know," she said softly, as if she were reading my mind. "I'm really trying to be better. Did I tell you I started getting acupuncture treatments? They're supposed to help you stay off drugs. Because I'm just taking way, way too many pills these days. I can't even keep track of them. And also, I've made a big, big decision—that I've just got to leave Michael. I'm like more addicted to him than anything. It's like, if I can break that habit, I can break all the others, you know?"

We were quiet a long time. I felt her hand against mine.

"Can't you just feel the poisons draining away?" she said. "Can't you just feel them leaving you?"

She sat up suddenly; I heard her cucumber slices fall—*plip, plip*—to the hardwood floor. "Tell me something, okay? Do you think I'm starting to look old?"

The candlelight shone on her face. Her hair hung in little

rivulets from her forehead, and her lips glistened, parted. She still looked like a scared little baby to me.

"No, you don't at all. You look like an angel."

"Because, see, I'm twenty-six now. And like, I went to visit Babette in jail last week. She's been there almost two years. You know, she had to kick everything cold turkey when she got there —heroin, coke, speed, everything. Can you imagine, living for years in a dark little room with bars, and nothing to ever make you feel better? She looked so sad and weak, and she looked so ancient. I never want that to happen to me. I never want to look that way."

She began to cry. I put my arms around her and rocked her softly, shushing in her ear. I would have done anything for her that night. But I didn't know where to begin, or what I could possibly do.

Two weeks later, Desi made good on her vow. The last straw came when Michael stole some jewelry her grandmother had given her, and she had to go to a sleazy strip joint in Times Square to buy it back from a guy. She packed her stuff in a bag, clutched Alexis inside a sweater, and moved in with her Russian girlfriend Tamara. Tamara was living in a loft on the edge of Soho with a band of punk Russian filmmakers, but they planned to find a place of their own soon. They slept each night in a big round window, because the sun came in each morning and warmed them up.

That first weekend, they began their quest for an apartment. For weeks, Desi delighted me with tales of their search. They called about a place near the Bowery and were told to be there in five minutes. When they got there, fifty people were lined up —"for a one-bedroom apartment with no windows!" There was a place on Second Street that seemed okay—it was only $400, since it didn't have a kitchen or a bathroom—but when she and Tamara walked outside, the police were talking to the super about a garbage bag full of blood they'd found on the sidewalk. They ended up searching the building for a body. Even though nothing was found, Desi and Tamara decided this was a bad sign.

There was something half-hearted about Desi's apartment search. For one thing, she seemed to relish telling how spectacularly horrific they all were. And beneath her bright outlook there seemed to lurk something regretful and sad. One night she went to a little club where Tamara was going to be singing some Billie Holiday songs. When Tamara began performing, Desi suddenly flashed on the scene in *Lady Sings the Blues* when Diana Ross freaks out. So Desi began to freak out. "I started crying, and I couldn't stop," she said later. "I felt worse since it was during her song, so I cried even more. I just sort of lost it. I almost fell on the floor. I was there with this guy, and he didn't know what was going on." She was also having casual brushes with Michael. She'd go back to the apartment "to pick up some clothes," or "to check on Sunny," or to do Michael's hair. Finally, I guess inevitably, she moved back to Avenue B. "Michael's calmed down a lot," she said. "We haven't had one single fight in four days now."

There comes a time in every hopeless affair when you begin to give up on it. I gave up on Hilary when I first moved to New York. Now, for the first time, after Desi moved back with Michael, I began to give up on her. I'd expended so much energy on her, gave her so much support for so long, and yet she never seemed to change or even really want to. The worst part was, she knew she needed to straighten out if she was going to survive. On top of everything else, she was finally beginning to worry about AIDS. Some of her friends had already died of it. She'd been exposed to nearly every risk group, so her only safety lay in not being a hemophiliac. But even this new danger failed to alter her behavior. When Michael made himself scarce, she still had run-ins with shady guys. Her use of drugs, her tendency to shoot up now and then, her drinking, none of these things slowed down. Her attitude toward me was changing, too; she called less and less frequently. Once she said she was avoiding me "because I don't want you to hate me. And I think I just let you down all the time."

Later that summer, there was at least one positive development. Michael left for good. He got involved in some drug deal that went sour, and he ended up holding a lot of cash. He decided to make a big score and skip the country. All he told Desi was he might go to Mexico, or maybe Greece. And then he was gone.

"All that money," I said. I'd gone to her place when I heard the news. "Did he leave you any trinkets?"

"No." Desi was stunned, lifeless, curled up on her loveseat. Then she glanced up. "Oh—well, he did leave me something." She walked slowly over to the closet, like a grieving widow, pulled something out and turned around. It was her big leather jacket, the one he'd stolen from her, the one she'd been so proud of nearly five years before.

"That's great!" I said. "Maybe it'll bring you luck. Maybe it's what you've needed all these years."

She folded the coat over her arms and hugged it to her. She looked absolutely lost. "I thought he'd take it," she said. "I really wanted him to take it. But he said he was through with me. He didn't want any part of me anymore." I sat beside her, but she was a thousand miles away. I could offer her no solace because she already knew she had lost me, too. I was only a week away from moving back to Texas. I felt like I was abandoning Desi, betraying her. When I said good-bye to her a week later she was so strung out, I don't think she even knew what I was saying.

In February 1987, I was going around the country for *Playboy* magazine, interviewing people about their fear of AIDS. While I was in New York, I looked up Desi and took her to dinner. I hardly recognized her—there were deep circles under her eyes, she was pale as a ghost, and more wasted away than she'd ever been. She said she hadn't slept in three days and hadn't been eating much lately. We went to a place called Nighthawks on First Avenue, and I ordered her a huge plate of food.

"I can't eat it," she said. "Maybe I'll just get a salad."

"No, it's okay. You can pick at it."

A couple of nights earlier, she'd hooked up with a punk band at the Pyramid Club. She'd been partying with them until just a few hours before. "I think I may have gotten married the other night," she said. "I remember I had to go back to my place for my white veil and my Nazi coat, so I could go to a wedding. But I don't remember much after that." She lifted up her sleeve and showed me a large red wound. "Look, I got branded. I'm such an idiot. I was with the band in some place, I think in Tribeca, and they were making sandwiches on this plate on the stove, and I said, 'Why don't you just burn me?' And I got it. That's what happens when you open your mouth too much."

I returned to Dallas almost wishing I hadn't seen her. As Desi would say, it was just too, too terrible. I wanted so much to remember something good about her, and I had an awful feeling that I might never see her again. That summer, the phone woke me up one night. I fumbled for it, and it took a few seconds for me to realize who was calling. It had been a long time since Desi called me, in the middle of the night or any other time, and I guess I didn't wake up as fast as I used to.

"Did I wake you?" she said. She sounded hazy, far away, but in gentle good spirits. "I'm doing real good. Do you remember that young guy Andy, the skater who lived in my building and used to hang out with me and Babette? I've been seeing him, and I have to stay on my toes all the time, so he won't think I'm a loony. I don't want to lose this one, you know? Andy is so straight, you wouldn't believe it. He hardly even drinks."

"That's great. That's really great, Desi." I asked her how New York was.

"It's warm. I really love the summer—it's nice because it's so pretty and people smile on the street. Yesterday I walked down to the river and went in the park, and I was in a swing, I was swinging, and there were all these little girls. I taught one of them how to swing. She was only two or three. She was with her father. Oh—a real good thing. I had a dream, finally, where that guy who kills everyone, he died. Now maybe I won't have those dreams anymore. Isn't that true? Is that how it works? If someone dies in your dream, doesn't that mean they can't come back?"

Not long after that, Desi disappeared. There was no answer at her apartment for two weeks. I called a gallery where she'd been working, but they said she didn't show up for work one day and they hadn't heard from her since. I called Lee and asked him to go by her building, but no one answered the buzzer. There was no one else to call—I didn't know Andy's last name, and there was no telling where Tamara was. A month passed, then two. I wondered if it was possible for someone to vanish forever, just like that. I'd feared for a long time that something would happen to Desi, but I thought I'd be called upon to do something—rush to her bedside, spring for bail, at least know what became of her. Instead, it seemed that one day she just went away. Nearly six years earlier, I had grown to accept it when Desi's postcards never arrived in the mailbox. But I would never be able to accept this. I would always worry and wonder about her, always feel guilty that I hadn't found a way to help her toward a better fate.

I moved back to New York in November 1987, and a few days after I arrived, something happened whose odds were eight million to one. I ran into Desi on a sidewalk.

I nearly crushed her with hugs. "Where the hell have you *been?*" She was laughing, closing her eyes and kissing me back. She looked wonderful. There was meat on her bones, her cheeks were pink and healthy, her eyes sparkled with a life I hadn't seen in years.

"Let me tell you, let me tell you," she said. She grabbed my hand and we walked down the street. "Do I look good? Can you tell a difference?"

"Are you kidding? You look incredible! But where have you been? I've been frantic for months!"

"Oh, hiding out. Incognito. You won't believe all my news."

Andy, the quiet young skate punk who lived in her building, had become her savior. He'd moved her into his place and tried to cut her off from the life she'd led with Michael. "I wanted him to. I begged him to, even though I gave him hell about it." Finally, he convinced her that it was time to be brave, and he went with her to check into a detox center—something I'd never been able to get her to do.

"I haven't taken any pills at all in nearly three months," she said proudly. "All I do anymore is still drink a little. Well, really a lot. But it's all I do, I swear. Oh, and the best thing, while I was in the hospital, I decided why not do everything scary at once. So I had an AIDS test. And it was negative, can you believe it?"

"Good for you, Desi. I'm so proud of you."

"Yes, Andy's so amazing. I think he might be Jesus. He's really raised me from the dead." She laughed and took my hand.

There was one other piece of good news: Desi was painting again. She'd gotten a tiny studio space in the public library on Avenue C, and she was working there every weekend.

We stopped in front of a gallery—she'd moved on to a new job too. She weaved just a bit, steadying herself against the archway. She must have had wine with lunch—but at least she'd eaten lunch! It was a funny image: Desi taking paper sacks to work with her, a sandwich inside, maybe a little bag of Fritos. The idea pleased me so much I hugged her again.

"So what are you doing here?" she asked. "Are you working?"

"No, looking for an apartment."

"You're moving back here? That's really great!" We began discussing apartments, and she kidded about giving me her old list to work from. Something began to trouble me. I was glad to find Desi and to find her so unbelievably well. But we were chatting like old friends, old acquaintances. She'd greeted the news of my return almost casually. Whatever poignance and emotion I'd once aroused in her was gone.

"Say," she said, "are you going to be here next Thursday?"

"Thursday?"

"You know, it's Thanksgiving."

"Yeah, I guess I am. I won't be going back to Texas that soon."

"Well listen—will you come for Thanksgiving dinner with me and Andy? I'm making a turkey for the first time ever. It'll be way too big for just two of us."

That was my first Thanksgiving away from my family, and it will always be my sweetest and most memorable. When I arrived, Andy was out buying ice cream for the pumpkin pie.

"He's shy about meeting you," Desi said. "He's so sweet, but you know, when he was young he went through a lot of shit in his life. Most people like that turn out so screwed up, but he's just amazing. He's one of the eight wonders of the world. He knows just when to crack the whip with me and when to ease up."

"And he's obliterated Michael."

"And he's obliterated Michael." She looked at me levelly, thinking about that sentence. Maybe it was the first time she'd realized it. Just then Andy came to the door. I'd imagined him as the polar opposite of Michael, but he really wasn't. He was lean and strong, with a short mop of blond hair, and he had an unmistakable air of street smarts about him. But he had a soft side that revealed itself easily. When Desi introduced us, she was so pleased she fell into his arms and burrowed her face in his neck.

"Isn't he wonderful? Isn't he a dream?" she said, beaming up at him. He laughed, embarrassed, almost blushing. But he cradled her protectively for a moment, his hand cupped gently against the curve of her back, and I could picture Desi rushing up to him like that a dozen times a day. He seemed used to holding her; he had saved her, after all.

It wasn't exactly a Norman Rockwell Thanksgiving. Desi had crammed a Smirnoff bottle in the turkey "to stretch it out," because stuffing was Andy's favorite. Then she cooked the turkey for five hours before she realized it was on "defrost." The corn bread came out kind of like soup, and her pumpkin pie was a color not found in nature. ("Darnit, I knew I shouldn't have tried it from scratch.") With each succeeding funny disaster, another bottle of cheap champagne was popped. The three of us toasted

Desi's wonderful meal and dug in in late-night darkness, telling stories until nearly dawn. There were new kittens at Desi's feet, and she smiled at me, clasping Andy's hand in hers.

Later, as I said good-bye at the door, Desi leaned close to me. "Do I look happy?" she whispered, "I can't remember, but I think this is what it feels like when I'm happy." I kissed her and looked at her drowsy, dreamy eyes. Of all the things I wanted to say, all that came out was "Good-night, Desi."

I walked back across town feeling a little sad, but not sad exactly. The streets were empty and quiet; even the Korean market was closed that morning. The city had that rare aura of benevolence that comes with a holiday dawn. Christmas decorations hung from the street lights, silver and gold paper stirred in the gentle breeze. I felt a pang of regret that I'd never been able to do for Desi what Andy had, that I hadn't helped her get straightened out and be rid of Michael years before, and saved her from many bad things. When I was leaving, she seemed to sense I was troubled; she brushed it aside with a kiss on each of my cheeks. "Come see us soon, okay? Ciao! See you! Ciao!" Now I could hear her voice, like music, as I walked for blocks and blocks in the early morning light.

the gods of
padre island

It can happen anytime. A kid is towing his raft out toward the surf, skipping on his toes across the hard, sandy floor of the Gulf of Mexico, and just before he reaches the safety of a sandbar a four-foot wave rolls over him and shoves his raft away, sucking him back in the undertow, filling his mouth with salt water. He comes up and gasps, choking, the salt water burning his throat, but before he can get a breath, a second wave crashes over him and he's trapped in the boiling water, in over his head, breathing horrifying lungfuls of water, rolling over and over in the undertow until the Gulf claims him as its own and drags him miles out to sea. It doesn't happen very often on the beaches of the South Texas coast; the surf and currents that lap against Padre Island aren't as rough and dangerous as those off, say, Southern California, where some lifeguards ride in helicopters up and down the coast and pull in as much as $18,000 a year. But people can drown in the Gulf as easily as in the Pacific, and that's not all a lifeguard on duty at Padre Island has to worry about: fistfights, shark attacks, stingray punctures, Volkswagens floating out with the tide—a hundred things can happen at any moment. Weeks may go by without a serious incident, but the guards can never let up, never take their eyes off the people in the surf, because it can happen anytime. And it can happen very fast.

On the Sunday morning of Memorial Day weekend, Doug Evans woke up wondering where the hell he was. He was lying on a flat, hard mattress, a roof stretched ten inches above his face, and from outside came the sound of rolling waves and crying seagulls. He tried to sit up and bumped his head, and when it all came back to him he wondered again if he hadn't made a terrible mistake. He had arrived in Corpus Christi three days before, with most of his possessions stuffed in the back of a Toyota pickup with Nevada plates, and he had immediately driven over the causeway to Padre Island and then 20 miles south to Malaquite Beach, on the Padre Island National Seashore. It was late in the evening and Malaquite was nearly deserted. Doug walked down to the water, felt it rush up and slosh between his toes, felt the wind blowing cool and clean off the Gulf, felt exhilarated.

He had spent the summer of 1981 guarding the beaches of Lake Mead, Nevada, a national park area nestled against the lake that sprang up with the construction of Hoover Dam. Lake Mead was a pain. A lot of the beachgoers there were rowdy drunks from Vegas coming out to raise hell and drown. He and his six associates were referees as much as lifeguards. For every near-drowning, there was a handful of fistfights, flashing switchblades, and rumbles between motorcycle gangs. Up in his steel lifeguard tower at Lake Mead, where temperatures could reach 118 degrees and the desert wind coming off the lake could dry-roast a man, Doug used to dream about working a beach with surf, waves, and an ocean wind. Through the National Park Service, he landed a job at Malaquite in May. He took his last music class at the University of Nevada–Las Vegas, said good-bye to his girlfriend, and drove to Texas. Now he was living in a tiny trailer on Malaquite Beach that the lifeguards used as a first-aid shelter, waiting for a paycheck that wouldn't come for weeks, worrying that he'd never find an apartment in Corpus this late in a busy summer season.

At nine a head popped in at the doorway to the trailer. "Hey, how's it going? You must be the guy from Nevada." Mike Solis introduced himself, and the two lifeguards were soon walking down the beach, Doug firing out questions. Mike knew the answers; he'd lived in Corpus Christi all of his twenty years and had been surfing and sailing off Padre since he was fifteen. He told Doug that the surf rolls over three sandbars on its way up to the beach: a shallow one twenty-five yards offshore, one about five feet deep fifty yards out, and another nearly a hundred yards out that is usually six or seven feet deep. The sand keeps the water murky most of the year; it doesn't turn blue until it's hundreds of yards out in the Gulf. If the wind is down and the water is calm, the waves might be just one foot high, but when gusts blow in the afternoon they can curl over at four feet or higher—safe for swimmers, but pretty slim pickings for surfers. In Malaquite's fourteen-year history no one has ever drowned while lifeguards were on duty, so keeping the record intact will be a piece of cake. "You just have to pay attention," Mike said. "You'll be all right if you assume that something *could* happen at any moment. The rest of your energies can be spent watching half-naked girls on the sand."

Down the beach, a hundred yards from Malaquite's four-hundred-foot-long cement pavilion, Doug and Mike came across a Portuguese man-of-war that had washed ashore. The jellyfish resembled a misshapen blue balloon with a mass of dark, curly tentacles dangling from its underside. Mike showed Doug how it could be picked up by its blue, inflated bag; he pointed out the stomach inside and then showed Doug the fresh scar on his side that he'd gotten by spilling out of his catamaran and brushing against the tentacles of a big man-of-war.

"The first time you get stung is the worst," Mike told him. "It feels like a bad bee sting, a real sharp pain, and then your skin just tightens up all around the sting. It'll go away in a couple hours if you don't do anything to it, but putting meat tenderizer on it makes it feel better right away." (The poison in jellyfish stings, like cobra venom, is protein-based, and meat tenderizer breaks down protein, so relief is usually immediate.) He pointed up and down the beach. "Sometimes the tide will come in real strong and there'll be dozens of these all over the place. That's when you get lots of business at the trailer."

Mike and Doug walked back to the trailer, where they met a muscular, curly-haired guy wearing a white T-shirt with LIFEGUARD stenciled on it. At nineteen, Jim Matthews was a veteran Padre Island lifeguard. He had worked the previous two summers at Nueces County Park's Bob Hall Pier, a less attractive, overcrowded beach 10 miles up the island. Malaquite has a long, wide stretch of clean white sand leading down to the water. The county beach has a thin stretch of hard-packed brown sand usually populated by locals who tend to make more noise, drink more beer, and cause more trouble than the tourists and families who predominate at Malaquite. Like Doug, Jim was starting his first day at Malaquite Beach. The three lifeguards went over their schedules and worked out shifts for the rest of the day—rotations from the single lifeguard tower in front of the pavilion to the first-aid trailer to the task of roving up and down the beach, torpedo buoy in hand, looking for trouble.

Whistles and T-shirts may make them all look alike, but in reality there are three kinds of lifeguards: those who work at private swimming pools (country clubs, hotels), those who work at public swimming pools, and those who guard the surf. A lifeguard's status, his mystique, increases in the same order. Swimmers tend to regard private pools as their turf and may resent a lifeguard's remonstrances. Swimmers in public pools are less familiar with the environment, but for the most part they are screaming, splashing kids who ignore lifeguards anyway. On the beach, lifeguards are transformed—they seem to have a magical aura of immortality. They become omnipotent guardians of the people in the waves, cool and indifferent and powerful in their stations high above the sand, surrounded by life-giving totems: the rescue surfboards resting on their stands, the torpedo buoys stuck in the sand, the blue, sun-bleached tower rising from the ground beneath them. People fear unseen things in the surf and find the presence of a lifeguard reassuring. The lifeguards up in a tower seem more disinterested and in control than swimming pool guards, since they don't whistle and yell every time a kid runs or splashes. A beach guard causes a commotion only when someone is drowning or being eaten by sharks.

Even though it was after 5:30 on a Wednesday afternoon and the crowd had thinned to just a couple of dozen families, Jim was in the tower paying attention. Lifeguards tell stories about working a long, boring shift only to encounter, just before climbing down and going home, a panicky moment of danger. The three guards at Malaquite approach danger differently: Doug keeps a cool head, plays it by the book, and Mike coasts confidently along, ready to solve anything as easily as he kayaks rapids in the

Guadalupe or scales rocky hillsides in Colorado, but for Jim the sea is a constantly threatening force of evil, something to fear. Especially on days like today, when he had been working all by himself while Mike and Doug took the day off. He had no one to back him up, no one to point choice girls out to, no one to share responsibility with. Working the beach alone makes the job scarier.

Jim was an Air Force brat who had lived in Corpus since 1974. In another age, he might have been affectionately called a big lug or a palooka. He was strong and tough, but he was also the kind of guy you couldn't imagine ever hurting anyone. During the school year he went to Texas A&I, where he was working on a degree in electrical engineering, and hardly a day went by when he didn't spend time with his girlfriend, Laura Martinez, a Texas A&I cheerleader he had dated since high school. But that didn't stop him from watching girls at the beach all day long, like Doug and Jim and every other male lifeguard worth his salt.

The sun was dipping behind the pavilion, shining through the slats in the tower to warm Jim's shoulders. He leaned back in his seat, put his feet up on the ladder, and watched two boys wrestle as they bobbed in the surf thirty yards offshore. He brushed a bit of sand from his knee, away from the boomerang-shaped scar left over from his football career at Richard King High School in Corpus. The sound of the waves seemed to grow louder as the noise of the beachgoers diminished. He could be stowing everything in the trailer now, getting ready to go home, but the two boys in the water were keeping him up there, reminding him of something from the past.

Two years before, on his first weekend as a lifeguard at Bob Hall Pier, Jim had been stationed atop the bathhouse, sipping a Coke. He had just graduated from high school, had gotten his lifesaving certification only months before, and had been told by the other lifeguards to expect a slow, boring job. All the guards together were expected to make only a handful of rescues all summer.

There were two kids, about fifteen or sixteen years old, out beyond the second sandbar, splashing around playfully—but maybe not so playfully. Jim was thinking of going out to check on them when one of them went under. Jim stood up. The kid came up from a swell, gasping, and Jim watched anxiously to see if he was just fooling around. He went under again without shouting. Jim jumped down to the beach, grabbed the rescue surfboard leaning against the bathhouse, and ran toward the water. A gust of wind caught the board and pushed him back; he pointed its nose into the wind and ran into the surf twenty-five feet up from the boy, so the current wouldn't push him uselessly away from the scene. When the water reached his waist he lay out on the board, curled his toes behind the end, and shot his hands back underneath the board, holding his head up to aim at the kid, who was floating face down now just beyond the second sandbar. The waves were rough as Jim crossed the bar; when two in a row broke right on top of him, he pushed his face into the fiberglass and held on tight, riding them out. He might have gotten out faster if he had left the board and taken just a buoy, but there wasn't time to wonder about that now.

He slid off the board and found the kid's arm in the water, then pulled him halfway onto the board and flipped him over. His eyes were closed, his jaw was clenched shut, and his lips were a deathly blue. His friend was treading water a few feet away, screaming at Jim hysterically, "If he dies, I'm gonna kick your ass!"

Jim lifted the kid's head back to clear the throat for mouth-to-mouth, but his jaw stayed shut like a vise, something that's not supposed to happen. A swell caught them and rolled them a few feet toward shore; Jim's toes touched ground briefly. He put his mouth over the boy's nose and blew in a breath. The chest rose and stayed there, so Jim pushed the boy's stomach with the flat of his hand. He heard a gurgling sound and looked up to see a small amount of mucus and water escape the boy's lips. The jaw stayed shut. He blew another breath into the nostrils, watched the chest rise, pushed the stomach more firmly this time, and the boy vomited a lot of salt water, then wheezed and coughed. His eyes shot open and stared at the sky, the pupils reacting to light. He kept wheezing, so Jim backed off to let him breathe on his own. The boy's friend was hanging on to the board now, yelling, "Come on! Come on!"

Jim yelled at the boy's friend, telling him to help kick the board toward shore. To his surprise, the kid obeyed. The two other guards were trying to control the crowd, to keep gawkers at a distance. When Jim and the two kids got to the beach they had to elbow through to get to the ambulance—one was stationed at the beach every holiday weekend—until a deputy sheriff yelled through a loudspeaker for the crowd to back off, and soon the ambulance was zooming away toward Corpus Christi. Jim got under a shower to rinse the vomit off himself and climbed back up on the bathhouse to finish his shift.

Jim never heard about the kid again, except for a news item on TV that night that said there had been two near-drownings on Padre Island that day. Nobody thanked him. The next day his supervisor told him he'd done a good job and not to worry about it, but someone had filed a complaint about his handling of the rescue. "It's nothing," the supervisor told him. "When these things happen, people get all upset about everything."

He remembered all this vividly and had come close to going through it again several times, so he felt relief when the two kids finally came ashore that Wednesday. He looked at the clock back by the trailer: 5:55. Miller time.

"Excuse me. Can I ask you something?"

Jim looked around for the voice—it came from behind the tower, from a thirtyish Baptist youth minister wearing a floppy white T-shirt that made his skin look tomato red by contrast. Around him were several teenagers, all wearing white T-shirts, all resplendently sunburned. One of their group, the youth minister explained, was missing; she hadn't been seen for two hours. They had searched the women's dressing room, the pavilion, the observation tower, and the beach with no luck. She was fifteen and was wearing a light blue bathing suit, beige sandals, and a white T-shirt. The group, nervous, wondered if she might possibly have floated out to sea.

Jim picked up the binoculars. Half an hour earlier, a couple had come looking for their sixteen-year-old son. Jim climbed onto the roof of the tower and scanned the north beach to see if this was only a coincidence. It wasn't. Three hundred yards away, their images wavering dreamily in the sunbaked air, the two teenagers were walking up the beach together, holding hands.

"Hey, Clint!"

"Yeah?"

"Got another customer for you." Mike helped a little girl into the trailer, and Doug put down another in a long line of peanut butter sandwiches to break out the meat tenderizer. Doug couldn't understand why everyone was suddenly calling him

Clint—he didn't think he looked at all like Clint Eastwood. But Mike and Jim thought he did, and they thought he acted like Eastwood's spaghetti-Western characters: a guarded, soft-spoken man of action.

Park ranger Charles Pearson, who worked out of the ranger station a mile up the island and had supervised Malaquite lifeguards since 1975, had made Doug the head lifeguard because of his experience and history with the park service, and for the first few days Doug had been apprehensive about coming out of the deserts of Nevada to order these two Padre Island boys around. But they had all gotten along well, and soon Doug established a routine: get to the beach at nine, do lifeguard drills, run a mile down the beach to the wood post barriers and swim back north against the current, divide up duties and trade them off throughout each day to keep everybody alert and happy. At night the three guards often hung out together at Cooper's Alley, a downtown Corpus bar frequented by suntanned sailboat racers and girls with eyes as blue as the water miles out in the Gulf. Doug had finally moved out of the first-aid trailer and into a ramshackle, un-air-conditioned garage apartment in Flour Bluff. As he sprinkled Adolph's on the little girl in the trailer, he looked around and found himself almost missing it. Almost, but not quite.

Mike walked back to the tower, glancing at his Aquadive watch to check the time left on his shift. A boy was sitting next to the seat in the tower—the snack bar cashier whose father had once dated Farrah Fawcett in high school. He was there to ogle the girls getting tans on the sizzling sand, and before Mike sat down the kid had hungrily pointed out half a dozen especially nice ones. Male guards scan the beach for girls diligently, as if it were in the normal course of their duties, but they're cooler about it than cashiers. On watch, they flick their gaze across the waves and occasionally glance down the beach to check on certain girls who may have turned over recently or undone their bikini straps or gotten up to walk the lifeguard's way. Sometimes a covey of nubile teenagers will lie down near the tower, stretching out on their backs in a long row that calls to mind the idle battleships lined up innocently at Pearl Harbor. When the wind is just right it rushes across the girls' brown, oiled flesh and breezes past the lifeguard, carrying with it the scent of coconut oil and Aliage. The girls at Malaquite are the lifeguards' Christmas presents in

July. They walk down to the beach in sundresses or T-shirts and short shorts, with their sultry, slinky limbs and their long, wavy golden hair, and unwrap themselves to reveal cute, brown bodies. Which one would be the summer's best: The delicious blonde with the tiny white knit bikini? The six-foot-tall brunette with the one-piece suit slit down the front to the waist? The fifteen-year-old Christie Brinkley look-alike in the burgundy sarong?

The only bad thing about Malaquite is its status as a tourist and family beach. Most of the girls whose beatific images filter through the lifeguards' binoculars turn out to be what the guys call Trouble. They're fourteen-year-olds on tour with a Methodist youth choir or sixteen-year-olds sunning beside their mothers and fathers. None of the guys wanted to be working the Huntsville prison pool in 1983. Anyway, Jim and Mike both had their girlfriends in Corpus, and Doug had unresolved ties in Nevada. What happened at Malaquite as July approached rarely went beyond the where-are-y'all-from kind of flirting, and the guys considered that just part of their job. Keeping up the image.

By midsummer, things at the beach had fallen into place. Mike, Jim, and Doug had developed a routine, a sometime car pool, and a shared wonder at how time was breezing by. Jim and Doug joined a health spa in Corpus, where they lifted weights a few nights a week. They went down to the beach before their shifts to help park-service naturalists release endangered ridley sea turtles. Working Malaquite had become as simple as breathing: each day, each crowd, each situation was different, but that was part of the routine, too. And so, especially for Doug, the job became something they could do without even thinking about it. The guards moved with ease and boredom. They were becoming old salts—beach guards.

A Saturday, hot and busy. Portuguese men-of-war had been washing up all day, faster than the guards could pop them, bury them, or drop them carefully into trash cans. A person could soft-shoe on the floor of the first-aid trailer, so much meat tenderizer had been shaken out during the day. Mike was sitting in the trailer drinking a Pepsi and thumbing through the 1965 Cape Cod National Seashore *Lifeguard Handbook,* listening absent-mindedly to the hand-held two-way radio propped in the trailer's window. The dispatcher was talking to a park ranger who had just ticketed a man for urinating right in front of the ranger station. Another ranger was trying to find a Polish man who had left his three Polish friends on the beach while he went to change clothes in his car; his friends hadn't seen him in three hours and none of them spoke English very well. Mike didn't know it, but within half an hour he would be putting in his own call to the ranger station.

Doug spotted the boat first. It was coming down from the north, a shrimper, riding fast and close to the shore between the second and third sandbars. Doug stood up in the tower and trained the binoculars on the boat—it was riding with one of its two nets in the water. He could see shiny mullet jumping in the net, and so could a hundred seagulls who were keeping pace with the boat, swooping down for the easy prey.

"Jeez, he's moving fast," Mike said, standing beneath the tower now and squinting up the beach. "That close in, I'll just bet he's going after brown shrimp, and that's illegal. Hey, we *swim* that close in."

Doug looked up and down the beach. Nobody was in the boat's path, so there wasn't any real danger, but he still wished he could do something. Boats aren't allowed in waters shallower than two fathoms—about twelve feet—along the national seashore. Any closer than that and they risk being battered to splinters on the sandbars.

The shrimper's engines grumbled as it passed, trailed by the screaming gulls, and everybody on the beach stopped to watch it go by.

Then Doug spotted the surfers, three teenagers who now were out past the second sandbar, a hundred yards south of the tower, right in the path of the boat. They were down in the water, arms out on their boards, treading water out of fear or maybe just curiosity.

The shrimper's pilot saw them too late to steer around them. He cut his engines and drifted to a stop, turning his bow out to sea. The boat slipped past the surfers and revved up again, but it was caught in the waves breaking over the second sandbar and scraped bottom. The current pounded the boat back. The pilot turned it straight out to sea and tried again, but a series of three- and four-foot waves knocked it back off the second sandbar, freeing it but sending it perilously close to grounding. The engine was open full throttle now; the boat moved over swells only to be knocked back by waves until its stern smacked down on the first sandbar. Doug, looking through the binoculars two hundred yards away, could hear the crump of ship against sand. After several agonizing minutes—all of them gleefully taken in by the lifeguards and the shrimp-boat survivors on the beach—it finally freed itself and went out a respectable distance before heading south down the island.

Mike radioed the dispatcher at the ranger station and told her about the incident. She asked for a correct spelling of the boat's name and wanted to know its home port, which is usually printed on the stern. "We didn't see it, but I think it was coming down from Port Aransas," Mike said. Pearson told them a citation would be waiting for the shrimper when it pulled into port.

Mike was having trouble being twenty. Going to Del Mar College near Corpus, planning to attend A&M later and then become a computer systems analyst, he had his future mapped out and had someone to share it with: his girlfriend, Della Gonzalez, a twenty-year-old from Corpus Christi he'd been dating for more than three years. But he felt that adulthood and its responsibilities were creeping up on him, smothering the fun in his life. He was by nature a freewheeling, devil-may-care guy, and his relationship with Della and a rapidly encroaching career were making him nervous. He was spending most of these summer nights not with Della, but with his friends from high school, a rowdy mix of upper-class Corpus surfers, University of Texas frat rats, and wild, raunchy A&M carousers. They had money and they lived fast, and Mike was moving in their lane. He drove a Fiat Spider his father, a general contractor, had helped him buy, and his garage apartment behind his parents' house was stocked with expensive stereo equipment and a color TV. His catamaran was just outside his door. When he was out with the guys, all of them Freixenet-fed self-proclaimed "butt gods," he felt most secure and sure of who he was. They partied in $200,000 homes when someone's parents were out of town; they roared around in Trans Ams missing parked cars by *this much;* they got wasted and watched Joan Jett on cable TV; they took wild, hotel-smashing road trips to Austin and Nuevo Laredo.

Mike's nightlife sometimes caught up with him at Malaquite, where he occasionally dragged in late after oversleeping to find that Doug and Jim had already set up the tower and done morning drills. Jim, who spent most of his evenings with Laura, watching TV at her house or going dancing, was being cool toward Mike one day late in July after Mike had committed just such an infraction.

Late that afternoon, Mike came up to Jim at the tower and asked him if he'd seen a blonde walk out of the dunes behind the beach, about two hundred yards to the south. "She walked in there with a towel and a basket and stuff, wearing a bikini with a T-shirt over it."

Jim looked toward the dunes. "No, I don't think I've seen her. How old is she?"

"I don't know. Twenties. Look—I bet she's in there naked."

"Oh, yeah?" Jim said, laughing. "Why don't you go find out for sure?"

Ranger Pearson had told them about finding a lot of women sunbathing in the nude over the years. The bottom line was that it wasn't allowed, but you didn't have to bother them unless someone complained. Ranger Pearson's nude sunbathing stories were some of his best, ranking right up there with his gory World War II tales and his vignettes from beach party drug busts in the seventies. But for the guards, a naked woman on Padre had been just an abstract idea until now. As Mike walked toward the dunes, he felt the invigorating rush of destiny, of history about to take place.

He stepped carefully up each steep dune, going back down and climbing the next one when he didn't see anything, pushing scrub brush aside soundlessly, trying not to kick up sand that would blow over the dunes. The nearest person on the beach was a hundred and fifty yards away. Mike heard his heart beat.

And then he saw her. About seventy-five feet away, in a low spot between the dunes, she was lying on her back on a huge white towel, naked and asleep.

Mike raced back to the tower and told Jim what he'd seen. Jim didn't believe him, and he could hardly believe it himself. They'd spent the whole summer watching girls and wondering what they'd look like out of their suits in the bright summer sun, and *here it was.* He wished he'd gotten closer, looked longer.

Mike climbed up the tower while Jim went to see for himself what all the fuss was about. Technically, he could walk right up to her and tell her that nudity wasn't allowed on the National Seashore. But instead he merely stood in awe, not twenty feet above her, gazing at her golden, unashamed beauty. She was still sleeping; her blonde hair fell back from her forehead and spilled across the white towel like spun gold. The wind was blowing a fine layer of sand across her oiled skin. She had no tan lines. Baby oil and paperback books—probably D. H. Lawrence and Anaïs Nin—anchored each corner of the towel. This was no fifteen-year-old Methodist soprano. This was Venus, Aphrodite, the goddess of light. This was an Austin girl.

When Jim came back with reverent close-up reports, Mike knew he had to go back for a closer look. This would be the best sight of the summer, better even than the time he and Jim paddled out past the third sandbar on the rescue boards and swam right into a school of jumping, playful porpoises. And the six-foot-tall brunette? She paled, she paled.

Mike walked up on the dune, following Jim's footprints, and froze like a statue. She was sitting up now, awake, about fifteen yards away, facing the beach. He couldn't move—he looked straight ahead, trying to affect nonchalance. His heart was pounding with amazement and the fear that she would see him. He pretended to be a nature lover surveying the dunes, and he slowly glanced to his left, toward the girl.

She was looking right at him.

"I got *this* close to saying something to her," he told Jim minutes later at the tower. "But I couldn't."

"What would you have said?"

"I don't know. Just hello. That's all it would have taken. I tried to say it, but it got caught in my throat. Nothing would come out."

"So what did she do?"

"Nothing. She didn't say anything. She just sat there looking at me. She didn't try to put her top on or anything. And so I just left."

Cursing himself, Mike wondered how his life might have changed if the girl had said something like "Hi." To sit beside a bronzed, bare goddess in the setting Padre sun . . .

"Hey, there she is," Jim said. The girl was running out of the dunes and toward the water. She wore a bikini with a bright flower pattern, and her yellow hair was flying in the wind behind her. She ran into the water, waded out until it was up to her waist, and swam around like a seal, rinsing the sand from her skin, diving into a wave to wet her hair. Then she got out and walked down toward the south beach. Mike and Jim stood beneath the tower, taking turns watching her through the binoculars until she passed the barriers and they couldn't see her anymore.

"You have to worry about drunks," Doug said from the tower, pointing at two bearded men in cowboy hats drinking beer out of cans and bobbing around in oversized inner tubes. "They get out there, get their arms and legs moving, and the oxygen level in their blood is so low anyway, then they pass out or fade out and go under. They don't yell, they don't struggle, and that's it."

Doug took a sort of Zen approach to lifeguarding, concentrating all his energies on watching people in the surf with the same single-mindedness he employed when practicing the tenor sax line from Coltrane's "Naima" over and over again.

"Lifeguarding requires you to concentrate for long periods of time on something that's basically boring," he liked to say. "It's like meditating, in a way. You have to concentrate on the water and the victims. People can either be too stupid or too smart to do this, but if you can master it, the job can make you mentally tough. You're working out every day as well, and that makes you physically tough. And since life can be tough in general, lifeguarding makes you ready for it."

Life was tough for Doug in Flour Bluff, a wind-bleached stretch of motels, seafood restaurants, and hardtack neighborhoods between Corpus and the island. His garage apartment wasn't exactly a swinging bachelor pad—it was furnished in late-'50s schlock and the neighbors had scores of dogs tied up in their yards at night. Doug kept a pile of oyster shells outside his door to toss at them when their barking woke him up. He left electric fans blowing in the place all day to keep the temperature bearable. Doug's home represented him as a man who wasn't planning to stick around very long. Musical instruments were crammed in everywhere: an electric bass, a flute, a clarinet, an alto sax, a harmonica, two enormous amplifiers he used as temporary end tables. Doug made the best of what he had. He stocked the tiny kitchen with fresh vegetables, brewed herbal tea so he could sip hot cups of it on the breezy steps outside while he read long, earnest letters with Nevada postmarks, got up at 7:30 each morning to make a lunch of boiled eggs, tuna salad, and grapefruit for the beach. He had been hanging out with a couple of women who worked for the park service, drinking quietly at Snoopy's Pier on the island and Neely's in Corpus, and pursuing a deeply tanned Malaquite regular that Mike and Jim called the Coppertone Girl, but most of his nights he spent at home, practicing on the flute and bass, reading, listening to jazz tapes. Doug said he used to be a romantic, used to have a lot of dreams and hopes, but that was all gone now. He figured it was just from getting older. He was twenty-four.

In September he'd probably move to Vegas and get a job lifeguarding at a big casino hotel, where he'd hand out towels and lawn chairs, take tips, and try to get a band together. Doug could already anticipate his regret at leaving Malaquite behind. It didn't have the ugliness of his old job at Lake Mead, where the guards put butterfly bandages on bikers' knife wounds and where Vegas nightclub singers took hookers out on boats and brought them back to the marina, hours later, black and blue. At Malaquite, there were no brawls or bikers or roving gangs of switchblade-wielding punks. Lifeguarding was reduced to its purest level here: the only enemy was the sea and what the sea kept hidden, and it was a beautiful enemy, cool and fast and rushing white where it broke over the bars, smelling of salt and fish and life.

Doug leaned back to pick up the binoculars and climbed onto the roof of the tower to sit on the edge a dozen feet in the air. From the tower, the deeper blue water of the Gulf seemed even farther out—perhaps a mile, perhaps just half a mile. Then it continued, dark blue and smooth, to the horizon, where Doug counted eleven offshore rigs jutting up like whiskers before the clouds. How wide was that stripe of blue water? Two miles? Ten? Twenty? And beyond the horizon lay Cuba and the Caribbean and the Florida Keys. Doug thought about those places he couldn't see for a long while, until a little redheaded girl riding a raft shaped like a bottle of tanning lotion kicked herself out beyond the second sandbar. Then he picked up the heavy glasses and went back to watching the kids in the waves.

Swimmers had been "harassing the wildlife" all day that Sunday. Mike and Jim had just finished treating a naked, screaming two-year-old for sea lice stings when they stepped out of the trailer to talk to a guy who was leaning against a cement pylon. He was about twenty-six, he wore a pair of borrowed corduroy op shorts, and he wanted to know if a lifeguard named Dennis Ramos was working at Malaquite this summer.

"No?" he said. "That's too bad. I haven't seen him since he left for Mexico, and I was kind of hoping he'd be back this year. We used to work this beach together. My name's Brice."

Brice Pennington first worked Malaquite in the summer of 1974, right after graduating from W. B. Ray in Corpus. In those big-budget days, five lifeguards worked the beach under the supervision of Ranger Joe Sewell, who would come to Malaquite on hot summer mornings to blow whistles while he ran the guards up and down the beach, sending them out in the surf to slosh through knee-deep water. A hardball player, Sewell. Charles Pearson came on in '75, and the Prussian drilling atmosphere relaxed to a laid-back shuffle. After Brice graduated from Southwest Texas State, he still came back each year to help finance his M.B.A. in international trade at Laredo State University. He worked his last summer in 1980, until August 9, when Hurricane Allen blew in, putting an end to Malaquite for that season. The lifeguard shack was destroyed, one of the two towers was washed back into the dunes, and Brice never worked as a lifeguard again.

After trading lifeguard stories for a while, Mike asked Brice if he wanted to go out in the water with him—way out. It was after five, and Mike was going to swim out to the blue water—something he'd been trying to do for a week. Andy Ashmore, a fifteen-year-old competition swimmer who rented floats in the pavilion, was going out with him, and Mike was going to tow a torpedo buoy behind him in case they got in trouble.

"Do you know how far out that blue water is?" Brice asked him, smiling indulgently.

"Not as far as it looks. We almost made it yesterday, but a shrimper was coming right at us and we had to head back."

Brice agreed to go out on one of the rescue surfboards to watch for jellyfish.

It took fifteen minutes for the three of them to make it past the third sandbar; the surf was very choppy, and the buoy roped to Mike's right shoulder was catching like an anchor as the waves rolled over him and sucked it toward shore, scraping skin from his shoulder. He and Andy had both swallowed mouthfuls of salt water, which burned in their throats, but still they swam out, going from the crawl to the breaststroke and back again, until they passed the waves and reached deep water that chilled like ice around their ankles. The blue water was straight ahead, almost close enough to touch.

Brice sat up on the surfboard and yelled at Mike and Andy to grab hold. They all looked back at the beach. The pavilion looked like a toothpick, and the people scrambling around on the beach were dots of red and blue.

"See those fish jumping out there?" Brice said. "They're feeding."

"Another fifty feet and we're there," Andy said. "See how close the blue is?"

Mike noticed Brice's concern. He was getting a little scared, too. "You want to keep going out?" he asked.

Brice smiled and shook his head. "If you ask me, I think you're both crazy."

"What, to keep going?"

"To be out even this far."

"Why?" Andy said. "Because of sharks?"

"Yes."

Mike looked longingly at the blue water. Just fifty strokes and we're there. But finally he gave it up. "Where fish are feeding, there's sharks. Let's race back to the beach."

Mike and Andy shot back toward shore, slowing down a few seconds later when they realized how tired they were—their arms felt like melted butter in the cold surf. Brice stayed behind to catch a few waves as long as he was already out.

Later, Brice stood dripping outside the first-aid trailer, listening to the steady rush of the surf, feeling the wind in his face on his first day at Malaquite all summer. He licked his lips and tasted salt. He was too busy to get out there as much as he wanted. Two summers after he last sat in that tower, Brice was now an account executive for an import-export company in Corpus. He spent three-fourths of his time behind a desk bathed in fluorescent light. He had to put on a jacket and tie to meet out-of-town clients. But you couldn't knock it, not really, because a good account executive could make as much as $25,000 a year. Those days of meager lifeguard's paychecks were over, along with the hot, boring hours on the tower, the awful snack-bar lunches, the sand in his hair and the Adolph's under his feet. That stuff was all behind him, thank God.

Doug came by to stow the torpedo buoys, Mike was making one last pass down the beach, and Jim was sitting on top of the lifeguard tower, scanning the kids in the water through the heavy binoculars. Brice held his towel over his shoulder and watched them from outside the trailer for a while. Then he turned and walked under the pavilion toward his car in the sunbaked parking lot beyond it. As he walked, he kept looking over his shoulder, as if he had lost something back there on the beach.

night life
in the age
of aids

Are you afraid of AIDS? If you're straight and you aren't, it's probably only a matter of time. In 1987, after a series of events —the deaths of Liberace and other celebrities, the controversy over AIDS testing and condom ads on TV, the passing out of free Trojans at a New England church and reports of increased AIDS cases among heterosexuals—people who'd rarely talked about the disease were suddenly talking about it constantly, in health clubs, in singles bars, at the office. In cities across America, local TV news crews turned their lights on in churning discos and asked heterosexuals, "Are you nervous about AIDS?" If they hadn't been nervous before, being asked the question made them think twice. And simply seeing those reports on TV made people wonder if they were in danger. Could making love to a stranger, or even a longtime lover, be an embrace with death?

It was bad. Then it got worse.

"You haven't heard or read anything yet," Health and Human Services Secretary Otis R. Bowen said that February, predicting that AIDS might make the black plague, smallpox, and typhoid epidemics "pale by comparison."

"I think the risk groups should be abandoned," Dr. Robert Redfield of the Walter Reed Institute of Research in Washington said that month. "There's really only one risk group—that's someone who has sexual . . . exposure to the virus" that causes AIDS.

Just weeks after those reports came out, I traveled to New York, Denver, and Los Angeles, talking with heterosexuals about AIDS. I went to places where single people meet—discos, parties, restaurants, neighborhood bars—and I heard some amazing things. Some people blamed AIDS on gays or a Commie plot or the wrath of God. Some wouldn't go anywhere without a condom. Some were angry; most men joked about it. But nearly everyone felt the danger looming on the horizon, and worried that it might only become greater with the passage of time.

new york city

I lived in New York two years before, right in the heart of Greenwich Village, where there may be more AIDS cases than any other neighborhood in the country. But like most heterosexuals, I hadn't worried about it personally. But this trip, there was no avoiding the subject—there were screaming AIDS headlines in the *Post* and the *Daily News* almost every day. Even the staid *New York Times* checked in—albeit in a mild-mannered way—with an amazingly frank Jane E. Brody column about condoms. It included such advice as "For disease prevention during anal sex, use the toughest condoms you can get, since ultrathin ones may not hold up."

I visited some of my old journalist friends. "You know what I think?" said a woman at Cable News Network. "It's only going to get worse. And as long as we live, it's never going away."

An editor at *Newsweek* said it wasn't fun anymore to go out in Manhattan. "Heterosexual angst has settled over every suck palace downtown," he said.

At midnight Friday night, the Limelight disco on Sixth Avenue had a waiting line fifty feet long. The crowd inside the converted eighteenth-century church was a microcosm of Manhattan: stockbrokers in Versace suits, coolly sipping Scotch; tough Brooklyn kids in suede jackets; Jersey girls applying lipstick in the half-dark; models and cabbies and nobodies and maybe a star or two, watching out for *paparazzi*. They moved around the dance floor, sat on the floor of a haremlike lounge, and smoked cigarettes at dark, low tables.

In the quiet bar near the back, I noticed four women sitting at a table, drinking and laughing, watching men walk by. They were eager to talk about AIDS. This is the same way every woman I talked with in every city reacted; I think women find it difficult to talk with men about AIDS, and they were glad to have the chance. One of the women asked me to sit down.

"I never worried about that stuff before, but now it's on everybody's mind," she said. She told me that her name was Irene, she was twenty-six, and she and her friends were all in advertising. "You hear about more and more people dying of it, and then all this stuff about the condom ads. I'm starting to wonder if maybe I should carry some around with me."

"Before, people would go out, they'd meet someone in a bar and they'd go home together," said Colette, a twenty-three-year-old who was visiting from Chicago. "Now you think twice about it. Jesus Christ, I go to the bathroom in a public place and I worry about it."

"And when you think about all those wild times you had in college," said Denise, twenty-five, "you're, like, 'Fuck!' You just go, 'Oh, those one-night stands!' You think about them now and it's scary."

I asked them if AIDS had changed the way people met and dated, and they all nodded.

"My mother's generation, the way they waited for marriage, that's coming back," said Colette.

"A few years ago, you might've just slept with a person and had a good time and that was it," said Irene. "Now more people are just starting to think, Stop it. Because you don't know."

They admitted that they'd done little to protect themselves from the disease short of holding guys off, since it's hard for them to ask men about their sexual histories or get them to wear condoms.

Colette stabbed my chest with her index finger. "Let's say you and I just met tonight. How would you feel if I said to you, 'Have you ever slept with a man?' Or if I said, 'Hey, let's go get some condoms.' Wouldn't that be insulting?"

She took a sip from her drink, rubbed a knuckle across her lips. "There was one time when I dated a guy"—she looked at her girlfriends—"I didn't tell you guys, but now that it's come up—

I went out with this guy a couple of times. And the first time that we were going to sleep together, he got up and got a condom. At the time, I was really dumb about it. I was impressed, because I thought he didn't want me to get pregnant. Then, the very next day, I read an article on AIDS. And I remembered he knew I was on the Pill. So I called him and said, "You son of a bitch, how *dare* you assume I'd have something you could catch?' I was very insulted. To me, that's *dirty*. I never saw him again."

Wendy was twenty-two, sweaty from dancing, maybe a little tipsy. "I think guys are hard up and wanna have sex. And a lot of girls won't care. What are you gonna do, ask a guy if he has a doctor's note? Guys wanna get laid. You think a guy who wants to get laid is gonna tell some girl that he has AIDS? No! And they won't wear condoms because it feels—whatever."

Colette sipped her drink and leaned closer to me.

"Look, I'm here for the weekend," she said quietly. "And, yeah, you go to another state, you meet somebody and, sure, you jump in the sack. You're on vacation, what the hell? It's not a big deal. But now it *is* a big deal. Because you may take something home with you that you're gonna live with, or die with."

Back out on the dance floor, three guys in suits surveyed the action. I cornered them in a hallway and asked if I could interview them. They laughed, scratched their heads, joked around.

"Well, I'm nervous about it and *he's* nervous about it," said one of them, a twenty-five-year-old attorney from Long Island named Mitch. He hooked his thumb toward one of his friends. "He's actually gay." They all laughed.

"Yeah," Mitch said, trying to keep a straight face. "I think most people are aware of it. Everyone jokes about it all the time now, because if you're not going to joke about it, the alternative is to live in fear. There's a lot of hype in the paper, and you wonder about the legitimacy of it all. Nevertheless, I'm concerned."

"But it's not a major topic of conversation, really," said Steve, twenty-five. He was from Long Island, too, where he worked for a car dealership. The third guy was a twenty-four-year-old named Frank, who lived in Queens and worked in the Garment District.

They said no women had ever asked them to use condoms, and they didn't seem to have the inclination to try them.

Would they be insulted if a woman asked them to pull on protection?

"I wouldn't be insulted, because I'd probably be worried the same way," said Mitch. "I might be a little disappointed, a little taken aback. But in the heat of the moment, you know. . . ."

"Condoms make it less pleasurable for women as well as men," Steve offered.

"Unless you use those big studded suckers," Frank said. "They're tough to carry in your wallet, though."

They didn't sense much change yet in the New York singles scene.

"I think it's going to take a few years until AIDS really hits home—with people who are close to people, their friends, their families," Mitch said. "Then maybe they'll listen up. But until then, I doubt it."

The next night, I was in my old haunt, the East Village. It's a strange, raw neighborhood full of old Polish immigrants and tough young punks, weirdo artists and transvestite junkies. It also has some of the best clubs in town.

I decabbed at Avenue A and Seventh Street, site of King Tut's Wah Wah Hut. A knot of punks jammed against the door, trying to get past the huge black bouncer, but he was counting heads —firemen had been coming around lately to enforce the club's capacity limit. I paid the $1 cover charge and squeezed in. It was seething inside, packed to the gills, but the drinks were cheap and the music great. King Tut's is a long, narrow bar that gets louder and hotter the farther back you go, and that's where I was going.

"I've sworn off sex for 1987," said a guy leaning against a column by the bathrooms. He had long black hair combed back from his forehead and wore a few black O-rings twisted around the watch on his wrist. Very cool, very New York. He said his name was Chris; he was twenty-four, lived across the Hudson in Jersey, worked as a cable-TV production assistant, and he was kidding about swearing off sex. But he was being careful.

"Bohemian girls in these downtown clubs are no go," he said. "Totally. Any girl with an artistic slant you have to stay away from, because she's definitely slept with bisexual guys. I'm only interested in a girl if she's from the suburbs."

I asked him about condoms.

"Even before the whole AIDS thing, I was always a big believer in condoms," he said. "I made up a little poem today for my friends. I'll tell you how it went." He pushed back his hair, concentrated. "Don't stammer and stutter/If you need a rubber/Ask Chris for a loaner/For something safe for your boner." He twirled around his beer, pleased. "I was shaving this morning, and I made that up. I always carry condoms with me for my friends, or for anybody."

Were his friends as worried as he was?

"My friends aren't that worried. They're much more cavalier in their attitudes than I. They're like, 'Oh, she's clean,' those clichés, you know? They really think a girl who might be kind of conservative is okay, but that's ridiculous. There's a little more animosity toward gays now, too. Something's wrong, something's kookie now. I'm an atheist, but there's some bad karma going on in the gay community."

At that point, a friend of his came up with a beaming Nabokovian vixen, who just might have been eighteen. She wore a brown bomber jacket, black tights, red Keds. "Hey, Chris, this girl wants to talk to you," his friend said.

"Okay." Chris leaned toward me and slapped me on the back. "I'm gonna go hang around teenagers," he whispered. "They're safe, too."

Near the fire exit, I ran into a girl I had met at King Tut's last year—a beautiful, fragile, tough little girl in a big leather jacket. Lisa was twenty-five; she led a very wild and often dangerous life, yet she managed to go to work each day as a receptionist uptown. She has known more than ten people who've died of AIDS, half of them gays, half drug addicts. The night we talked, two of her friends were close to death from it. I asked her if she was afraid.

"I don't know." She downed a little gulp of vodka. "There's so many other bad things that can happen to you, you know? It's, like, getting sick with some dreaded disease is not as bad as everyday stuff."

Lisa knows nothing about safe sex; she's seen a condom only once in her life, when a guy she met at Area used one with her. Usually, when she has sex, she's too far gone to think about such things. Anyhow, she thinks condoms are too weird.

I asked her if she ever thought about getting AIDS.

"No. This girlfriend of mine sometimes mentions it. We just, like, joke, you know? We believe in reincarnation and stuff like that. We believe we used to be together in a past life and every-thing, so we just keep on going, whatever happens."

I'd done the discos and braved the East Village—now it was time to check out the singles scene on the Upper West Side. Clark Kenowitz is the bartender at Amsterdam's at 80th Street and Amsterdam Avenue, which has long been one of the hottest pickup spots in Manhattan. When I got there, it was still warm from the lights of a TV news crew. "They were doing the same thing you're doing," Clark said. "All the people they talked to said they think about it now."

So the fear of AIDS had reached Amsterdam's?

"No doubt about it," he said, rubbing a twist around the rim of a glass. "In fact, we were half-joking about putting a condom dispenser in the bar on Friday and Saturday nights, when this place is unbelievably crowded and there's a lot of 'Hi, what's your sign?' things going on."

Do people talk with the barkeep about AIDS?

"Yeah. People will be standing around bullshitting, and it'll come up. It never did before. It's really been just the past six months. When I'm speaking with a guy, he'll be a little more open about it. A woman won't say, 'Yeah, I've been screwing Tom, Dick, and Harry, and now I'm only screwin' Tom.' But a guy will say the equivalent of that."

Lucy's Retired Surfer café was only a few blocks away, but there was a ten-below wind-chill factor to consider, so I hailed a cab and made the short, careening trip. Lucy's gets a younger crowd; it's a bit of California on Columbus Avenue, with "Hey, dude" bartenders and marlins and surfboards on the walls. I shook off the frightening March cold and encountered four handsome lads clutching beers near the door.

Three of them—Tim, Doug, and Chris—went to Villanova. The fourth guy, Mark, went to Georgetown. They were all from Brooklyn.

"At Villanova, the girls aren't that liberal," Tim said. "If we were going to school here, I'd be worried. But it would be pretty easy to tell which girls potentially had AIDS. Pigs are pigs. You have to know how to tell the pigs from the nonpigs."

How do you do that?

"A pig is someone who looks like a tramp. Someone who's easy to pick up. Which is, of course, what you're looking for." His friends all laughed. "It's a double-edged sword."

I asked them about condoms. This being the Upper West Side, Chris pointed out, "That's good stock to invest in."

"I agree," said Doug.

"I read an article in my school paper two weeks ago that talked about heterosexual AIDS cases," Tim said. "They were warning that you should use protection. And for a Catholic university, that's—" We all paused. We were clogging the main artery toward the bathroom, and a luscious young blonde needed to squeeze through. When she was past, Tim said, "Now, she is the type of girl who wouldn't have AIDS. And even if she did, I don't think I'd think about it."

So, were they scared of AIDS? Did they worry about it?

"It's like we're almost convinced that middle-class white Americans don't get girls pregnant," Tim said.

"You don't think it's going to happen to you until it happens," Mark agreed. "You know there's nothing you can do about it, so the best way to cope with it is to try to deny it."

I thanked the guys and went to talk with the blonde, the one Tim was sure did not have AIDS. She was sitting with a girlfriend at the bar; the bartender had given them little rubber whales and they were playfully batting each other with them. I ordered a screwdriver.

"Oh, do you want your mermaid?" the blonde girl said.

"Nope. It's yours."

She took the little plastic mermaid off the edge of my glass, licked the screwdriver drips off it, and added it to her little mound of souvenirs. She said her name was Sarah; she was twenty-one and went to Columbia. Her friend Julie, a girl with flowing brown hair and amazing hazel eyes, was twenty-one, too; she was a student at the Parsons School of Design. They were lifelong friends from a small town, who'd been sent to the big city for an education. And now their folks were worried.

"My parents have been sending me information about AIDS," Julie said. "They'd rather I be celibate. They'd rather I hadn't lost my virginity at all. But they know I have, so they're really, really hyper. They don't want a dead daughter on their hands. If you sleep with just two people, you can get it, because sleeping with one person can be like sleeping with twenty people. Who's to say? I've had a lot of boyfriends who slept around a lot."

"Plus, a lot of people around here are actors and dancers and stuff," Sarah said. "There's a high percentage of them who are bisexual, and that's a scary thing."

"I've pretty much abstained for the past month," Julie said. "I mean, my boyfriend left town and I stopped sleeping around. Before I had a boyfriend, I slept with whoever struck me. Now I'm waiting for another boyfriend, and even then, I would use condoms."

Like the guys across the bar, Sarah and Julie have friends who think their higher station is a barrier against AIDS.

"They don't worry about it," Sarah said. "They think it's a junkie and fag disease from downtown, and they're uptown, so it doesn't affect them. So they continue sleeping around."

When the girls left, they waved their whales at the bartender. "Thanks for the fish," Sarah yelled. Then they were out in the cold, and a cab appeared like magic to sweep them home. I sat at the bar. There were pictures of surfers on the wall, crates of Mexican beer stacked on the floor, blond guys with sunglasses doing shots for the hell of it. Shades of things to come.

los angeles

I used to think of L.A. as a crazy, sun-soaked land of Porsches and palm trees, surf punks and motion-picture executives. I've added another impression: Of all the places I've been in the past year, it's the most frightening place to be a sexually active heterosexual. It may not be statistically more dangerous than New York, but for some reason, the level of hysteria in L.A. seems strikingly higher. From the moment I arrived at LAX, I was inundated with the AIDS issue. It was on page one of the *Los Angeles Times*

S.F. LEADS WAY IN TRACING PARTNERS OF AIDS PATIENTS

I'd barely turned on the radio in my rented Pontiac when I heard a promo for a report on *Eyewitness News* about straights and AIDS. ("I like sex," a woman's pained voice said as I drove down La Cienega, "but I'm not willing to die for it.")

After the freezing weather in New York, at least it was warm in L.A. I had dinner that Friday at a Thai restaurant in Hollywood with my friends Tom and Barbara and a friend of Barbara's named Diana. Diana was single; she was involved in myriad film and video projects, with acting credits that included a role in the film *Reform School Girls*. She was wildly beautiful, with jet-black hair and striking eyes. Barbara had told me she had a very funny, caustic sense of humor. But it was hard to work humor into our talk that night.

Tom and Barbara had recently lost a friend to AIDS. They'd visited him over the months as he died a slow and agonizing death, and they described how their friend, who was gay, had wasted away before their eyes. I was struck again by how differently people feel about AIDS when they've known someone who died of it; in a strange way, they're not as hysterical about it. They're more compassionate, more serious.

"I've had seven friends die of AIDS," Diana said. There were many gays in her business—actors, singers, artists—and she'd forged close friendships with a lot of them. She's been aware longer than most people of the dangers heterosexuals face.

"I'm extremely nervous," she said.

"Did you used to have sex with anybody without even thinking about it?" Barbara asked her friend a tad jokingly.

"Yes, in the olden days," Diana laughed back. "Sex any time, with not just anybody, but, you know—when it was my choice. I mean, my tastes are peculiar."

"Do they run to bisexual men?"

"No, I hope not. The thing is, I'm more concerned about the partners of my partners than my actual partners. There are only a few men that I'm nervous might have been really wild men. I'd be real surprised if any guy I ever slept with was bisexual, and I just hope that people they've slept with have the same history."

An amazing thing about L.A.: Almost every woman with whom I talked had taken an AIDS test or was about to take one. Diana was on the brink.

"Well, someone was saying how inaccurate the test is. And how you can be free of the virus now and two months from now, it'll show up. I've thought about taking the test, but when I heard that, I figured—" Diana gripped the edge of the table so hard her knuckles got white—"just *hang on* and hope. I mean, it's not permeating my every thought."

I asked her if she'd changed her sexual practices, if she used condoms, had cut out casual sex.

"To be honest with you, Dave, I haven't gone out this year. And next time, I'm going to try something new. I'm going to employ the old-fashioned courtship before sleeping with somebody.

Women look at sex a whole lot differently than men do. I don't know many women who take it casually and just think of it as something to say, 'Hey, guess what I did last night?' Barring AIDS, I also just want to make sure the next time around, somebody feels strongly about me—not just here today and gone tomorrow.

"It's interesting how many heterosexuals have at this point not even thought they could get it," Diana added. "I spoke with a friend six weeks ago, and she'd been seeing this guy who was real sexual. After they'd gone out for three months, he wanted to introduce another man into their sexual situation. And I said, 'Casey, are you kidding me?' She said, 'I wasn't interested.' 'Well, this guy has had male relationships!' 'I think he's had only one or two,' she said. So I asked her if she used condoms, and we talked about AIDS a little bit, and she completely, totally freaked out. She was convinced she had it. They've since broken up, and she took an AIDS test last week. But, you know, it could still show up."

Later that night, I went to a party at a movie producer's place in the Hollywood hills. It was an amazing stucco house built into the side of a steep, high hill. The lights of L.A. were spread out like a winking carpet down below. My friend Tom, who's a screenwriter, wangled me into the party, and I became one of its themes: Go off to a back bedroom and get interviewed by *Playboy*. People treated it almost as a lark out by the bar, by the chips and dip, by the stereo booming a Los Lobos tape. But when I talked with people alone, they were, without exception, serious, concerned, and worried.

"The other day, I was driving," said a thirty-year-old shiatsu-massage technician named Jill. "And I suddenly felt this wave of fatigue. And I thought that maybe I had it." She noticed my surprise and laughed. "Really! It passed through my mind. I'm very aware of my immune system, and I felt something coming on. And I thought, Oh, God, it could be a possibility."

"Do you and your friends talk about it?"

"*Yes.* All the time. It's a terrifying notion that if you have an affair, you can get it. I think a lot of people are hesitant about getting into new sexual relationships. I am. I haven't bought condoms, though. Some of my friends have—both men and women. The responsible ones."

Jill said that single life in L.A. had definitely changed.

"It seems like there's just less of a sexual vibe being put out, by *everybody*. It's kind of neat, because people may show their childlike side, or their intellect, before they show their sexuality. It adds mystery. It's getting back to a kind of romantic innocence before having sex. I just wish we could have taken this turn without having a disease cause it."

Had she been tested for AIDS?

"I don't know where to go, and I hate getting needles in my arm. I want to get one, kind of. Everybody should have a test. They should have block parties and have tests, if only to lessen people's panic."

She said she was in a relationship right now but that if she had to start a new one, she'd be very careful.

"At this point, if a man told me he was a fabulous lover and he thought I was the cat's meow, I *still* wouldn't sleep with him. I'd want to *like* him. You know, his essence. So that when we got out of bed, we'd still have something. I wouldn't be embarrassed or hesitant to get an AIDS test with that person. My ex-boyfriend actually did that with this girl he wanted to have an affair with. The Red Cross people were at U.C.L.A. for a blood drive, so they gave blood and got tested together."

Robert, a twenty-seven-year-old carpenter in the film business, had a special insight about AIDS. All night people kept saying to me, "You should talk with Robert." "Go talk with Robert." So I went and talked with Robert.

"I'm worried, because my brother is gay," Robert said, smoking a cigarette as he sat on the edge of a bed, away from the noise of the party. "He's been active in the AIDS Project L.A. program. In my social circle, I know two people who've died of AIDS and another one who tested positive for it. My brother has worked with ten or eleven people who've died of it. We're going into retrograde homophobia. All of a sudden, it's back again: queer bashing, guys beating up guys just because they're gay. And now you're hearing jokes about gays and AIDS in regular conversation, from people you wouldn't expect to hear that from. I'm working on a movie right now, and the whole cast and crew, you can hear it in the way people are speaking."

Robert said he wasn't sure whether or not to be personally afraid of AIDS. He's wary of the media hype and he said he doesn't sleep around.

"The religious fanatics say that it's a plague that was predicted and will start and have no finish," he said. "I've heard people say that once it's on the college campuses, it's all over. The whole population will have it. It's like the Red scare all over again."

Do his straight friends worry about AIDS?

"No, it's sort of over there in the gray area. They aren't using condoms. It's like, 'Yeah, it's in the news, and it's topical—let's talk about it—but it's not going to affect me.' It's even like that in the homosexual community—people see their friends dying, and they still carry on the same lifestyle. All you have to do is go up and down Santa Monica Boulevard and you can see it's just a meat market, a mess. It's a place where people go, they fuck somebody; the next night they go, they fuck somebody else.

"I think that once it gets across to heterosexuals, it's going to be hard to stop. Because sex is the most powerful drug. Sexual attraction is like fire. And it's amazingly evident among my straight male friends that sex has to do with being virile and strong."

But Robert thought women were different. And he expressed, better than any woman with whom I'd talked, why women and men may be reacting differently to the threat of AIDS, why women may be so much more serious about it.

"Women have an innate sense of their physical being," he said. "They menstruate. They have these serious things going on in their bodies that men don't. We have this thing between our legs that doesn't change—it doesn't put us through any cycles; we don't have to have contact with our bodies. But women have to deal with their bodies all the time. Birth control generally falls to the women. And it's going to be women who put the brakes on, especially since it seems that it's the women who are being infected by the men, more than vice versa.

"I have a friend who has the best attitude about sex: He just says, 'Listen, I don't want it to fall off. You've only got one—it doesn't grow back. And I'm gonna know the girl before we have sex.' And he stands by it. It comes down to just being responsible for yourself."

I talked with others at the party: people who'd had an AIDS test, people who hadn't because they "didn't want to know," someone who'd heard rumors that the Russians introduced AIDS into the U.S. as germ warfare, a woman in her twenties whose father had given her a box of condoms and said, "If you're going to have sex, use these."

The weekend I was in L.A., *Carnaval* was raging in Rio de Janeiro. I went to a local version of *Carnaval:* a pre-Lenten Mardi Gras extravaganza held at the Palladium on Sunset Boulevard. Tickets were $25 a person, and still the cavernous night club was jammed with thousands of revelers.

There were scores of women walking around in dental-floss bikinis, with boa feathers rising from their hair. Dozens of musicians kept up an incessant samba beat, with whistles and cymbals screaming and crashing in the air. Everyone was drunk and dancing, gripping the hips of strangers and making long conga lines on the dance floor. It was hot and sweaty, but something was missing. I'd been there for an hour before I realized what it was: carnality. There was an amazing absence of sexual vibrations in the place. Sure, there was lots of flesh. One woman strolled around, a six-foot-tall blonde with only an excuse for a skirt, which blew off her ass with the slightest breeze, and a black fishnet top that offered a glimpse of her virtually naked breasts. Fat Latin men followed her around, showering her with light from their flash cameras. But all they did was look—the safest sex of all.

I noticed two women cruising the place, dancing slightly as they took in the spectacle around them, and I asked them to talk with me. They said they were both high-school teachers in their late twenties and, yes, they were afraid of AIDS.

"My friends and I talk about it a lot," said Carmen, who wore shiny black tights and a bright red shirt. "Because you don't know about the past of someone you sleep with. I've been very careful. I haven't been with anyone, unless it was a boyfriend, for eight months."

Her friend Stephanie said it was difficult to take steps to protect herself.

"I was going out with this guy, and I asked him if he was bi or a homo or if he'd ever had a relationship with a man. And he was quite pissed, insulted. He said, 'No, don't worry about it.' But he got over it, and then he asked me the same question, if I'd ever been with a woman. And I got pissed." She laughed. "But you have to ask that."

"Yeah, you have to now," Carmen agreed. "Because of the incubation period, I think more and more people are going to find out they have it. I can have it. Anyone can. I'm having an

AIDS blood test next week. I'm paranoid. I mean, I've had nine lovers in the past two years. I counted them, just because of all I've been reading. So I'm taking the test, just so I can be at peace with myself."

Her friend looked at her, stunned. "They have a blood test for AIDS? I didn't know that."

"It's to see if you carry the antibodies," Carmen told her. "My best friend just had hers. It takes two weeks to get the results, so she doesn't know yet. I'm getting it at the free clinic in Santa Ana."

"Oh," Stephanie said, shaking her head. "I wouldn't want to know."

By the end of the night, the star of L.A.'s *Carnaval*—the amazing blonde with the see-through fishnet top—had decided on a man. She'd been dancing for hours with him—a tall, very young guy with rumpled brown hair and a face as chiseled and perfect as something you'd see on a Greek statue. He seemed almost bashful, dancing with that statuesque, erotic woman—he must have known that every man in the Palladium wanted to be in his shoes. When I last saw them together, they were at a table off in a corner, mauling each other, her hands gliding through his hair, her white breasts visible even from a hundred feet away.

And then I saw her leave alone, stamping out in a huff. I looked around and saw the young man walking by himself. If I was going to talk with anybody, anywhere, for this story, it would be with him.

He told me he was eighteen and his name was Egas. He'd moved to L.A. from Brazil three years before and had just graduated from high school. And, yes, he couldn't believe his good fortune when that woman picked him up.

"Not bad, huh?" he said, ducking his head shyly and looking around. "Everyone was looking at her—everyone. I don't know why she picked me."

I asked him if he was nervous about AIDS.

"Yes, I'm nervous about it. I first heard about it one year ago. I thought it was just gays. Now I know it's dangerous. I know if you wear condoms, it reduces the risk, but still, it's dangerous."

"Would you wear a condom?"

"Yeah. I think everybody would."

I asked, as delicately as I could, what had happened with the woman. Why hadn't he gone with her?

"I'm kind of scared," he said, shrugging. "She's too anxious to have sex. Maybe she's got AIDS; I don't know. I just got her phone number. I'm gonna think about it."

Everywhere I went in L.A.—the beaches, the restaurants in Westwood, the comedy clubs in Hollywood—I heard the same things. Everyone was scared, many people were thinking of getting tested. And condoms, if they weren't being used, were at least the talk of the town. My last night there, I went to Pizazz, a singles bar in Marina del Ray. It was your basic "Hi, what's your sign?" disco—in previous incarnations, it had been called Popcorn and Big Daddy's. But it was still the same: polished bars, a dance floor, revolving lights, thumping Top 40 dance hits. I leaned against the wall near the dance floor and watched a young couple dance. She was a cute redhead; he was a handsome young guy with a tan and a John Travolta dance technique—very flashy, with lots of spins. They ruled the dance floor and even had a table that was connected to it, like a throne.

Now, throughout my research for this article, I'd avoided going up to a couple in progress, sticking my recorder in their faces and saying, "Hey, what about AIDS?" It seemed a sure-fire way to ruin a guy's line, to quell a burgeoning romance. I didn't want to bum out young lovers. But that night, I figured I'd do it. The worst thing that could happen was that I'd get knifed. I went up to the guy the next time he sat down and asked if I could interview him and his girlfriend. "Well, is there money involved?" he said. "Because if there's money involved, you'll have to go through my agent."

I broke the news to him—no dough—and he called his girlfriend over. His name was Jeff; he was twenty-one. His girlfriend, Katie, was twenty-two. We talked about the basic stuff: how some people were afraid of AIDS, how others continued to screw around without precautions, how it was hard to think about AIDS and safe sex in the heat of the moment. And then our talk took a sudden turn.

"If you're going to be promiscuous enough to sleep with anybody who comes your way," Jeff said, "for sex and not love, then you deserve to get it and you deserve to die."

I was stunned; I just kind of nodded.

"This is going to sound off the wall," he went on, "but I've done a lot of thinking about it. And I think that God has done this, because AIDS is contracted not only by people who are sexually promiscuous but by drug abusers—and people who abuse drugs heavily are thieves, prostitutes, rapists; they will do anything for money to buy drugs. God is doing this to eliminate homosexuals and drug abusers and people who are sexually promiscuous."

Katie disagreed.

"What about babies?" she said. "Babies are getting AIDS. That would be like God being like Hitler—killing people who aren't perfect. That's not right."

"But say I had AIDS, and I was sleeping with you and guys and everybody. And what if you got pregnant? That baby would have AIDS! That baby would be deformed; it would have one arm, whatever."

"But why would God kill that baby just because you were bad? It's not fair."

"It's like, Why does God allow abortions? Why does he allow miscarriages? Being gay is against God; it's against the Bible. And I think he started it by making it just in the gay populace, and now he's taking it to sexually promiscuous people. There are people who are bisexual—as disgusting as that sounds—who will go to a gay bar one night and sleep with a guy and come here the next night and sleep with a girl. And I think the people who are dumb enough to sleep with a guy like that should get it."

I told him it sounded almost as if he were glad about AIDS.

"I'm thankful for it," he said. "Because I've never been sexually promiscuous—I've slept with only three people in my life. And I think something should be done about people who are."

"I don't," Katie said. "It's going to kill a lot of innocent people, and I don't think it's fair at all."

"How can people be innocent if they're sleeping with a different person—"

"Because," she interrupted, getting angry, "if my husband went out and had sex with someone and brought it home to me and I got AIDS, and my children got AIDS, I'd be an innocent person, and my children would be innocent."

I sat back and watched them argue. Only a while ago, they'd been dancing, holding hands, looking into each other's eyes. Now they were shouting over the music about Hitler and rapists and anal sex, and this guy was espousing the kind of gay-bashing, fundamentalist attitudes I'd heard about at that party my first night in L.A. Jeff and Katie raged back and forth for maybe half an hour. I hadn't said anything in a long time. Then Katie looked at her boyfriend with a kind of resignation and said, "Honey, let's dance." And so they stood up, and they went back to dancing.

denver

By the time we were circling two miles above the Mile High City, I would have given anything for a break from AIDS hysteria. I'd have preferred to be on a tropical island, sipping rum from a coconut, flirting with native girls who'd never heard of safe sex. But I figured Denver would be at least a relief compared with New York and L.A. I'd picked it as my third city to visit because I'd heard that AIDS paranoia hadn't yet spread to the Rocky Mountains. Denver represented to me something robust, healthy, butt-kicking. It was a mountain town, a town of the West. It wasn't a media center or a place one associated with junkies or gay-pride parades. As we made our approach, I looked at the lights of Denver and hoped all was calm down there.

My first stop was Rick's Café, a restaurant/bar in the Cherry Creek area. Rick's had a healthy crowd for Thursday night— people stood around the long bar unwinding from work, smoking and drinking, a vaguely Yuppie crowd. At the tables, people were eating such things as salmon steaks with juniper berries, beef stew served in hollowed-out bread loaves—mountain food. Near the bar, two young women sat at a table, having a drink and talking.

"AIDS concerns me, but it doesn't concern a lot of people," said Beth, a twenty-five-year-old account executive for AT&T. "One of my real good friends just broke up with his girlfriend, and we were talking the other night. I told him, 'Hey, you'd better be careful.' And he said, 'Oh, I figure I have another couple of years to be promiscuous before I really have to start worrying.' So there are a lot of people out there who are aware, but it hasn't really sunk in yet."

Beth's friend Kim was also twenty-five; she worked for AT&T as a technical consultant. She said they both had steady boyfriends, but that didn't entirely ease their concern.

"Even when you start dating someone, you worry," Kim said. "You see these commercials they're showing in Europe that say, 'You didn't just sleep with her, you slept with the last ten people she slept with and that they slept with.' I think about that."

But their fear didn't seem to be a major force in their lives, as it was for women in New York and L.A.

"If I knew a guy, if I really trusted him and respected him enough to have a sexual relationship, I probably wouldn't ask him to use a condom," Beth said.

Not far down the road, I checked out the Pearl Street Grill. It was a wood-paneled pub, a cozy place to drink with friends or watch Broncos games. It was also a little artsy—writer types hang out there, and a foreign-film house operates a few doors away.

At the bar, a guy named Wes sat drinking an enormous glass of Watney's beer. He was twenty-two, a student at Denver University, and he tore himself away from the hockey highlights on ESPN to talk with me.

"The media play AIDS up so big," he said. "I don't know if it's as big a problem as they play it up to be. It's like drugs—when Reagan was after them for those short months, they played that up real big and made it more of a problem than it was. But AIDS is definitely a problem—we should be concerned about it. We're a little more sheltered out here than other people are, like in New York."

But Wes admitted that it was hard to ignore the hype completely.

"If I'm going out with a girl and I know her pretty well, I won't give it a second thought. But if I've just met her, I'll definitely take precautions, maybe by abstaining for a while. A couple of years ago, I would've been more likely to jump into the sack."

While I was talking with Wes, two women came in and claimed a table near the bar, causing quite a stir among the men in the place. I was the first one who got to them.

Maren, dressed in black, with a hammered-silver brooch at her neck, said she was a flight attendant. Her friend Jill worked in retail sales; they were both twenty-three.

"People are starting to talk about it," Maren said. "A friend of mine just died of AIDS. He was a hemophiliac—he got bad blood. That was the first time that it struck anybody I know. I don't do any drugs and I don't sleep around, so I don't have to worry about it that much."

"I don't know anybody who's really concerned about it," Jill said.

"I don't either." Maren took her drink from the waitress, took a sip. "I think when you're around people your age in college, and everybody's like you, it's probably like, 'Naw, nobody has it.' I think the only way to learn is the scary, hard way. People in New York and L.A. are a lot more afraid because they've had so many more people die of AIDS than Denver has."

By the end of the night, I felt an almost euphoric sense of relief. The people with whom I'd talked were aware of AIDS, but it wasn't a horrific abyss at the edge of their consciousness. I felt reassured. I felt safe.

The next day was perfect: The sky was a solid sheet of blue, it was 60 degrees, and I had the keys to a friend's Suzuki. I rode up into the mountains, went hiking, poked around some gold mines, paid my respects at Buffalo Bill's grave. I felt as if I'd escaped to a safer world.

But I was fooling myself. Within a few hours, I would talk with women who wished they could live on another planet, with men who had condoms burning a hole in their wallets. In a few hours, I would be at Neo.

Every city has its strips of singles bars where bright, hopeful young people meet to drink, dance, and pick up tropical sex diseases. In Denver, most of these clubs are in a small inner-city suburb called Glendale. My friend—the one who had lent me his Suzuki—said I had to go there, that I'd gotten the wrong impression. Scott was a news writer for the CBS affiliate in Denver, so I'd discounted his theories. Too many hours spent watching the satellite news feed, I figured.

We pulled up about a mile from Neo—that's how far it seemed we had to walk past parked cars to get there. It was a three-story boxlike place rising from a parking lot, with the letters NEO spelled out against it. Inside, everything was stylish: Italian lamps, black TV monitors, splashy new-wave art on the walls. Neo was packed with a Friday-night crowd that numbered around twelve hundred; it was shaking and mingling to the thump of Prince's "Kiss." Everywhere—outside the bathrooms downstairs, on the edges of the dance floor, on carpeted steps near the ceiling—people were on the prowl. I felt those strong sexual vibes, that raw sense of carnal possibility, that had been so lacking at the Palladium in L.A. It was like a time warp to 1979, this atmosphere. Wolf packs of single guys moved through the crowd, their eyes flicking from one girl to the next. Women in slinky dresses crossed their legs at the bar, tonguing the straws in their drinks and smiling. It was invigorating, unbelievable.

But it didn't mean that people weren't afraid of AIDS.

"I'm scared to death," said Kristi, twenty-three. She worked at a financial company in Denver with her twenty-one-year-old girlfriend Elise; they were sitting on one of those carpeted seats high above the dance floor, watching the goings on around them.

"I'm so scared of AIDS, I'm not even scared of cancer anymore," said Elise. "My whole family's had cancer—my mom, my aunt. I had cervical cancer when I was sixteen. But I don't think anything about that now. It doesn't frighten me at all. But I'll tell you something, if I had AIDS, I don't know what I'd do."

"Let me put it this way," Kristi said. "We're pretty good girls. It's not like we go to a bar and we take every guy home. But even if you do it once in three years, it stops you from doing that. Like that guy right there in the striped shirt, talking to that girl"—I looked over at him—"he could have AIDS right now. And it just really terrifies me."

Elise told me about the time, a month before, when she had slept with her boyfriend's best friend on the spur of the moment. It was something that happened once, but it's still affecting her.

"For three weeks afterward, I was so paranoid that he had diseases. I don't do it that often, but all it takes is once. And I thought, God, maybe he has this disease and he doesn't care."

"People are going to use AIDS to get back at other people," Kristi predicted. Then she told me this horrifying story. A guy she knows—a friend of someone she works with—met a girl at a club named Josephina's. He flirted with her, she responded; and before he knew it, they were at his place, having sex. He couldn't believe his good fortune. The next morning, he woke up alone, went to the bathroom and nearly fainted. There, written in lipstick on his mirror, was a note the girl had left him. It said WELCOME TO THE AIDS FAMILY.

"That's murder," Kristi said. "That girl murdered that guy. He knows her name. I think he should take her to court. Two days later, he was scared and he took an AIDS test, and he had AIDS. He just sat in his apartment after that for three days. He said, 'I might as well kill myself. I don't want to go through it.'

"You know how they talk about the atom bomb? If AIDS really spreads, I think it'll kill us off before the bomb does. Why make bombs? By the time you use them, there may be only thirty people left on earth. I wish that I could get into a spaceship and go to another planet and start over. This world sucks, it really does."

Shaken from that talk, I went to the bar and did a shot. Jesus Christ. I looked around at the hundreds of people and began to feel scared again. Maybe more scared than I'd felt the entire time in New York and L.A.

Later, near the DJ's NASAlike control center, I talked with a blond guy named Jake. He was twenty-five, very handsome and stylish-looking, and worked for a movie theatre. He wore a black sweater, gripped a cold beer. We had to shout over Big Audio Dynamite's "Bad Rock City."

"Condoms are a big thing now," Jake said. "I know girls who never even saw one before, and now they want you to have one before you even talk to them. That's no lie. It's pretty damn recent, too, just in the past couple of months. I never heard of a woman carrying a condom, but they are now. I am, too. It's something I never had to deal with before. You're insulted at first. But I understand why, after talking with some girls. I think women are more worried right now. I don't see any problem with it. If they don't mind, I sure don't."

Was the fear of AIDS changing things?

"Oh, definitely. People are being a lot more cautious, a lot more discriminating. If you don't look your cleanest, your best, they make a prejudgment right there."

So people were having casual sex less often?

"I think so. Unfortunately." He smiled. "But a place like this, I don't think it makes much difference. People are here for basically one reason. They take as many precautions as they can—they know the risks in coming to a place like this. But other places, and as far as dating goes, I think it's getting a lot more cautious."

I asked him if he was trying to be careful. He gave his head an aw-shucks scratch.

"Well, you know, old habits are hard to break," he said. "A man needs a woman, you know what I mean?"

I had a troubled sleep that night and woke up Saturday morning to this page-one story in *The Denver Post:*

AIDS TESTING CLINICS SWAMPED BY CALLS

AIDS-testing clinics in several cities, including Denver, are being swamped by heterosexuals who fear they have been exposed to the deadly disease, health officials said Friday.

In Colorado alone, the number of AIDS tests administered state-wide has doubled since December, officials said. . . .

Health officials in Los Angeles, Long Beach, Atlanta, San Francisco, Boston and Florida concurred. They told The Associated Press that the trend probably is the result of stepped-up education programs and wide publicity about Liberace and other victims of acquired-immune-deficiency syndrome. . . .

"We're swamped here on the phones," said the executive director of the Boston AIDS Action Committee, Larry Kessler. "For February, we had more than 4000 calls; 3000 were asking about the test. It's a whole different scenario, because 80 percent were calls from heterosexuals, highly anxious people."

I went to a party my last night in Denver. It was no different from parties I'd been to in L.A. and New York—I tried to talk with people about AIDS, and it got out of hand. Within ten minutes, half the party was in the kitchen, arguing about AIDS testing, about how you could get it, about whether or not people who have the disease should be quarantined. I heard that lipstick-on-the-mirror story again, not once but twice. Later on, I would hear that the same story was circulating around New York and Texas. It's an urban myth, like alligators in the sewer system—an expression of people's deepest fears. It's also a perfect illustration of the way things stand right now for heterosexuals in America and their fear of AIDS. They may be nervous, they may be scared, but the vast majority of them lead lives untouched by the disease. They have to make up strange, quirky stories to feel some connection to the deadly illness, which has already claimed thirty thousand lives in the U.S. I guess that all we can do is hope things stay that way, that we never reach a time when we all have true stories of our own to tell.

10

the no decade

One night last month I stood in aisle 31B of my neighborhood grocery store in Dallas, trying to look invisible. I mean, this was *31B*—a no-man's aisle full of tampons, contraceptive foam, and feminine napkins. I had been on 31B only once before in my life, on an errand of mercy for a girlfriend who waited at home, watching "Moonlighting" with a heating pad clutched to her abdomen.

But this time I was there on my own, a few paces to the left of the tampons, staring nervously at racks and racks of condoms. I had just returned from a month-long trip around the country, writing about heterosexuality and AIDS for *Playboy* magazine, and I had developed a certain calm, quiet terror.

I tried to relax, to close my eyes to the horrors that lay before me. I scanned the brands for a plain, simple, no-nonsense box, one the checkout girl wouldn't recognize. Fourex Natural Skins were the most unobtrusive looking, but the sheep on the box disturbed me. Just above them were Excita Extra Ultra-Ribbed with Spermicidal Lubricant and Reservoir End (Extra Pleasure for Both Partners). All the others had pictures of stunning couples embracing on beaches, kissing and laughing in golden sunsets. I wondered: Why are they smiling?

I wasn't. I felt a sudden rush of anger. What the hell was I doing on aisle 31B? Why should I, a nice little North Dallas WASP boy, have to buy a box of rubbers? That was the kind of thing my *dad* and his friends had to do back in World War II. Those were things you used to carry in your wallet when you were sixteen and throw away your first week in college. What forces of nature and man had caused me to load a cart with Ragu, Bounty paper towels, and peanut butter merely to cover my purchase of a dozen Sheiks? I stood there on aisle 31B, and my anger grew. I know AIDS is a serious national issue, something that demands responsibility and caution from everyone. On a rational level, I can accept that. But on another level, I was steamed.

I didn't want to buy any damn condoms.

I guess that, like a lot of people, I had been pushed too far. Ever since 1980, it's as if some ominous conspiracy has tried to make Americans behave, to homogenize our actions and morals, to make sure nobody has fun anymore. You can't have sugar in your gum, caffeine in your cola, or salt on your steak. You can't have a beer without thinking of Mothers Against Drunk Drivers. You can't have a beer at all if you're under twenty-one, as the minimum drinking age rises across the country. You can't smoke a joint, because the president has declared a national war on drugs—every night on TV, a newly dried-out football star says, "Just say no." You can't get a job without someone testing your urine or run for office without getting a "moral report card." You can't buy *Playboy* at 7-Eleven or ride a motorcycle without a helmet. You can't smoke anywhere. A no-drinking-while-driving bill just cleared the Texas Legislature, so you can't tip back a cold one on the way home from work. The Federal Communications Commission ruled in April that radio DJs can't do blue material, even if they steer clear of profanity. You can't join the armed forces without submitting to an AIDS test, and if you test positive, you can't get in. You can't even drive without wearing a seat belt in the '80s. And on top of all that, you can't have sex with strangers, because it might end up killing you. This is why, that night on aisle 31B, I felt trapped. But I bought the condoms anyway, hiding them beneath my Tostitos, blushing when the checker had to run the Sheiks back and forth, back and forth, over the scanner before it beeped and I could flee.

To understand why I'm so mixed up and bitter, you have to understand my generation. Many of us feel cheated for having missed the '60s, when things were jumping, alive, bursting in all directions instead of meekly forming one line. When we graduated from high school in 1975, Jimi Hendrix, Janis Joplin, and Jim Morrison were all dead, and so was their era of rock and roll. We came of age after Vietnam and before Reagan—we were the last, gasping breath of the baby boomers. Our older brothers and sisters had been in the thick of the '60s—they were sent home from high school for wearing moratorium arm bands, they bought the "White Album" when it first came out, and they were tear-gassed at their universities. They helped fight for and win the Sexual Revolution and made great gains in the women's movement and the struggle for civil rights. The history was still beating up dust, still echoing in the streets of Chicago and Watts.

But by the time my friends and I went to college, we accepted those freedoms, that way of life, as if it were the way things had always been. That was how fast the '60s changed America. At that time it seemed like everything in our culture was based on the word "yes": Yes, you can have all the sex you want—that's what the Pill is for. Yes, you kids can live together without getting married—your parents will even help hang the drapes. Yes, you can read *Hustler* or see *Wanda Whips Wall Street*—the Constitution guarantees it. Yes, Yes, Yes—it's a free country. Have a good time; enjoy yourself. But we're in a different decade today, and it's based on a different word. If the '70s were the Me Decade, then maybe this is the No Decade.

Today I talk to college kids in night clubs and feel relieved that at least I wasn't in the class of 1986. They're coming of age in the No Decade, surrounded by limitations and shrinking possibilities, being told what not to do at every turn. The *New York Times Magazine* recently dubbed them the "Unromantic Generation": they're so damn *serious*, so obsessed with planning, with their careers, with staying on track, that they have no time for anything fun.

I describe to them what it was like to be at UT-Austin in the mid-seventies, and they can't believe it; it sounds like ancient history to them. Those were loose, free, thrilling times, I tell them. Most of my best friends—Rich, Lee, Peggy, Jack, Monika, and Jess—grew to adulthood between classes and parties in that great ex-hippie town of hills, lakes, and barefoot girls. It was the perfect college life. Ther were radio-TV-film classes in which students turned in erotic films as term projects: artsy, soft-focused shorts starring friends from Jester dormitory. There were trips to the country for cactus buds and psilocybin mush-rooms, sandaled walks around campus, and communal life in co-ops, where everyone shared the chores and eventually slept with everyone else. There were steamy affairs with stained glass artists, punk band drummers, and clear-faced clerks in health food stores who sunbathed topless at Barton Springs. There was dancing to reggae at the Armadillo on hot Saturday nights and summertime skinny-dipping at Hippie Hollow.

That was the way we lived ten years ago, and I think we were typical of our generation. We indulged in party drugs and friendly sex—we might swallow a Quaalude and go to a pajama party, where we'd nurse a beer through the night and look for a twenty-four-hour romance. But it didn't mean we were drug-crazed sexual deviates. We turned out all right, became doctors and journalists and teachers, cable TV subscribers, even moms and dads.

I guess the last year things were that free was 1979. I was a rock-and-roll critic for the *Dallas Times Herald* then, and most of my UT pals had moved back to Dallas. We lived in a ragtag, ethnically rich neighborhood around Lower Greenville Avenue, amid Mexican movie houses and bohemian bars, a kind of mini-Austin. We settled into our twenties, some of us having strings of two-week affairs, others living with lovers in a few spare rented rooms. We worked hard and played hard in our little chunk of Dallas, miles from the condos and singles apartment villages that sprawled to the north. North Dallas weirded us out —people our age were turning preppy up there. But under the skin we were all the same. We were young and hot-blooded, and we didn't have to fight for our right to party. We smoked grass on our porches at twilight, with cats maneuvering between our legs, and we flirted with people at parties, at Bar Tejas, after *Casablanca* at the Granada Theatre.

But while my friends and I were wrapped up in ourselves, having a blast, the country around us was restless and troubled.

On a deep level something was terribly wrong—too much had changed since the early '60s. Back in those days, America seemed like a simpler place. There were absolutes, things everyone could count on: Mom was in the kitchen, Dad was in charge, and "Father Knows Best" was a prime-time show. The '60s began with June Cleaver doing dishes in a cocktail dress and pearls; they ended with Jane Fonda in Hanoi. That's a long way to go in ten years, and it sent the country reeling, anchorless and lost, for the ten years that followed. By 1979 we were living in a world as dark as anything Yeats had imagined. Things were falling apart, the center wasn't holding, anarchy had been loosed upon the land. It was a world of moral relativism, a maelstrom of hard-core porn and pregnant teens, of crazed terrorists and sixth-grade dopers, of heavy metal and meaningless sex. People were floundering; they were living in a time when there was no right and no wrong. They had lost the ability to show self-restraint, to rein things in. Jimmy Carter presided over all this confusion and to his lasting regret labeled it a national malaise.

Nobody wanted to hear that. Once the president had confirmed our darkest fears, he was history. America needed someone who would say, "Don't worry, it's all right, things are fine," a relic of the days of Ike, someone who could represent what we felt we had lost. We found that someone in Ronald Reagan. Voting for Reagan was like voting no to the country we had become, like voting no to where the '60s and the '70s had taken us.

To some, Reagan's landslide defeat of Jimmy Carter in 1980 was a joke. We had put an actor in the Oval Office—a co-star to a chimp! Reagan was a perfectly uncynical, uncomplicated man who couldn't be accused of being an intellectual—he saw things in black and white, and he was relentlessly optimistic. So we embraced him. Something about Reagan reassured people that there really was a right and a wrong. He said it, he believed it, and we believed him. Reagan would give us back the absolutes that had been missing since the end of Camelot in 1963.

And so the No Decade was born. Since people could no longer rely on themselves for moral certainty and self-control, substitutions were made. Bureaucracy, legislation, and reforms began setting the limits that had disappeared, redrawing the lines that had faded to gray.

In December 1980, before Reagan even took office, the symbol of the new decade hit newspapers across the country. *Newsweek* ran a story about teenage sexuality that upset a sixty-five-year-old Denver grandmother named Barbara Aiton. A member of the Pro-Life Commission of the Catholic Archdiocese in Denver, she sprang into action, printing up five hundred buttons that simply said NO. They were distributed to teenagers, and Aiton was interviewed by the Associated Press. Her story was mentioned in a Dear Abby column, and within weeks eight thousand chaste teens were wearing NO buttons on their chests, and sixteen thousand more buttons were on order.

There were other sudden changes. TV evangelists people had once laughed at over late-night popcorn suddenly became nationally respected ideologues. Jerry Falwell and his Moral Majority, Pat Robertson, Jimmy Swaggart, and Oral Roberts wanted moral fiber back in the American diet. They wanted women back in the homes raising kids, state-sponsored prayer back in the schools, and gays back in the closet. They wanted smutty magazines like *Playboy* and *Penthouse* banned from the marketplace. Amazingly, they faced little outspoken opposition, unless you counted Larry Flynt and Bob Guccione. It seemed as if the only people involved in a movement in the eighties—the only people with commitment—were those on the fundamentalist far right. And it seemed as if all they were waiting for was a sign.

On August 2, 1982, at supermarkets, bookstores, and 7-Elevens across America, that sign appeared: a cover story in *Time* magazine with a screaming, bloodred headline that read,

HERPES: TODAY'S SCARLET LETTER

Herpes had been around for thousands of years and had been identified as sexually transmissible as far back as the late '60s. But in the summer of 1982 it was a trendy topic. It had been in the news for months, slowly creeping toward page one, and when it appeared on the cover of *Time* it caused a national panic.

The herpes simplex virus, the magazine reported, was a recurrent skin disease that caused cold sores on the mouth and small, blisterlike eruptions on the genitals. The outbreaks healed in about a week, only to break out again later. Some people had herpes once and never again; a few had outbreaks as often as once a month. From a medical viewpoint, it was a relatively harmless disease except during childbirth. Reduced to simple terms, genital herpes was just a cold sore in the wrong place. But in other terms, it was a *sex disease* that would *never go away*.

That was how it was presented in the *Time* story. Herpes horror stories were told: a pregnant housewife wanted to cut away her skin when she learned her herpes might be passed to her baby in childbirth if the virus was active; one man caught it on the only one-night stand of his life; a cab driver was so terrified of giving it to someone that he had become celibate; co-workers of a woman who had herpes circulated a petition to ban her from the office.

Time said that as many as twenty million Americans had genital herpes that summer and that as many as half a million more might get it within a year. The story was summed up in perfect No Decade style: "Perhaps not so unhappily, [herpes] may be a prime mover in helping to bring to a close an era of mindless promiscuity. The monogamous now have one more reason to remain so. For all the distress it has brought, the troublesome little bug may inadvertently be ushering in a period in which sex is linked more firmly to commitment and trust."

Across the country, people read the *Time* story and panicked. The twenty million people with genital herpes suddenly felt like lepers. There was even talk of tattooing the letter H onto their foreheads. Few people stopped to ask, "What's all the fuss about?" Those who did, writing in the *New Republic* and the *Nation,* accused *Time* of fanning the herpes scare, of pressing forward a national agenda to crack the whip and make folks behave, no matter what the cost.

Naturally, the Moral Majority saw herpes as a gift from heaven. Sermon after sermon, in nearly every church and denomination across the country, included references to herpes as God's answer to our country's recent sexual debauchery. The good Lord was putting an end to the Sexual Revolution, trying to instill morals back into the American way.

Did it work? All I know is that my friends and I were terrified —it was all we talked about that summer: "You shouldn't go out with him. I've heard he has herpes." "You slept with that girl from the party? You're crazy! Weren't you afraid she might have herpes?" We discussed not-so-subtle ways of asking dates whether they had it. "Do you have herpes?" was suggested as an icebreaker.

"I don't have to worry about it," my friend Lee would gloat, nodding toward his house, where he lived with his girlfriend of two years. "But *you* guys," he shook his head. *"You* guys are in trouble."

Herpes didn't really end the Sexual Revolution. But it did put a germ of doubt in most people's minds, one that hadn't been there since the early '60s. For the first time since the Pill was discovered, having sex wasn't worry-free.

That summer, when herpes was being called the plague of the '80s, I came home one day with a sack of groceries, and—I remember this very clearly—I turned on "All Things Considered," a news program on National Public Radio, and started putting away my frozen pizzas. I had tuned in to a story about an immune disease that made people unable to fight off simple illnesses like colds or the flu. They invariably ended up getting cancer or pneumonia and dying. The odd twist to this disease was that it affected only homosexuals and Haitians. That's weird, I thought. But at least it wasn't something I had to worry about.

It's funny, but back in '84 and '85, I still clung to the belief that the '80s were *great*. Even though it was a decade of IRAs and condo time-sharing, of Saab Turbos and imported water, I had decided to be different. I focused on one of the few groups that hadn't fallen in line, that didn't own suits or do aerobics: the kids in the cool scene in Dallas, who hung out every night at Tango, On the Air, the Starck Club, and Club Clearview. I had cut myself off from how people were really living and thought I was in a time of glitzy, post-punk excess. In my world, girls in rubber dresses danced to British new wave, their lips painted white, their hair a dazzling stack of mousse. Guys wore baggy trousers and black leather jackets; they wore flattops or long, wild locks. These were cool kids, and they were like my extended family. We danced to the Cure, New Order, the Clash. We puffed clove cigarettes and did flaming shots at the bar. In the daytime—which most of us disliked—you could be anything. You could be poor, rich, sixteen, stupid, brilliant, portly, plain, on the run from the law. But nothing stopped you from being hip and in the scene on '80s nights.

The summer of 1985 was the last time I held onto my delusions, and they were at their richest, their most deluding. That summer we were all on Ecstasy. CBS News called Dallas "the

Ecstasy capital of America," and it was true: at the Starck Club on Saturday nights it seemed as if a thousand people were on the then-legal designer drug. You could buy an aspirinlike tablet of X for $10 or $15 and be in a delirious mood for hours. Everyone loved everyone else on X; it was like the free-love '60s or those laid-back days in Austin. Sex was great on X, and it was bountiful. For a short time the '80s seemed like the time to be alive, the most partying decade since the Roaring Twenties.

But the morning after X, blood pumps through your body like Karo syrup, and your brain feels like a bag of gravel. You're sullen, tense, anxious. You want to lie down, even if you're supposed to be at work, even if you're supposed to be the best man at someone's wedding. I would feel that way and think it was just a designer hangover. But it was actually reality setting in. One cold X hangover day I came to grips with the truth. I wasn't living the '80s life—I was trying to escape from it. So I swore off X, cut down on drinking, even began staying home a few nights a week.

I did this, and something occurred to me: by swearing off X, I was saying no to *myself*. Everyone rebels, everyone has to learn to grow up. There's a time when you slow down your partying and start to strive in your career, when you settle into a monogamous relationship, maybe get married and have kids. And in each stage of the process, you grow a little, you gain a certain strength and character. That may be the worst thing about the No Decade. It denies people all those stages of growth and change. When simply forced on the masses, rules can't possibly mean as much. Being told what to do at every turn robs us of our right to choose—to decide when we want to say no for ourselves.

Before last winter, few heterosexuals had worried about AIDS. But then came the controversy over condom ads on TV, dire warnings from the surgeon general that AIDS was a threat to everyone, and another cover story in *Time*. But now, no one accused the magazine of blowing things out of proportion. If anything, people wondered why they hadn't been warned before.

THE BIG CHILL—HOW HETEROSEXUALS ARE COPING WITH AIDS hit the newsstands February 16, 1987. Inside was the grim latest news. Heterosexual infection accounted for nearly 4 percent of the AIDS cases in the country, a figure expected to rise to 5.3 percent by 1991. That was only the number of heterosexuals who had developed the disease, which has an incubation period of six months to several years. The number of straights carrying the virus could only be estimated. More than one million Americans were thought to be carriers, and more than 90 percent of them didn't know it. This was not a disease that caused a little cold sore and went away. This was a disease that killed you.

According to *Time,* 85 percent of the callers reaching an Atlanta AIDS hot line were heterosexuals, and 40 percent of calls to a similar hot line in Chicago were from frightened women. "Most say, 'I had too much to drink, and I went home with this guy,'" said the Chicago hot-line's director, Mary Fleming. "I hear stark terror in heterosexual women, who are deciding to be celibate."

This is what led me to aisle 31B of my grocery store that night. The guys and I feel awkward and uneasy about the whole thing; we've never had to be responsible about sex. The Pill let us off scot-free. In the old days—say, 1982—we'd careen around town in a 1966 turquoise Tempest, getting royally stewed and talking about women. But now, in 1987, our boys' nights out are relatively somber, almost funereal. We agree to meet someplace, and we arrive separately, strapped in our cars by seat belts. By our second drink we think compulsively, "Let's see, was that my second or third? It's just been thirty minutes. . . . Better eat some fries or something to keep that old blood alcohol below point ten." More than likely, we go to only one bar. And instead of salivating over the luscious brunette at the bar, we're more likely to dive into desperate AIDS talks, much the same as our herpes talks of five years ago. Someone might say, "Have y'all ever slept with a girl who's been with a bisexual?"

Everyone grips the table, stares into space, reels their memories back across their twenties, into their late teens. Bells ring: "Oh no! That girl Denise, in the dance department at S.M.U.! She always went out with—gulp—ballet dancers!" Or "Remember Sally? You know that guy she broke up with to go out with me, the one with the blow-dried hair and the real fresh breath? You don't think—no. *No!*"

Suddenly, the bill has arrived. Men and women are equal partners, and we have to do the right thing. But what is it? The idea of safe sex, of monogamy, of rejecting casual encounters, goes against our very grain. How are you supposed to brag in the locker room in 1987? "Hey guys, guess what happened to *me* last night? I met this hot blonde babe and got her to my place, and as soon as she's inside, she strips to the *skin.* " "Wow! What did you do?" "I told her to put her clothes back on. I looked at her and said, 'Just say no, Trixie, *just say no!'* " Is that what it takes to be a he-man in the No Decade? Will this be the new machismo?

Women seem to feel less ambiguous about it. Evidence shows that men are much more likely to give women AIDS than vice versa, so women heterosexuals are those who are really most at risk. My women friends are very concerned, very scared. When the *Dallas Times Herald* published a six-week study called "Sex in the '80s: Coping with the AIDS Scare" in its March 29, 1987, edition, one of my friends talked to me about it, waving the front page as if it bore the news of her best friend's death.

"Did you read this?" she wailed. "It has these safe-sex guidelines—it says to use Saran Wrap for oral sex. It says you shouldn't brush your teeth before sex because it can make microscopic cuts in your mouth. But that's the one time *everybody* brushes their teeth. Condoms, sheets of latex, rubber gloves, spurting tubes of nonoxynol-9—guys aren't going to do all that."

Another friend of mine—let's call him Dan—was the first guy in my gang to face facts. His girlfriend read a cover story in the February *Atlantic* called "Heterosexuals and AIDS: The Second Stage of the Epidemic" and called him at work, flipping out.

"We've got to use condoms from now on!" she screamed.

"Huh?"

"Condoms, condoms! They're the only thing that can stop you from getting AIDS."

Dan and his girlfriend had been monogamous for nearly a year, but she was worried about the legions of young women he had entertained for six years before that. Any one of them could have harbored the deadly virus, and using a condom was the only way she could be sure she was safe from Dan—if he hadn't infected her already.

"What about you?" Dan shot back. "What about all the guys you've dated?"

"If you're going to insult me," she said, "I can hang up the phone right now."

Things have been going downhill for a long time, but now life in America is taking on the quality of a Fellini film. How are we supposed to live in times like these? I wonder what famous romantics would do if they lived in the '80s. Can you imagine Marc Antony grilling Cleopatra about her sexual history? Or Elizabeth Barrett Browning asking Robert to use a Sheik? King Edward abdicated the throne of England for the woman he loved, causing the greatest romantic scandal of the twentieth century. Can you picture him winding Saran Wrap around Wallis Simpson the night they first made love?

Many people are trying to find something good in AIDS. They say it's bringing back romance, putting an end to casual sex, setting America back on the moral track. But they're ignoring that it is part of a larger picture. Throughout the '80s there have been more and more encroachments on our social freedoms, our civil liberties. Why haven't people protested? Why does no one charge the barricades? Even liberals merely grouse and complain when magazines are yanked from convenience-store shelves and when congressmen's wives argue for the censorship of rock and roll. They complain, and then they accept it all. I think it's because, deep down, maybe we *wanted* a No Decade to happen. In an uncertain world, being told what to do can be comforting. It's like having a strict father. We may complain, but we rely on him to make sure we don't go too far, that we don't go wrong, that we're safe. But this year, for the first time since 1980, cracks have begun to appear in the No Decade's fragile foundation. From Irangate in the Reagan administration to reports of wife-swapping and call girls at the PTL ministries, the institutions that have led us down a righteous moral path are crumbling.

Today I walk through the dark, echoing streets of the Deep Ellum district of Dallas at night, watching people pass me from Club DaDa toward the Prophet, kids who laugh and hope there's more fun around the corner. But it's hard for me to find much joy in it. I stand on Main Street, the quiet block between the bar-dotted blocks of Elm and Commerce, and I can hear the competing sounds of bands, the tinkle of distant, breaking bottles, the giggle of girls smoking grass in a parked car. Once I would have been thrilled by the action, by all that possibility, by the fact that at 1 a.m. the night was still young. But I've been to New York and L.A. lately, and I know what's coming: that chill dread, the fear of AIDS. You can already sense a collective feeling of resignation and defeat spreading across the singles scenes of Texas. It's unavoidable. Things are never going to be the same again.

11

a today kind of marriage

We called ourselves the Austin Mafia. Nearly all of us had gone down to the University of Texas and come back to Dallas to take up our lives, some of them ruinous and some successful. But Jack and Peggy and Lee and Hancel and Rich and Anne and I had always stayed together, hanging out at night and going to drive-ins and loaning each other money. We were all sort of shiftless, younger than our years, incapable of more than two consecutive serious thoughts. Marriage and babies? They were almost inconceivable, to none of us more so than Jack and Peggy. Jack was a brilliant, passionate goofball who put "boy scientist" on his IRS forms and made a meager but satisfying living repairing calculators, doodling with computers, and playing drums for a band called the Shitty Beatles. He was a jokester, a private stand-up comic for our gang, a twenty-seven-year-old going on fifteen. The idea of some baby's calling him Daddy would make your sides split with laughter—or your palms sweat with fear.

We were at a burger place called Hunky's and Jack was eating a hot dog when he dropped the bomb. The hot dog was dripping chili and onions and he put it down, swallowed the bite bulging his cheeks, and said, "Peggy and I are eloping to Hot Springs tomorrow night. She's pregnant, and we're going to have our honeymoon at Graceland."

Everyone laughed but Peggy. Some of us had been friends as far back as grade school; now we were in our late twenties, grabbing dinner together and listening to another one of Jack's colossal jokes. But he soon convinced us it was no joke. For once in his life, Jack wasn't kidding.

"It's true," Peggy said. "We really are." We looked into her solemn, wistful face and realized that Jack and Peggy—the least likely candidates of us all—were going to be the first to bite the dust and set up housekeeping.

We weren't so surprised about Peggy. She was a quiet hipster who taught fifth-grade English at a private school and who had, more than any of us, settled into a nice life for herself. If we all got together to eat dinner or watch "Hill Street Blues," we'd usually end up at Peggy's. If we really needed someone to talk to, Peggy would wake up in the dark and answer our phone calls. She hadn't always been happy: That had come with Jack. For a couple of years, she'd lived with a Polish-American novelist/ dishwasher in Ohio, where she'd gone to get her master's. But she missed Dallas and the gang, and her boyfriend seemed to us, on the one occasion we met him, to be the gloomy cause of a pall that had fallen over her for a long time. When Peggy moved back to Texas in 1983, she and Jack began hanging out together, and they finally faced us one night with the astonishing, embarrassing admission that they were going steady. Jack's high jinks brought Peggy to life; she became straight man and yukster to his constant stream of goofy observations and roadhouse antics.

They were fun to watch. They were both so alike and so different from everyone else. They liked drive-in movies, antique clothes, Busch beer, and the *National Enquirer.* They loved baseball and everything in pop culture; Peggy had a *master's* degree in it, which put a cool curve in the short stories she wrote and in the way she taught her fifth-graders.

They did have some differences—Peggy's family was fairly wealthy (she wore Neiman-Marcus underwear beneath her Salvation Army clothes), while Jack cared little about money, career, ambition. And now here they were, noisily sucking the last drops of milk shake from their cups, with a one-way ticket to Preg City.

We all wished them good luck. "Luck? We don't *need* luck!" Jack said expansively. "We have the whole world in the palm of our hands!" He held up his palms, pretended to fumble the planet on the restaurant's linoleum floor, and went, "Oops!"

the happy couple returns

The Monday after their weekend elopement, Jack and Peggy screeched up my driveway in Jack's '66 Tempest. They looked like they'd just done something illegal and were going to let me in on it.

"I had my finger up her butt crack the whole dang time," Jack said, closing the car door. Peggy got out on the other side, swinging the Newlywed Gift Pak they'd gotten at the courthouse three days before, protesting this account of their wedding.

"Not *up* it," she said. "I had a dress on. It was *on* my butt."

"I was goosin' her, was what I was doing. The whole dang time."

Peggy rolled her eyes. "I almost missed my cue to say 'I do.' I was too busy swatting his hand away."

They'd driven straight to Hot Springs Friday and gone to the courthouse, in one of those sleepy Southern squares where World War I veterans sit on benches watching the traffic. Inside, their first sight was a holding cell full of prisoners. ("We figured that was a good sign," Jack said.)

Peggy held up the Newlywed Gift Pak. "Look at all this neat stuff," she said. "Tide, Massengill disposable douche, Scope mouthwash, Midol—"

"Yeah," Jack said. "I picked up the Midol and waved it around in the courthouse and went, 'Hey, honey—no excuses tonight!' "

Peggy rolled her eyes, which she did with amazing regularity. "It was like 95 degrees that day—we'd just driven all the way there, we were hot and sweaty, and our faces were all red."

I winced. "Sounds romantic."

They went to a justice of the peace, who spent most of the brief ceremony talking about himself. "And he slipped some Jesus stuff in the vows, which we really didn't want in there, but what could we do?"

"I paid the J.P. twenty bucks, too," Jack said, "which means with the marriage license, Peggy still owes me a total of twenty bucks. Actually, you don't have to pay the J.P. anything, but he was looking at me with ten-dollar signs in each eye. I wanted to rabbit-punch him a few times."

This all left me a bit pained—my picture of weddings is a little more idealized. I think of weddings like they are in '30s movies, or like the one between Prince Charles and Lady Diana back in '81, when the whole gang got together at 5 a.m. to watch it. We scattered black-and-white portable TVs all around my place and munched on wedding cookies and cheap champagne while the royal couple kissed outside Buckingham Palace. This Hot Springs wedding just seemed to be missing something.

"Did y'all kiss then?" I asked. "You know, like you're supposed to?"

"Sure," Jack said. "The J.P. smiled and said, 'You can go ahead and *score* now, Mr. Turlington—you're married! You can get some of the sweet stuff!' "

Peggy rolled her eyes.

The rest of their wedding weekend went along those same lines—they motored to Little Rock for their wedding night and called their parents from a "cheap, clean hotel room with free HBO."

"Yeah, my mom started bawlin'," Jack said.

"My mother wasn't there," Peggy said, "and my father didn't believe it. He just started laughing and hung up." The next morning, they went to Memphis, so they could always say they'd honeymooned at Graceland. They barely had time to drop fifty bills at Elvis gift shops and catch a few dog races in West Memphis before it was time to head back to Dallas. On the way back, they had their first argument: Since Peggy was keeping her last name, what would the baby's last name be? Peggy, who has no brothers to carry on the family name, voted for Norvell. Jack insisted on Turlington, traditional this one time. They finally came up with a way to settle the issue when they got home—they would decide who got to name the baby by playing chicken with their cars.

"Well, how does it feel?" I wanted to know. "To be married, for life?"

Peggy shrugged. "I have to admit, it felt a little shocking to wake up in Little Rock, Arkansas, married."

"I guess it was like . . . real, real beautiful," Jack said, affecting an angelic glow. "Here we were, married in Little Rock, married as shit, and I woke up, the little lady still asleep, so cute and precious, all curled up and snorin' like a sawmill, and I thought —*Yeah. Yeah.* This is it. This is *perfect.*"

They drove off to break the news to Jack's roommate, the lead singer of the Shitty Beatles. The group had just released a single, though it had never had a gig, and Jack was afraid that John would take the news hard. And they still had to convince Mr. and Mrs. Norvell that they'd actually done it. I watched Jack's Tempest sail around the corner at the end of the block, with Jack and Peggy inside, heading off together, married as shit.

finding a love nest

"Well, what do you think?" Jack pulled an ottoman from the bed of his old pickup and gestured back toward the house. It was something, all right—two stories tall, sixty years old, with a long, open porch and French windows all across the top. Just a block down Swiss Avenue, in the historical district, houses like this had been fixed up into mansions years before and went for a million dollars apiece. But a lot went downhill in a block: Here the sidewalks were cracked, half-naked children ran around squealing in Spanish, and a crumbling apartment house across the street advertised rooms for rent by the week.

"Dream home, huh?" Jack said. *"Dream* home!" We clomped up the wooden steps and went inside, where Peggy and a few friends were touring the high-ceilinged, oddly painted rooms. There was a lot of work to be done, but the house was enormous, and it had possibilities. They'd decided to rent it, with an option to buy in a year or two if things worked out.

I asked Jack how Peggy was doing—she looked tired.

"It's morning sickness," he said. "She's in E.N.S.—the Early, Nasty Stages. Hey, look at this." He picked up a crumpled sheet of paper, smoothed it out. "Peg and I were talking about baby names, and she asked me to write down ten names, in order of preference."

His list went like this:

1. Dale
2. Dale

3. Dale
4. Dale
5. Dale
6. Dale
7. Dale
8. Dale
9. Bud
10. Special Ed

Jack had had a thing about the name Dale ever since he saw a commercial in the '60s in which a teenager goosed his girlfriend's mom by mistake at the bottom of a pool and came up sputtering, "I'm sorry—I thought you were Dale!" He had magazine subscriptions sent to him in that name, and it was his dog Sam's nickname. So it was natural that he name his kid Dale—it kept the joke going. But there were people who would see this list as a danger signal. This was no joke to Peggy—she could no longer smoke, she never so much as sipped a beer, and she was looking more and more ragged out every day. Some of us in the gang, now that we'd had time to fully realize that Jack and Peggy were actually married and expecting, were wondering if they would be okay. Jack, who could be deadly serious about things like politics (he subscribed to the *Klan Watch Newsletter*), seemed to be dealing with married life on a comic level. Sooner or later, it was bound to hit him—he would wake up and realize where he was.

"Did you hear about Sam?" Jack asked me, sitting on a just-moved-in couch and rubbing down his old mutt's shoulders. "We heard that sometimes dogs can get jealous of newborns, and you can deflate the situation by getting a doll, carrying it around the house, kissing it and showing it to Sam, giving him some attention, too, to sort of break him in. So we did that, and then we went out to a movie. When we got home, the doll was scattered in a million pieces all over the house, and Sam was in the corner, growling and foaming at the mouth, with the doll head hanging out of his jaws. And we went, 'Uh-oh. . . .' "

Later on, our friend Rich came over and the three of us drove in Jack's pickup to Sears, took the escalator to major appliances, and walked up to a Kenmore. The house didn't have a refrigerator, so Jack and Peggy had bought this one, on sale. We helped get it loaded in the truck, and Rich and I stood gripping its sides as Jack careened back toward Swiss Avenue. We had a great time, just like in the old days of a month before, cutting up like high-school kids. Buying a *refrigerator* at *Sears!* Suddenly, the whole thing seemed so ridiculously bourgeois it was absurd, and we were goofing off all through East Dallas, as if it were really just a great big joke.

jack gets a curfew

Mr. and Mrs. Norvell seemed to adjust fairly well to the idea of Peggy as a suddenly married, expectant mother. None of their four daughters had ever been very predictable, anyway: They'd been in punk bands, designed wild clothes, cracked up cars, gotten into various levels of heartache and trouble, and one of them had even married a forest ranger. Yes, the Norvells could handle this all right. A month after the wedding, they gave a reception for the newlyweds, sending out engraved invitations and preparing a feast at their mansionlike North Dallas home for an odd mix of guests (teachers from Peggy's school, old family friends, some of the old rowdy crowd from Austin, the rest of the Shitty Beatles). Everything went smoothly, though Jack bridled when Mrs. Norvell insisted that he and Peggy pick out a china pattern and get it registered at Crate & Barrel. ("It's stupid," Jack said, before caving in. "If people can't think of a present, they can just give us stacks and stacks o' cash!") At the party, only a few people brought dishes. Jack and Peggy's favorite gift by far was a five-foot-long plastic airplane that had hung on the wall outside the Jet-Away Lounge on Cedar Springs, until the place was being torn down just as Rich happened by. Now Jack was running his hands back and forth over the jet's shiny gray surface, his vision blurred by joy, as a dozen discarded blenders and toasters lay strewn at his feet. "This," he said reverently, "is going over the mantel."

As the night progressed, the quiet crowd stayed in the house, munching veggies and listening to Mr. Norvell's big-band albums, while the rest of us bopped in the huge yard out back, downing long-necks and catching up on stuff with the Austin kids. Things got sort of hazy after two or so, and I wasn't really aware of things until Rich called me the next day with incredible news.

"You won't believe this," he said. "Last night, Peggy gave Jack a curfew."

"No!"

"Yep. He got in real late, and she was real mad, and so he has a curfew now."

"What is it?"

Rich didn't know. Whoa, boy. This was too much. This was great. I tracked down Jack to get the scoop.

"Well, you know, I hadn't seen a lot of those guys from Austin in a long time," Jack said, "and Peggy got tired pretty early, around 2, and said she wanted to go home, and I told her to go ahead, that I'd be home before too late."

"When did you get home?"

"Uh . . . 5:30. And, boy, was I in the doghouse. Peggy was thinking, Oh, no, shades of things to come. And I thought, Hmmm, this isn't really atypical behavior for me. *What have we done?*"

After a moment of seriousness, Jack was laying on the sarcasm. "Oh, God, what have I got myself into? A woman who doesn't like to party at all—she only stays out till, like, 2, 2:30 a.m., that's it. She gets tired and can't even knock off a twelve-pack; she stops after eight or nine beers! What a wimp! What have I *done* to myself? A gilded cage is a cage all the same!"

Jack's curfew was a joke, too—it was officially set at 4:30 a.m. —but at least it was a goal, something to shoot for. Two weeks went by and I heard nothing else about that night, until one day I had lunch with Peggy, alone with her for what I realized was becoming a very rare time. Peggy had gotten over her morning sickness and looked pretty chipper. "I'm feeling great," she said. But when I made a joke about Jack and his curfew, she didn't laugh.

"That's not really how it happened," she said, after staring at her plate a long time. "It wasn't that I was mad at him; I was more hurt than mad. I really wanted him to go home with me from the reception. I wasn't feeling too well, and I get real sleepy these days—I can't stay up all night like I used to. But he wanted to go out with his friends—which is fine, I can understand that, he never gets to see them anymore—so I went home. I watched part of an old movie on the VCR, then I went to bed, but I couldn't go to sleep. I started crying at 4 and kept it up till he got home at 5:30. I'd cry for a while, stop, then start crying again.

When Jack came home, my face was all swelled up, the tears were starting to sting, and I think he was really shocked. He felt real bad, and he put his arms around me and said something like, 'Once we get all settled in, things will be all right again,' and I felt better, but then I thought, Bullshit! and started crying again. I didn't say anything about him needing to act like a father, because I thought he was uncomfortable with that. I just said, 'You can't *do* this to me!' " She took a breath, looked around our table. "Then he said something like, 'Yeah, I oughta start becoming more responsible,' or 'I'm a family man now.' He's never said anything like that before, and I think he really meant it."

Peggy and I talked about things the rest of us had all discussed but had been afraid to bring up with her—what kind of father Jack would make, whether he'd be able to take it seriously.

"Sometimes I'm scared," she said. "I was scared that night. You know that movie, *St. Elmo's Fire*, where Rob Lowe plays a kid who's a terrible father? I was afraid either I was gonna have to deal with something like that or else I'd strap him down so badly that we would both be miserable. But so far, that hasn't happened—he's begun to accept it all gracefully."

"Do you ever talk about the baby?"

"Not really . . . it's . . . it's not exactly a taboo subject, but neither of us quite believes it yet, I think. I mean, until lately, I felt so sick, and I guess I thought, How could I be happily pregnant and have this wonderful creature inside, and feel so sick? I don't think either of us has really faced it yet"—almost imperceptibly, her hands dropped toward her stomach—"we just don't think of it as *real.*"

babies at the baseball game

A wet diaper has a certain inescapable smell, even when it's in the back seat of a '66 Tempest hurtling along Interstate 30 with all the windows down. Sitting in the back of Jack's car, I knew the baby beside me had loaded his pants, but obviously Jack hadn't noticed—he had one elbow out his window, his palm slapping the hood to the beat of a Ventures tape, and beside him, Peggy was adjusting a cool six-pack of Busch in her lap, probably thinking about how much she'd like one. We—Jack and Peggy and I—had made a date to go see the Texas Rangers drop another game at Arlington Stadium, and at the last minute, Peggy decided to bring her nephew along, to see what taking care of a baby in public was like. It would be sort of like a dry run.

"Will is wet!" I yelled into the wind.

Jack jerked his head around. "Gosh dang it, Will!" he said. "Quit acting like a baby!"

Will played with his tennis shoes in his car seat and chewed a wad of gum, perfectly content. He wasn't quite two and rarely understood anything Uncle Jack said. Sometimes, Jack would explain complicated algorithmic theorems, then stop midway through, feigning impatience, and say, "Why . . . why . . . you're not even paying *attention!*"

"He'll be okay till we get to the game," Peggy said, reaching back to check Will's diaper. "What's that on your shoe, Will? Gum?" She pointed to a tiny dot of green on the heel. "Gum? Gum?" Misunderstanding, Will pulled the gum from his mouth and spread it out on his shoe.

"Will, act your age!" Jack yelled.

Actually, Jack seemed happy to have Will around on the rare occasions when Peggy's sister brought him up from Pasadena. He treated him as a toylike, miniature man, pointing out busty women on the street, offering him cigars, suggesting improvements for his car seat ("When we drive him in the pickup, we can make him a little pickup baby seat, with an itty-bitty gunrack").

We slowed down behind a mile of cars, which made no sense. Only a handful of people ever went out to see the Rangers get shelled. "Maybe there's a special promotion tonight," Jack said. "Maybe it's Saab Turbo night." Peggy asked the folks in the next car and found out that everyone else was going to Six Flags Over Texas, right next door to the ball park, to see the New Edition in concert.

"Watch this," Jack said when we'd stopped completely for a moment. He reached over the seat, tenderly touched Will's little chest. "Hey—what's that on your shirt?" Will looked down, and Jack flipped his fingers up to catch his nose. "Haaaa! Gotcha! Betcha he falls for that for the next five years."

It wasn't Saab Turbo night. Jack assured the ticket tearer that he'd read all about it in *The Dallas Morning News,* but no dice. Just when it looked like Jack was going to give up, his face brightened. "Oh, *now* I remember," he told the guy. "This is *Krugerrand* night."

We went way up in the cheap seats in time to see the bottom

of the second. Peggy spotted Cal Ripken of the Orioles popping his glove near second base. "Ooo, Cal Ripken!" she said. "If I don't go home with you guys tonight, I'll be with him."

We guys—including Will—couldn't let that pass. We began looking around for dames. Jack tried to teach Will to say, "Hi, girls!" and by the fourth inning, he would go, "Hi, girsh!" if either of us even nudged him.

"*Now* I remember what tonight is," Jack said as six cute teenagers made their way up our section. "It's Nude Teen Night! Will —when they come by, say, 'Hi, girls, drop 'em!' "

Will popped a bite of hot dog into his mustard-coated mouth and squealed, "Hi, girsh, doppim!" Jack patted him on the back, glowing, as proud of his young nephew as if the kid had just discovered a cure for cancer.

"Hey," Jack said in the middle of the fifth, "this is already the fifth inning, and I've only had, what, fifteen beers? C'mon, Will, let's go get us some brews." As he led Will down the aisle, he leaned down and said, "Remember, if you get lost, you're in Plaza Box Level seating, section 414, row G, seats 11 through 14. Got that?"

At the concession stand, Jack ordered a Texas-size Budweiser for Will, a pretzel for himself. The ladies behind the counter made a big fuss over Will, and Jack ate it up, proud as a poppa. "Yeah, he's a really good kid," Jack told them, picking up Will and nudging his chin with his fingertips. "Now, if he could just do something about that horrible, horrible drinking problem."

Deep in the eighth, Peggy was sitting next to me, dying for a beer and a binocular view of Cal Ripken's buns as he went into his batting stance. She looked beautiful these days—her complexion had that clear, beatific radiance pregnant women sometimes get. She was always in a good, tranquil mood, too. She looked beside her, where Will was dozing off in Jack's arms. "He *loves* Jack," she whispered to me.

On the way home from a rare Ranger victory—about the only one we saw all year—Will got restless and cranky, started bawling. Jack pulled a pen from his pocket and said, "Will! Hey, hey, Will! Look at this!" It was one of those action pens, with a picture of Graceland at the top. "Look, Will, what's that hiding behind that bush? That bush right there?" He tipped the pen over. "Why . . . why . . . it's *the king of rock 'n' roll!*" The rest of the way home, he sang "Are You Lonesome Tonight?", until Will was asleep in his car seat, exhausted from another eventful night out with Uncle Jack.

dressing down the shitty beatles

In a big booth at Campisi's Egyptian, an Italian pizza place, the gang was eating Thursday night out. Jack and Peggy had been married nearly three months and something remarkable had happened—Peggy was starting to look pregnant. I mean, there it was, right there. You couldn't miss it. Before, it had always seemed so abstract, something to be concerned about, to fret over. But as Peggy's belly began ballooning like a soccer ball, it all suddenly seemed so simple.

Our waitress raced over, tugging at her apron. "Who had the Lite beer?"

"Yo!" Jack said. "Tastes less." Jack and Peggy were wearing matching plaid Bermuda shorts—both Jack's. ("They fall down around my hips, but they're starting to fit better," Peggy said.) Peggy had been to the doctor that day, but she could hardly describe it, because Jack kept butting in. He'd gone, too.

"Yeah, we listened to the little guy's heartbeat," he said. He pointed at his wife's stomach, and we all looked. "It sounded like electronic music. We were waiting a long time, so I decided to be indiscreet. I said, 'Doc, as long as we're waiting, I've got a butt problem.' "

Everybody groaned and threw garlic toast at him. This was becoming his 1,000th Reagan-operation joke.

"I said, 'Maybe you could check it out . . . I may have a polyp or something. I'm pretty sure I have a really huge butt polyp.' "

The waitress saved us by coming with our orders. Jack and Peggy were splitting a plate of linguine; money was getting pretty tight for them. The rent and bills on the big house were higher than they had thought they'd be, and besides, they'd been making baby purchases. Just that day, they had bought a baby car seat at Storkland, and earlier in the week, Jack had bought a crib at a garage sale. They weren't rich, but they looked happier than I'd seen them in months.

"Hey, have y'all heard me and Peggy's latest get-rich-quick scheme?" Jack said, wolfing down a last forkful of pasta. "A nude teen petting zoo! It can't miss! Work a few extra weekends a month! We'll do testimonials: Hate your boss? Tired of forty-hour weeks? Be your *own* boss! Open a nude teen petting zoo! I earned $400,000 my first weekend, tax-free!"

As we walked outside into a glittering blue twilight, Peggy pointed at three enormously fat women waddling down Mockingbird Lane. "That's what I'm gonna look like," she sighed.

Jack snorted. "What do you mean, *gonna?*" But then he put his arm around her and patted her back. They were going off to a Shitty Beatles rehearsal—Jack's band had its first real gig ever that weekend, at the wedding of a friend of a friend in Wimberley, Texas. Peggy was going along, which had the makings of trouble—it was no secret that Dennis and John, two AAA salesmen who were the other Shitty Beatles, thought this marriage business was a bunch of baloney, an aggravating inconvenience to the future of the band. If Jack wanted to leave a practice before midnight, they'd say stuff like, "You mean you let your *wife* tell you what to do?"

Later on from Peggy, I heard what happened that Thursday night. Something about the visit to the doctor—listening to the baby's heartbeat, hearing and seeing tangible reasons for sacrifices he'd made for months—had really seemed to get to Jack. Just the way he walked with Peggy the rest of the day, putting his hand on her elbow, acting protective, seemed to suggest a change in him. Then, during a business discussion with the band, Jack did something he'd never done before, at least as far as Peggy knew. Dennis and John wanted to invest all their $300 fee for the gig back into the band. "No hotel rooms," said Dennis. "We'll just sleep on people's floors and save the money."

Peggy was in the bathroom when she heard Jack do it—he stuck up for her and the baby. "But Peggy can't *do* that!" he yelled. "She's *pregnant!*"

Peggy left in mid-practice; she had to be up at 6:30 for school. When Jack got home, about midnight, she was already half-asleep. He walked right up to the bed, stretched out beside her, and reached out gingerly to touch her belly. His breath was sweet in the air from a few cans of Old Milwaukee, and Peggy lay awake, watching as Jack slid down and put his ear against her stomach, trying to hear that tiny heartbeat again. It was a moment, the most romantic seconds of their lives. Then Jack shook his head and looked up at her.

"Peggy," he said sadly, as if what he was about to say caused him to feel all the sorrows of the earth, "you don't really want to name him Dale, do you?"

Peggy gathered him up in her arms, tousled his dark mop of hair. "Yes, I do," she said. "Just as long as we can give him other names, too."

They went to sleep that way, with Sam chewing a Frisbee at the foot of the bed, with firecrackers popping in the alley out back, with sirens in the distance and their whole lives ahead of them. They went to sleep, lulling each other toward Storkland, snoring like sawmills. They had no idea what was going to happen to them, any more than the rest of us did, but they were almost absolutely sure that when it did, they would be there together.